PENELOPE WARD

First Edition, August 2016
Copyright © 2016 by
Penelope Ward

Cover Design: Letitia Hasser, RBA Designs
Illustration by: Sarah Jane - @illustriousjane
Proofreading & Interior Formatting by Elaine York, Allusion Publishing
www.allusionpublishing.com

PROLOGUE

When his car pulled up outside of our apartment, my stomach sank. I just knew. The past several weeks had felt like a storm was slowly brewing. Don't ask me how, but for some reason, my heart sensed tonight was the night it was going to get shattered into a million pieces.

It had been slowly breaking anyway.

Elec hadn't been the same since returning from his father's funeral in Boston several weeks ago. Something changed him. He'd made every excuse in the book not to sleep with me. That's right. My boyfriend—love of my life—with the voracious sexual appetite suddenly just stopped wanting me. It was like a switch had gone off inside of him. That was my first clue, but there were several other signs that the guy I'd thought was my soulmate had somehow fallen out of love with me.

Since returning, he'd spend his nights writing like a maniac instead of coming to bed—anything to avoid me. His kisses, which used to be filled with passion, were now merely tender, sometimes chaste.

While I knew *what* was happening, I hadn't a clue *how* or *why* it had happened. I'd *believed* he loved me. I'd felt it for so long. It was genuine. So, how could things just change so fast?

The door slowly creaked open. My body stiffened as I sat up on the edge of the bed bracing for the worst.

Elec took off his glasses, placing them on the desk. He then slowly and nervously slipped his hands into his pockets. I doubted I'd ever feel those hands caress my body again. His eyes were red. Had he been crying in the car? Then came the words that started the unraveling of any trust I'd had in my own judgment.

"Chelsea, please just know I tried everything I could not to hurt you."

The rest was all jumbled, masked by the enormity of the pain and sadness building in my chest and numbing my brain.

I didn't know how I was going to ever recover from this hurt, how I was ever going to trust in love again. Because I truly believed he loved me. I believed love was indestructible.

I was wrong.

CHAPTER **ONE**

Supersonic Hearing

My little sister is such a drama queen. *Literally*. Jade is an actress on Broadway.

She clapped her hands together, applauding the students who'd just bravely put themselves out there to try out for *Joseph and the Amazing Technicolor Dreamcoat*. "You all did such a great job today! Tomorrow we cast the roles and start our first rehearsal. This is gonna be epic!"

Jade had come out to the Bay Area to visit our family for the week and offered to volunteer at the youth center where I worked. Since there wasn't enough time to produce an entire play, Jade decided to direct the kids in one key scene from the musical that would be performed later in the week.

I loved my job as director of the arts at the Mission Youth Center. It was just about the only thing going right in my life. The only downside was the fact that these walls were haunted by memories of my ex, Elec, who used to be a youth counselor here. That was how we met. He'd loved his job, too, until he quit so that he could move to

New York after we broke up. He moved to be with *her*. I shook my head to shoo away thoughts of him and Greta.

Jade grabbed her purse. "I need to go back to your place to use the bathroom and have a quick bite."

I'd just moved into a new apartment that was only a few blocks away from my job. The lease had finally run out on the place I'd been renting with Elec across town. Even though my ex sent me his half of the rent for the remainder of our lease after he'd moved out, I couldn't wait to vacate that place; every corner of it reminded me of him and of the miserable months that followed our break up.

My place was right in the south central section of the Mission District. I loved the culture in my new neighborhood. Produce bins and a variety of cafes lined the streets. It was also a mecca for Latin culture, which was great, except for the fact that it reminded me of Elec, who was half Ecuadorian. Little reminders of the guy who broke my heart were everywhere.

Jade and I strolled down the sidewalk, stopping at a fruit stand so that she could buy some papayas for an afternoon smoothie she planned to make back at my apartment. We also ended up getting two coffees to go.

I bent back the opening on my coffee lid as we walked. "So, little sis, I never thought we would be in the same predicament at the same time."

Jade had recently been dumped by her musician boyfriend.

"Yes. But the difference is, I feel like I have way more distractions in my life than you do. It's not that I don't think about Justin. It's not that I don't get sad, but my performances keep me so busy that it's almost like I don't have time to wallow in it, you know?"

"I told you I've been doing these phone therapy sessions, right?"

Jade took a sip then shook her head. "No."

"Yeah. I found this psychologist who specializes in trauma from failed relationships, but she's in Canada. Anyway, we do phone sessions one night a week."

"Is it helping?"

"It always helps to talk things out."

"Yeah. But no offense, you don't seem any better for it. Anyway, you can talk things out with Claire or me. You don't need to pay big bucks to talk to a stranger."

"Nighttime is really my only time to talk to anyone. You're performing at night, and Claire is too wrapped up in being a blissful newlywed. Besides, she's never had her heart broken. She listens, but she doesn't get it."

Our older sister, Claire, married her high school sweetheart. Even though the three of us were close growing up in nearby Sausalito, I'd always felt more comfortable opening up to Jade.

When we arrived at my building, my sister stopped to sit on one of the benches in the corner of the fenced-in courtyard. "Let's sit for a bit, finish our coffees." Her gaze wandered across the grass to my shirtless neighbor. "Okay...who's the hottie in the beanie defacing the property?"

"What is it with you and beanies?"

"Justin used to wear one. That's why I love them. Isn't that sad?"

"That *is* sad."

5

"This from the girl who still sleeps in her ex's shirt."

"It's comfortable. It has nothing to do with Elec," I lied. It was the one thing I allowed myself from him. It made me sad, but I wore it anyway.

"So...who is that guy?"

I didn't know my neighbor's name, but I'd see him once in a while doing spray paint art along the wrap-around concrete wall that surrounded the property. It served as a vast canvas. His spray painting was true art, definitely not what would be considered simple graffiti. It was an elaborate mix of celestial and geographical images. This guy just kept adding different artwork to the wall gradually. It was a work in progress. I could only assume he planned to paint the entire circumference of the property, as much as the wall space would allow.

"He lives in the building, next door to me, actually."

"What is he doing? They allow him to do that here?"

"I don't know. The first time I saw him out here, I thought he was vandalizing the property. But no one seems to care or stop him. Every day, he adds to the mural. It's actually quite beautiful. But it doesn't match his personality."

Jade blew on her coffee. "What do you mean?"

"He's not very nice."

"You've talked to him?"

"No. He's just not friendly. I've tried to make eye contact, but he walks right by me. He has these two big dogs, and they're pretty mean. They bark all of the time. He walks them every morning."

"Maybe he's like a savant. You know, really good with art. Or maybe he's a genius but with limited social skills. What do they call that...Asperger's?"

"No. He communicates just fine. I've seen him yelling at a few people. I'm pretty sure he doesn't have that. This guy is just not friendly. He doesn't have Asperger's. He's just an ass."

Jade chuckled. "I think you should totally stop by his place with some warm muffins wrapped up in a basket. It's the neighborly thing to do. Maybe he'll loosen up...or loosen *you* up."

"Muffins, huh? What's that code for?"

"Muff...muffins. Same thing. If I lived here, I'd be all over that. But I *don't* live here. You do. And you totally need a distraction. I say...he's it."

I admired the guy's broad shoulders and tanned muscular back as his arm moved the spray can up and down. "God, doesn't he remind you of Elec, though? Arm tattoo...dark hair. Artistic. Basically, that's the *last* type of guy I'm going for at this point."

"So, if someone looks like or seems similar to Elec, then they're automatically disqualified? They're destined to do the same thing Elec did? Is that how you think? That's just stupid rationale."

"Maybe that's fucked-up. But the last thing I want is to be with someone who reminds me of him in the least."

"Well, that's a shame, because Elec was freaking hot, and this guy...is even hotter."

"Can you remind me why we're discussing this? The dude doesn't even say hello to me. He's not signing up to be on this delusional version of *The Bachelorette*. He's not interested."

Neighbor Dearest suddenly wiped the sweat from his forehead, took off the mask covering his nose and mouth, and dumped the spray cans into a black draw-string sack. He slung it over his shoulder and just when I thought he was going to walk away and out of the court-yard, he began to walk in our direction. Jade straight-ened in her seat, and I hated that my pulse raced a bit.

His eyes were focused on me. I wouldn't call it an angry stare, but he wasn't smiling. The sunlight beamed directly into his blue eyes, which glowed and really stood out against his tan skin. Jade was right; this guy was tru-ly gorgeous.

"Blueberry are my favorite," he said.

"What?"

"Muffins."

"Oh."

Jade snorted but stayed silent, letting me take the brunt of this humiliation.

"And I'm not anti-social or a savant. I'm just a good old-fashioned prick...with supersonic hearing."

He smirked and walked away before I could say anything.

When he was safely out of earshot—for real this time—Jade sighed. "Angry guys are the best in bed."

"You just can't stop yourself, can you? Haven't you done enough damage? I've always told you that you're loud when you think you're whispering. Now there's proof...at my expense."

"You'll be thanking me later when you're screaming out in orgasm as the angry artist is Van Goh-ing down on you."

"You're crazy."

"That's why you love me."

"It is."

CHAPTER **TWO**

Barking Orgasm

A week later, and Jade was gone back to New York. I already missed her like crazy. The only reason I hadn't gone to visit her was that Elec lived there now with Greta. While it was extremely unlikely that I'd run into him, I wasn't ready to visit their territory just yet.

Angry Artist and I had not crossed paths since the incident when Jade was visiting. Even though I hadn't seen him around, his dogs woke me up almost every morning barking their heads off. Since I worked the afternoon program at the youth center, my mornings were free. I often had trouble sleeping at night and needed the mornings to catch up on some shut-eye.

It was seriously to the point where I couldn't handle the barking anymore. If one dog wasn't barking, the other one was. Most of the time, it was a chorus of yelping in unison. I didn't care how intimidatingly good-looking he was; I needed to address it with my neighbor.

Tuesday morning, I pulled myself out of bed and threw on some sweats. I dabbed on a little bit of under eye concealer before walking over to his door and knocking.

He opened, wearing a fitted white t-shirt. His hair was disheveled from sleep. "Can I help you?"

"I need to talk to you about your dogs."

"What? No basket of muffins?"

"No. I'm sorry. I wouldn't have the energy to bake, given that I can't sleep because of your animals' incessant barking."

"There's nothing I can do about the barking. I've tried everything. They won't shut up."

"What are the rest of us supposed to do in the meantime?"

"I don't know. Get some earplugs?"

"Seriously. There must be something you can do."

"Aside from putting a muzzle on them—which I won't do—no, there isn't. Anyway, do you hear them barking now?"

For some reason, they'd stopped.

"No. But it's rare that they're ever quiet like this in the morning, and you know it."

"Look, if you want to complain to the landlord, go right ahead. I can't stop you. But there's nothing I can do to keep them from barking that I haven't already tried. They have minds of their own."

"Well, then that's what I'll have to do. Thank you for making me resort to that. Thanks for nothing." I walked away and heard his door slam behind me soon after.

Almost the second I returned to my apartment, the barking started up again.

Lying back in my bed, I knew there was only one thing I could possibly do that would help me relax enough to sleep amidst the barking. Despite not wanting to resort to it, I grabbed my Bose noise-reducing headphones and placed them on my ears to block out some of the sound. Even though there wasn't any music playing, they did help. But I slept on my side. They were only a solution if I was lying on my back. The only time I ever lay in that horizontal position was when I masturbated. And why was I suddenly thinking about the angry artist? Sadly, the thought of touching myself immediately brought on unwanted images of him. I didn't want to think of him that way. He was a jerk; he didn't deserve to be the object of my lust. But he'd smelled so fucking good, like spice and musk and man. We don't have control over what we fantasize about. The fact that he was mean and unattainable made him that much more likely to be an object of my forbidden thoughts. Just like I learned in psychology class back in college, thought suppression often leads to obsession. If you tell yourself not to think about something, then you'll think about it even more.

Slipping my hands down my pants, I began to massage my clit. God, I didn't even know his name. This was sick, but at the moment it didn't matter. I imagined him over me, pushing into me, fucking me angrily. All the while, the hint of barking was still in the background as I rocked back and forth, bringing myself to one of the most earth-shattering climaxes I'd ever experienced.

I collapsed back and managed to fall asleep for an hour.

The mid-morning sun streamed through the window. Blinking my groggy eyes open, I noticed the barking had stopped. The animals must have been out for a walk.

I had a couple of hours before I was due to report to work, so I decided to look up the phone number for the building owner. There was a management office in the building, but the woman who worked there was pretty lax. Suspecting she wouldn't take my barking complaint seriously, I figured I'd go straight to the top. I'd only ever dealt with the woman in the rental office and had never spoken to the landlord.

An internet search pulled up the name D.H. Hennessey, LLC. There was a phone number to contact them, but it opened to a general voice mailbox with an automated greeting. I wanted to talk to someone in person, so I hung up without leaving a message. I noticed that the address listed was on the first floor of this building. Deciding to head down there, I slipped on a dress and some shoes and brushed my hair.

Knocking on the door, I took a deep breath then waited. When the door opened, the sight of him nearly made me fall over.

Angry Artist was standing there, shirtless and wearing that damn beanie again. My heart was pounding. Sweat was pouring down his chiseled chest, and I swore my mouth actually watered.

"Can I help you?" It was the same thing he'd asked me when he opened his apartment door. This felt like déjà vu, an episode of *The Twilight Zone* or a bad dream where no matter which door I opened, he would be there.

"What are you doing here?"

"This is my place."

"No. Your apartment is next door to mine."

"That's right. That's my apartment. This is my *place*. My art studio and gym."

"This was the address listed for the landlord."

A wry smile spread across his face. Suddenly, I felt like the stupidest person in the world as it dawned on me: he *was* the landlord. That was why the prick had encouraged me to issue a formal complaint.

"You're D.H. Hennessey..."

"Yes. And you're Chelsea Jameson. Excellent credit, great references...chronic complainer."

"Well, this explains a lot...how you're able to get away with defacing the property and being an overall asshole to your neighbors."

"I would hardly compare my creating *art* to defacing property. Have you not looked around this entire neighborhood? It's an art mecca. Mine is far from the only mural. And you're overreacting about the dogs. So, the real asshole in this situation? Debatable."

Behind him, I could see multiple canvases of spray-painted artwork as well as a weight bench and other workout equipment.

"Where are the dogs now?"

"They're napping."

"Dogs nap?"

"Yes. They nap. They're catching up on sleep because your bitching kept them up this morning." He cracked a smile. That made me realize just how much this exchange was actually amusing him.

"Clearly the D stands for dick?"

He didn't immediately respond, and a little staring contest ensued before he said, "The D stands for Damien."

Damien.

Of course he had to have a hot name, too.

"Damien...like from that movie *The Omen*? Fitting."
I looked around. "Why do you list this space as your address for tenants?"

"Oh, I don't know. Maybe I don't want crazy people who compare me to the anti-Christ showing up at my residence at all hours."

I couldn't help but laugh a little. This was a lost cause. "Alright, well, clearly this visit was in vain, so enjoy your workout."

♦ ♦ ♦

That afternoon, members of the San Francisco Symphony paid a visit to the youth center. They put on a small performance just for us. Watching the smiles on the kids' faces as they toyed around with the fancy instruments served as yet another reminder of how much I loved my job.

While everyone was focused on our guests, I noticed one of the teens, Ariel Sandoval, hiding crouched down in a corner with her phone. Wireless devices were against center rules, since this was supposed to be a place for learning. The teenagers with phones had to leave them in a bin at the front desk and retrieve them on the way out.

"Ariel, is everything alright? You should really be engaging with everyone else."

She shook her head no. "I'm sorry. I know I'm not supposed to have my phone. But I need it. And no, I'm not okay."

I sat down on the ground next to her. The floor was cold against my butt. "What's wrong?"

"It's Kai. I'm stalking Facebook now to see if any-one's tagged him."

Her boyfriend, Kai, was also a regular here and played on the center's basketball team. He was the object of more than one girl's affections. When I discovered Ariel and Kai were dating, it worried me, not only because of their ages—they were both fifteen—but because of Kai's popularity.

So, it came as absolutely no surprise when she said, "I think he's seeing someone else."

"How do you know?"

"He hasn't been coming here after school for the past week, and my brother said he saw Kai at the mall with a girl."

My heart sank. I wanted to tell her that she was probably right about him, but I wasn't sure she was emotionally ready to hear that.

"Well, don't jump to any conclusions until you confront him, but you should definitely talk to him. Better to know these things than to be blindsided later. You don't want to waste your time with someone who isn't honest."

Didn't I know that.

Even though Elec hadn't technically cheated on me physically, he had emotionally cheated.

Ariel wiped her eyes then turned to me. "Can I ask you something?"

"Sure."

"Whatever happened between you and Elec?"

My stomach dropped. I wasn't expecting her to bring him up, and it was way too long of a story to rehash.

Elec used to be everyone's favorite youth counselor. When he left the center, the kids were devastated. It had been common knowledge around here that we were boyfriend and girlfriend; everyone had gotten a real kick out of that.

"You mean you want to know why we broke up?"

"Yeah."

If I was going to sum it all up in a single sentence, there was only one response. "He fell in love with someone else."

Ariel looked confused. "How can you be in love with one person and just fall in love with someone else?"

Ah. The question of the year.

"I'm trying to figure that out myself, Ariel."

"I remember how he acted around you. It seemed like you guys were in love."

"I thought we were," I whispered.

"Do you think he really didn't love you at all...or was it just that he loved the other girl more?"

It was as if this fifteen-year-old girl had searched into my soul and picked out the one question that I'd asked myself the most. I wanted to be honest with her.

"I'm not sure if there are different levels of love, or if his leaving meant that he never loved me at all. I don't understand if it's possible to just stop loving someone. I'm trying to work through these very questions. But the bottom line is, if someone is cheating on you, they don't love you."

She stared off. "Yeah."

Nudging her with my shoulder, I grinned. "The good news, though? You are still so young, and there is plenty of time to find the right one if it's not Kai. You're at a very difficult age right now, probably the most difficult stage of your life. Both you and he are hormonal and just discovering who you are."

"What about you?"

"What *about* me?"

"Have you found someone else?"

"No." I paused, looking down at my shoes. "I'm not sure I will."

"Why not?"

How could I possibly shatter this young girl's hopes? How could I admit aloud that I didn't think I could ever trust another man again? That was my own personal issue, and I refused to taint her with my dark cloud of doubt.

"You know what? Anything is possible, Ariel." I smiled.

If only I believed my own words.

CHAPTER **THREE**

Hole in the Wall

"I just have a couple of minutes before I have to get my makeup done before the show, but tell me what's going on," Jade said.

I had texted my sister earlier: *You're never going to believe this. Call me.*

It was right after discovering the identity of my landlord.

"So, you remember Angry Artist?"

"You banged him?"

"No!"

"What is it, then?"

"Turns out...he owns the building."

"No way!"

"This is not good."

"Why not? I think it's great!" she said.

"In what way? Now, I'll never get those dogs to shut up."

"No, I mean when you guys start boning, you won't even have to pay rent."

"I'm not going to bone him. Because he's a jackass. And even if in some bizarre universe, I were doing that...I would *never* not pay my rent. That would make me like a whore."

She laughed. "Mmmm."

"What?"

"Angry sex is the best sex, you know."

"Yeah, you've said that before. I can't say I've ever experienced it."

"Well, when you have it with...what's his name?"

"Damien. That's his name. I'm not going to be having angry sex with Damien."

"Damien? Like from *The Omen*?"

"That's what I said to him! I mentioned that when he told me his name. He didn't seem too happy."

"When does he seem happy about anything?"

Snickering, I said, "True."

"That's hot, though. Shit...they're calling me. I have to go."

"Break a leg!"

"Fuck a landlord!"

"You're nuts."

"Love you."

"Love you, too."

Conversations with my sister always put me in a good mood.

With an hour to go before my phone therapy session, I decided to go grab some takeout. On my way downstairs, I ran into Murray, the building super. He was sweeping the stairs and whistling while the metal from the dozens of keys he carried attached to his belt clanked together.

"Hey, Murray!"

"Well, hello there, gorgeous lady."

"You don't normally work on Tuesdays."

"Going through a bit of a rough patch. Boss let me pick up some extra hours."

"By boss...you mean D.H. Hennessey?"

"Yeah...Damien."

"You know, I just met him. I had no clue that my anti-social, next-door neighbor with the barking dogs was actually the landlord."

Murray chuckled. "Yeah, he doesn't really advertise that fact."

"What's his deal?"

"You mean how does a young guy like that own this place?"

"Well, yeah, that, but also why is he so mean?"

"His bark is way bigger than his bite."

"No pun intended there?"

"Right." He laughed. "Deep down, Damien's good people. Lets me work extra whenever I need to and real generous at Christmas time...even if he does seem to have a stick up his ass sometimes."

"A stick? It's more like a pole." I snorted.

"Some days, yeah. But hey, he puts meals on my table, so you won't hear that from me." Murray winked.

"He's pretty talented, though," I said. "I'll give him that."

"Smart, too. Believe me. Rumor has it, he graduated from MIT."

"MIT? Are you kidding?"

"Nope. Can't judge a book by its cover. Invented something. Sold the rights to the patent apparently then used the money to invest in real estate. Now he just collects the rent and does what he wants...makes art."

"Wow. That's...pretty darn impressive."

"You didn't hear that from me, though."

"Got it, Murray."

"Fancy plans tonight?"

"Nope. Just heading to grab some dinner and bring it back to the apartment."

"Well, enjoy."

"I will."

Twenty minutes later, I returned to my apartment with tostones and arroz blanco con gandules from my favorite restaurant, Casa del Sol.

After scarfing down my food, I sat in my room and meditated for a bit in preparation for my phone therapy session with *Dr. Veronica Little: Relationship Trauma Specialist.*

At two hundred dollars per one-hour session, Dr. Little wasn't cheap. It was my mother who suggested I see someone to talk about my feelings. While I wasn't sure if it was working, I continued to go along with it every Tuesday evening at eight-thirty.

Perhaps, I should have forwarded the bills to Elec.

◆ ◆ ◆

I had my therapist on speakerphone while I folded laundry in the bedroom.

"You bring that question up a lot, Chelsea. Whether or not Elec truly loved you. I think part of why we can't seem to move forward from that can be explained by the concept of the unicorn."

21

"The unicorn? What is that?"

"A unicorn is something that is mythically beautiful and unattainable, right?"

"Okay..."

"That was what Greta was to Elec. He'd ruled out a possibility of love with her because she was forbidden. He was able to fall in love with you in the meantime. That love was quite genuine. However, when the unicorn suddenly becomes attainable, that changes everything. The power of the unicorn is extremely potent."

"So, what you're saying is that Elec really did love me but only when he basically thought that being with Greta was an impossibility. She was his unicorn. I wasn't a unicorn."

"That's exactly right...you were not his unicorn."

"I wasn't his unicorn," I repeated in a whisper. "Can I just—"

"I'm sorry, Chelsea. Our time is up for today. We'll explore this issue a little more next Tuesday.

"Okay. Thanks, Dr. Little."

Blowing out a long breath, I plopped onto my bed and tried to make sense of what she'd just said.

Unicorn. Hmm.

My body stilled at the sound of laughing.

At first I thought I was imagining it.

It was coming from behind my headboard.

I jumped up.

"Unicorn. What the fuck!" he said in his deep voice before cackling some more.

Damien.

He'd been listening to my therapy session!

My stomach dropped.

How could he hear all that through the wall?

"You've been eavesdropping on me?" I asked.

"No. You've been interrupting my work."

"I don't understand."

"There's a hole in the wall. I can't help but hear your hot mess phone conversations when I'm working."

"A...hole in the wall? You've known about this hole?"

"Yes. I haven't gotten around to fixing it. Must have been there before I bought the building. Probably used to be a glory hole or some shit."

"You've been listening to me...through a glory hole?"

"No. You've been subjecting me to asinine conversations with people who are ripping you off...through a glory hole."

"You are such a..."

"A-hole?"

CHAPTER **FOUR**

You Bacon Me Crazy

The following day in work, I couldn't help but obsess over the fact that Damien had been listening to my private conversations. Was that even legal?

The night before, I'd stopped our communication through the wall pretty quickly after his revelation, retreating to the living room and polishing off a bottle of Zinfandel with a side of cookie dough.

Thankfully, I was too busy at the youth center today to let it totally consume me, since it was the evening of the center's annual breakfast-for-dinner function. Once a year, the staff cooked a giant breakfast in the industrial-sized kitchen for all of the kids. My responsibility was frying pounds of bacon.

On the walk home, literally reeking of bacon grease, I resumed my obsessing over the hole in the wall. I'd noticed that the opening was actually right behind my bed. My only saving grace was that if my room was adjacent to his office, maybe he wasn't typically in there as much at night as he would have been if it were another room. Maybe he hadn't heard all of my sessions. Or maybe I was just kidding myself.

Exactly how much did Damien know? I got into some really private stuff with Dr. Little. Backtracking through it all during the walk home, I nearly knocked into a fruit stand.

Feeling fired up, when I arrived at my building, I impulsively passed my door and charged over to Damien's apartment. The dogs, who were normally quiet in the evenings, were barking up a storm for some reason.

Knocking frantically, I planned to demand that Damien tell me exactly what he'd heard through my wall. When he didn't open, I knocked harder. The barking intensified, but still no answer. Just as I was about to turn around and leave, the door flew open.

Damien's dark hair was drenched, and beads of water were dripping from his forehead down to his chest. He was completely wet. The carved V at the bottom of his abs was proof that all of that working out downstairs was paying off. A small towel wrapped around his waist was the only piece of fabric on his otherwise naked body.

Rippled muscular body.

Holy shit.

He was obscenely hot.

I pried my eyes upward. "What are you doing answering the door like that?"

"What am *I* doing? What are *you* doing, knocking on my door like a lunatic? I tried to avoid having to get out of the shower, but I thought there was something seriously wrong. And what the hell is that smell? That's not bacon, is it?"

"Yes. I was cooking bacon at work. I—"

"Fuck!" he growled through his teeth.

"I came to talk to you about fixing the hole in my wall, but clearly—"

Before I could finish my sentence, the two black rottweilers had charged toward where I was standing, pouncing on me as their weight knocked me onto my ass. They frantically licked my face, neck, and chest as I lay on the hallway floor. They were also biting at the material of my shirt.

Terrified, I managed to cry out, "Get them off of me!"

Damien struggled with the massive animals to finally remove them off my body. My face was sticky from slobber.

He forced them back into his apartment as their paws scratched and slipped against the hardwood floor. Damien then returned to the hallway and slammed the door behind him to lock the dogs inside.

He reached out his hand, and I took it as he slowly but forcefully lifted me off of the ground as if my body were light as a feather.

Speechless, I looked down at myself. A huge chunk of material was missing from the front of my shirt, exposing my bra.

He looked liked he was struggling with what to say. "Chelsea, I—"

"Are you happy now? Look what they did to me."

"Fuck. Really? No. I'm not happy. The dogs are obsessed with bacon, okay? It's like their catnip. That's why they jumped on you. Why the hell did you have to come in here reeking of it?"

"I need to go," I said, heading back toward my door.

He tried to stop me. "Wait."

"No. Please. I just want to forget this ever happened."

I retreated back to my apartment, leaving Damien standing there with his hands on his waist.

◆ ◆ ◆

After a hot shower, I'd calmed down a bit, starting to think that maybe I had overreacted in blaming Damien for the dogs' freak-out. He'd done his best to get them off of me quickly, not an easy feat considering he was also gripping his towel to keep from revealing his junk.

I was also pretty sure he was trying to apologize before I'd cut him off. Still, I had a bone to pick with him about the eavesdropping. But nothing was going to get addressed tonight. I was way too tired and feeling defeated.

Grabbing my purse, I decided to walk to the bodega and pick up something simple to make for dinner. Nearly tripping over a small bag on my way out, I bent down to pick it up and recognized that it was from Casper's, the funny t-shirt store in town.

Inside was a rust-colored shirt in size small with white writing. It said *You Bacon Me Crazy* and had a smiley face with lips made out of bacon strips.

There was no note inside, but I knew it had to be from Damien.

On the return trip home with my groceries, I kept thinking about how he'd gone out of his way to buy the t-shirt as a peace offering. Was I being a bitch and overreacting about everything from the hole in the wall to the bacon attack? I honestly didn't know. All I knew was that I didn't really like the overly sensitive person I'd become over the past year.

After making myself a quick dinner of spaghetti and marinara sauce, I went back to my room to read. Every time I sat up in bed, I couldn't help but wonder if Damien was on the other side of the wall.

When I thought I heard a noise behind me, I asked, "Are you there?"

After a brief pause came the deep sound of his voice. "Yes. I'm working in my office. I'm not eavesdropping on you."

Not really expecting an answer, my heart started to pound.

After a minute passed, I broke the ice. "Thank you for the shirt."

"Well, I owed you a shirt...and an apology."

"I know I really didn't give you a chance to apologize. I'm sorry."

He didn't say anything, so I continued, "What are their names? The dogs."

"Dudley and Drewfus."

"Cute. Where did you come up with those?"

"I didn't."

"Who did?"

"My ex."

Interesting.

"I see."

"Why are they so quiet at night...like right now...but so noisy in the morning?"

"They're not here."

"Where are they?"

"They're with her. We share custody. She drops them off here on the way to work in the morning, and I return them at night."

"Wow. I was wondering why I never hear them in the evenings. Now, it makes sense." I had to know. "So, you used to be married?"

"No. Ex-girlfriend."

"She used to live here with you and the dogs?"

"You know, for someone who didn't want me knowing her business, you sure are nosey as fuck."

"Sorry. But it's only fair, don't you think, after you've heard so much about me?"

He sighed. "Yes. She used to live here."

"What happened?"

"What do you think happened? We broke up."

"I know that. But I mean...why didn't it work out?"

"There's not always a clear answer to that question. It's not always as simple as..." He hesitated. "Someone fucking their stepsister."

Oh. My. God.

He's such an asshole!

He'd definitely been listening to more than just the last session. Feeling ashamed, I'd never told anyone except Jade and Dr. Little that the woman Elec left me for was actually his stepsister, whom he'd apparently been in love with for years—since he was a teenager.

When I didn't say anything, he chuckled. "I'm sorry. That was bad. I'm going to hell."

I remained silent, shaking my head in disbelief.

He continued, "That really happened? Sounds like something out of a bad book."

"Yes, it really happened. What else did you hear?"

"Christ, I'm not judging you, Chelsea. I could care less about all of it. It doesn't matter."

"It matters to *me.*"

"That therapist is ripping you off."

"Why do you say that?"

"She's pulling unicorns out of her ass just to get you to keep questioning everything so you keep paying her money. Tell me this. After all these weeks, are you any closer to feeling better, figuring it all out?"

"No."

"That's because sometimes there isn't a satisfying explanation for everything. You want an answer? Shit happens. There's your answer. People fall out of love, in love, fuck up. It's part of life. You didn't do anything wrong. Stop trying to figure out what you did wrong."

Closing my eyes, I let his words resonate. To my surprise, my eyes were welling up. Not because he was yelling at me, but because it was the first time it really sank in that there was nothing I could have done to stop what happened. And that maybe it wasn't all my fault.

I finally spoke again. "I wasn't always so insecure. It's just...the experience with him—with Elec—has really been a defining moment in my life because it's made me question everything. I thought I did everything right to make that relationship work. I believed he loved me, and I felt safe with him, saw my entire future with him. I would have bet my life on it. I just feel like I won't be able to ever trust anyone with my heart again. That scares me, because I don't want to end up alone. I really thought he was the one."

"Well, clearly, he wasn't. You just have to accept that and move on. I know that's easier said than done, but that's what it comes down to. You have no choice but to accept it, so it's up to you whether you want to waste more time living in the past, trying to solve an insoluble problem instead of moving on with your life."

God, he was right.

I cracked a smile. "How did you get to be so smart?"

"This is all common sense."

"No. Not just this. I mean...MIT?"

"How did you find out about that?"

"So, the rumor's true?"

"Yes. I went there, but it's not something I brag about."

"You should be very proud of yourself. That's amazing."

"It's not that amazing. People fighting for our country...kids battling cancer...those are amazing people. Sitting in a physics class with a bunch of other nerds is hardly amazing."

"You're hardly a nerd, Damien."

"Not on the surface, no."

"I would have never guessed based on..."

"Based on what?"

"How you look...that you went to MIT."

"Why? Because I have ink and work out?"

"No, it's not that. It's just you're..."

Effing gorgeous. And no one as hot as you could possibly be equally as smart.

"Never mind," I said.

I closed my eyes again, relishing the new clarity brought on by his straightforward advice.

After a long moment of silence, he said, "I'm headed out. Murray's coming to patch the hole in the wall to-morrow afternoon. If you're at work, he'll let himself in."

"Thank you."

Oddly, I wasn't sure I minded the hole anymore.

CHAPTER **FIVE**

Burnin' Down the House

My landlord followed through with his promise. The very next day, Murray had plastered over the hole, thus killing any chance of future impromptu therapy sessions with Dr. Damien.

In fact, an entire week went by without a single altercation between D.H. Hennessey and me.

The dogs were still barking every morning, but I didn't dare go near them long enough to complain. Now that I knew his ex dropped them off, if I happened to be up, I'd watch from the window to see if I could catch a glimpse of her.

One day, I managed to look out at just the right time, spotting a girl around my age with short brown hair racing into the apartment building with the two rottweilers. I then ran to my door, cracking it open a bit to spy as she passed down the hallway. She'd whizzed by so fast that I really didn't get a very good look, except to see that she was curvier than me.

After five minutes, I could hear her footsteps as she left his apartment. Watching from the window as she ran through the courtyard, I wondered what type of a relationship they had now, whether it was amicable, whether they ever still had sex. I wondered who ended it. I also wondered why I was thinking about something that wasn't any of my business—why as of late, I was constantly thinking about Damien. One thing was for certain: it was a hell of a lot better than constantly thinking about Elec.

That same afternoon on the walk to work, I noticed that Damien had added quite a bit to the mural since last check. There was now a section depicting a bunch of pyramids.

Chills ran through me as I marveled at his talent and all of the intricate details of his work, the way the colors all blended and faded into each other. I wondered if there was any significance to the scenic images. Damien Hennessey was one complex human being.

When I arrived at the youth center, Ariel was waiting in my office. She looked like she'd been crying.

Shit.

Even though I knew what had likely transpired, I asked, "What happened?"

"I was right about Kai. He *was* cheating on me."

"I'm so sorry to hear that."

After letting her vent for the better part of an hour, I finally said, "There's a reason for the serenity prayer, Ariel. You ever hear of it?"

"The one about praying for the strength to accept the things we can't change? Yeah, my mom taught it to me a long time ago."

"Yes. That's the one. I'm still working on that my-self, but really, we have no choice but to accept certain things. All we can do is try our best to move on."

I smiled to myself, realizing that I was basically giv-ing Ariel the same advice that Damien had given me. It was so much easier dishing out that advice than adher-ing to it.

On the walk home that night, for some unknown reason, I felt more at peace than I had in a long time. I decided to pick up one of my favorite frozen individual lasagnas from the organic section of the market. I'd bake it and have it with some wine, maybe watch something on Netflix. I was getting excited about it.

Boy, my life was pretty pathetic.

After I arrived at the apartment, I placed the lasa-gna into the preheated toaster oven. It would take forty minutes to bake all the way through. That would leave me just enough time to take a bath, shave my legs and maybe read a little in the tub.

It was probably the most relaxing bath I'd ever tak-en. Surrounded by candles, I immersed myself in an ad-dicting book Jade had gifted me. It was actually a ménage romance. I didn't normally read such kinky stuff, but she was adamant that I would love it, especially since it was about two men and a woman instead of the other way around. I ended up getting really into it—so much so, that I somehow fell asleep after pleasuring myself to one of the hottest scenes.

The sound of the smoke alarm, and the smell of burning cheese caused me to jolt up from the tub. Grabbing a towel, I ran to the kitchen to find flames shooting from my toaster oven. It was on fire!

Panicking, I grabbed a bowl and began to fill it with water. Before I had a chance to dump the water onto anything, my door burst open. The next thing I knew, Damien was charging toward me with an extinguisher and yelling at me to get back.

Everything happened so fast. I just stood there numb, clutching the towel around me as he doused the flames.

When the fire was fully out, Damien and I both stood there in silence looking at the charred remains of my beloved toaster oven. The damage was mostly contained to the oven itself, but the countertop looked like it might have been charred a bit, too.

I coughed from the smoke.

"What the fuck," he muttered, still staring at the scene of the disaster.

"I'm so sorry. I'll pay for whatever damage was done to the counter. I—"

"How did this happen?"

"Frozen lasagna...it burned."

"No. I mean...*how* did it happen?"

"I was reading a book in the bathtub and—"

"You were reading in the tub," he interrupted, gritting his teeth. "You were READING in the tub while you were also cooking something that almost burned my goddamn building down?"

"No. You don't understand. I—"

Damien started to charge toward the bathroom.

"Where are you going?"

"I want to see what book is so important that it nearly cost you your life."

Fuck.

No.

Fuck!

It was too late. He'd already picked up my Kindle off the floor. My heart was beating faster than it probably ever had.

After he took a look at the title and swiped through a few pages, he turned to me and laughed incredulously. "Nice. Real nice. The apartment was about to burn down while you were in here reading about two guys drilling a girl in every orifice," he huffed before tossing the Kindle aside. He was half-smiling when he said, "You little perv."

Mortified could not even begin to describe how I was feeling. I wanted to cry, but I was too frozen in shock to form tears.

"I fell asleep. I'm sorry. I didn't mean for this to happen."

"What would've happened if I wasn't home?"

"I don't know. I don't want to even think about it." The shock must have worn off a bit, because the first teardrop fell from my eyes.

Damien let out a deep breath when he noticed me crying. "Fuck. Don't cry."

"I'm really sorry about this."

Damien left the bathroom and began going around and opening all of the windows. Still dressed in only a towel, I followed him around like an idiot.

"The apartment needs to air out. It's not good to breathe this shit in," he said.

"Okay."

"Do you eat pizza?" he asked.

That was a random question. He was so unpredict-able.

"Yes."

"Get dressed then come next door. Give the smoke a chance to dissipate."

Damien grabbed the extinguisher and left the apartment just as fast as he'd barreled through it.

Did he just invite me over for dinner after I almost burned his building down?

Coughing, I ran to my room and changed, choosing a tiny black sundress. I felt stupid for even attempting to get dolled up when Damien was just offering me shelter and food after my near-disaster. But for some reason, I wanted to look good.

Could this night have been any stranger?

♦ ♦ ♦

My palms were sweaty as I stood outside his door.

Get it together, Chelsea.

Knocking lightly, I took a deep breath in.

The door opened sooner than I was ready for.

"Well, if it isn't Firestarter," he drawled. "Come on in."

"*Firestarter* and *The Omen*...between the two of us, we make a couple of terrifying old movies. Did you invite me over here to mock me, by the way?"

Damien lifted his brow. "Did you expect anything less? Yet...you still came."

He'd changed into a fitted gray sweater and dark jeans and smelled like he'd just sprayed on a fresh coating of cologne.

"You changed," I stupidly said.

"Well, I smelled like a chimney. So, I kind of had to."

"Right."

He wasn't wearing the beanie anymore, and for the first time, I noticed that his dark hair had a slight curl to it. He also had some sort of white powder on his cheek.

"What is that all over your face?"

Wiping his cheek, he said, "It's flour."

"I thought you were ordering pizza." I looked over at his kitchen counter and saw some chopped up vegetables and jarred sauce. "Wait...you're...making it?"

"Yeah. Homemade is better and healthier. I use whole grain dough and low fat cheese."

"So, are you like a health nut or something? You do work out a lot. I know that much."

"I try to take good care of myself, yes."

"Me, too. I try. I don't always succeed, but I try."

"Right. Frozen lasagna and all." He winked. "I'd say that was an epic fail all around."

"I'd probably have to agree with you."

We smiled at each other. I was relieved that he was making light of everything. When his eyes lingered on mine for a few moments, I felt flush. It actually became uncomfortable because I worried that my attraction to him was somehow transparent.

Needing to distract myself from his gaze, I looked around and said, "It's so quiet here without the dogs."

"I know. I don't like it." Damien walked to the other side of the counter and began pouring sauce over the rolled-out dough.

"You miss them when they're gone at night?" I asked, taking a seat on one of the stools.

"Yeah."

"I've seen her dropping them off. What's her name?"

He hesitated then said, "Jenna."

"Hmm."

He stopped what he was doing for a moment. "What, Chelsea?"

"What do you mean?"

"You look like you want to ask me something else."

"Nothing...it's just...what happened between the two of you?"

"For the record, she *isn't* my stepsister."

Jerk.

"Well, thank God for that."

"She's my cousin." He laughed.

I reached over, took a little of his flour and flicked it at him. "Clearly, you don't know how to be serious."

"I *was* being serious when I told you how much I miss my dogs when they're not around."

"You know what? It's none of my business."

"What do you want to know?"

"Did you break up with her?"

"Yes."

"Why?"

"She wanted things I couldn't give her."

"Like what?"

"She wanted to get married and have kids."

"You don't want those things?" When he didn't answer, I asked, "Or you didn't want them with *her*?"

"It's complicated."

"Okay. Like I said, it's none of my business."

"The bottom line is...when I first met her, she told me she didn't want those things. Then, over time, she changed her mind. I didn't want to keep her from living the kind of life she envisioned for herself."

"So, you broke up with her."

"Yes."

"Did you love her?"

"I honestly don't know."

I stared off into space a bit. "Okay. If you have to think about it, you probably didn't."

"I know what you're trying to do, Chelsea."

"What?"

"You're trying to analyze my situation to somehow find answers to your own shit. Not all guys are the same. We're fucked-up for different reasons. I hope you stopped seeing Dr. Fuckwad, by the way."

"Actually, I did. I took your advice. She wasn't making much sense toward the end."

"Good. You should be looking forward, not backwards, anyway."

"That's what I'm trying to do...you know, when I'm not accidentally burning down buildings."

"You said it, not me," he said, placing the two round trays into the preheated oven. "These are going in for a half-hour. What do you like to drink?"

"Anything you have is fine."

"Rhubarb Juice Concentrate, then?" he teased.

"Ugh...no."

"What do you *like*?"

"Wine."

"What kind?"

"Any kind is fine."

"Do you have a problem saying what you want or something?"

"Seriously, any kind is fine...except Moscato."

"See...now, what if I'd opened up Moscato? You would've drank it and been miserable."

"Probably."

"Don't be afraid to say what you want. Life is too short."

"Okay, then. Do you have Chardonnay?"

"No."

"White Zinfandel?"

"No."

I laughed. "What do you have?"

"Beer."

"Beer..."

"You can't always get what you want. But don't be afraid to ask."

"Water is fine."

God, I needed a glass of wine.

CHAPTER **SIX**

The Dating Game

Steam filled the kitchen as Damien took the two pizza pies out of the oven. I couldn't help admiring the curvature of his ass as he bent down.

Digging my teeth into my bottom lip, I said, "That looks really good."

"Wait till you taste."

I bet.

Stop where your mind is going, Chelsea.

I cleared my throat. "Pretty confident in your cooking skills, huh?"

"Pizza is like sex. It's hard to fuck it up."

Chuckling, I said under my breath, "I don't really remember."

"That long, huh?"

Heat permeated my cheeks. "I didn't even realize I'd said that out loud."

He pointed to his ears. "Supersonic hearing, remember?"

"That's right."

"So, it's been a while?"

"Well, it's going on a year since my breakup. I haven't been with anyone else after him. And I've only been with two men in my life."

"Both at once, I take it?"

"No." Grabbing the napkin next to me, I rolled it and threw it at him. "It was only a book, Damien!"

"You mean you don't really want to be blindfolded and fucked in the ass with a cock in your mouth?"

"No, I truly don't."

"I'm just messing with you. If we were all really representative of the things that help get our rocks off, I'd be one pretty sick fuck."

"I don't want to know." I shook my head and sighed.

"What's that sigh for?" he asked as he placed a plate of pizza in front of me.

"You know way too much about me, Damien Hennessey."

"By accident, yes."

"Still." I blew on the pizza and took a bite. "You owe me. I want more dirt on you. Tell me something I don't know."

"Your rent is going up in January."

My mouth was full. "Are you serious?"

"Actually, I am. The property taxes went up significantly. I have no choice but to raise it fifty bucks across the board."

"That sucks. But that wasn't the kind of information I was hoping for. Maybe we can negotiate." The way the words had come out of my mouth made it sound like I was propositioning him. That was not how I meant it.

God, I hoped that didn't sound bad.

He chuckled and blew on his pizza. "You know what you are, Chelsea Jameson? You're like pizza. Hot...but bad for me in large doses."

I tried to sway the conversation, but the only thing I could think to ask was, "You think I'm nuts, don't you?"

"Nah. I know you're not really crazy. When I called the youth center to confirm your employment, I couldn't get them off the phone. They wouldn't stop talking about how wonderful you are with the kids there. I figured you were good people. So, even when you were being a pain in the ass about the dogs, I never thought you were a bad person."

"I didn't realize you called my job."

"I check everyone out thoroughly before giving them a place here. I don't want the stress of having to evict people. But even good people sometimes take advantage."

"Like not paying their rent?"

"Yeah...but it's one thing if they can't afford it. What pisses me off is when they're late and just bought a brand new car, or they're going out to eat every fucking night. That's one of the advantages of living in the building you own. I can see the shit that goes on. If you've ever seen me lose it on someone, it's only because they're bullshitting me, telling me they can't pay their rent when they're fucking driving a better car than I am."

"I used to think you were just being mean. I made assumptions about you before I knew certain things. I'm sorry for that."

"Oh no, I quite liked being called Angry Artist."

I almost asked him how he knew about that term but soon realized that would have been a dumb question.

His stare burned into mine once again. I found myself having to look away.

I suspected there were many layers to Damien. I wanted to peel them slowly. It had been so long since I'd wanted to know everything about someone. It scared me how much he knew about me, though.

"Do you think I'm pathetic?" I suddenly asked.

"Why would you say that?"

"After all the stuff you overheard?"

"No. I really don't. You have every right to be upset by what your ex did to you. The guy told you he loved you. He led you to believe certain things. He promised you something, and he faltered on it. You don't do that to someone."

"You never told Jenna you loved her?"

"No. I didn't. And I never promised her anything, either. I don't make promises I can't keep. That's the difference between him and me. The thing is, you're letting his mistakes reflect on you somehow. You didn't do anything wrong but be a loving girlfriend. He didn't deserve you."

My heart suddenly felt heavy. "Thank you for saying that."

"But you need to move on."

His words were sobering. Of course I knew I needed to move past my issues about Elec. It was just easier said than done.

"I guess I don't really know the best way to do that."

"Stop focusing on it. Stop giving it power. You need distractions to do that. You have to put yourself out there. You need to get in the dating game."

"That's what I mean by I don't know how to do it. I haven't ever dated."

Damien squinted in disbelief. "How is that possible?"

"I'd just broken up with my high school boyfriend a few months before Elec started working at the youth center. Elec and I became friends, and then it eventually morphed into something more. So, I went from one serious relationship right into another. I've literally never dated. I don't even know how people go about dating nowadays. Do you go to bars? What do you do to meet people?"

"What do I do...or what do most people do? All I need to do is just...be. Women flock to me."

"Seriously?"

"I'm kidding. Sort of." He winked. "Someone like you? You should do online dating. But only meet people in public places. Otherwise, it's too risky."

"I wouldn't even know where to begin."

"It'll take ten minutes. You just need a picture of yourself to create a profile." He suddenly got up.

"Where are you going?"

"Getting my laptop. We'll do it right now."

Hit with an onslaught of disappointment, I hoped my face didn't give me away. I hated that I felt this way, but it bummed me out that Damien was so quick to pawn me off. It basically closed the door on any potential interest in me before the door really even opened, I suppose.

"What are you...my pimp?"

"No. But you seem clueless, like you could use some guidance. So, I'm offering to get you started. Unless you don't want my help."

Hell, if he wasn't interested in me, I might as well let him help me.

"I guess it couldn't hurt."

"Alright, then." He pulled up the site and spoke as he typed. "Your user name is Chelsea Jameson, and your password is fire3...since you like threesomes."

"Thanks a lot. That will be easy enough to remember." *Jackass.*

He continued entering information. "Name...Chelsea. Age..." Damien looked at me for clarification.

"Twenty-five."

"Height?"

"Five foot four."

"Weight?"

"They ask that?"

"They do, but you don't have to put it down."

"Skip...on principle."

"Bra size?"

"They ask that?"

"No."

"Jerk." I smiled.

Damien continued entering my information. "Hair... blonde. Eyes...blue. Okay, now they're asking personality questions. Hobbies and interests?"

"Reading..."

"Of course. Reading ménage!" After typing that in, he tapped on the keys to delete the last part. "Okay. Reading. Anything else?"

"Working with children, taking walks, and travel."

We continued going down the line as I tried to make myself sound as least boring as possible. The last question was the most superficial one.

"How would you rate yourself on a scale of physical attractiveness from one to ten?

"I can't rate myself."

"Ten," he quickly answered.

"Ten?"

"Yes."

"Are you just saying that?"

"No, I'm not. But here's the thing...even if you don't think you're a ten, you should still put down ten, because that exudes confidence. Confidence is sexy. But in your case, you really are a ten. You're beyond beautiful."

Feeling like I was melting into my seat, I said, "Thank you."

"You're lucky that's the case, too. It helps balance out the crazy." He winked.

"Thanks," I laughed then cleared my throat. "What next?"

"Your profile is done. We just need to upload a picture. Do you have one in your phone you want to use?"

I sifted through the photos, and to my surprise, I hadn't taken one good picture of myself alone in the past six months. All of the decent shots, where I was smiling or made up, were with Elec.

"I like this one, but he's in it." I said, handing him the phone.

"That's him?"

"Yeah."

"Hmm." He scratched his chin as he examined the photo then said, "You could do better. Anyway, I'll crop him out."

"Can you?"

"Yeah. It's easy." Damien started messing around with it. "Okay. Done. See?" He turned the phone toward me. "You'd never know he was there except for that piece of black. It looks like a sweater over your shoulder."

It gave me a strange sense of satisfaction that Elec had been reduced to a mere garment of clothing.

"So what do we do now?"

"Now you have to figure out how to use it. I'll create an account if you want, and we can pretend to connect, so you can see how it works."

Pretend to connect. Was I a fool for thinking we were somehow already connecting?

"That would be good. So I don't make a fool out of myself later."

"Well, that very well may still happen."

Watching Damien as he input information about himself, I noticed he often licked the side of his mouth whenever he concentrated. Each time his tongue moved, I felt a tingle run through me.

I definitely wouldn't mind licking that spot for him.

He flipped the computer toward me. "Okay. I just made both of our accounts active. It's a free trial for thirty days. After that, it's forty-five dollars a month. You use this computer. I'll use my iPad."

A notification popped up on my screen. "Did you just poke me?"

"No."

"Someone poked me!"

"Believe me. You'd know it if I poked you."

"Seriously. Someone just poked me."

"Ignore him."

"Why? I see him now. His name is Jonathan. He's not that bad looking."

"You literally just became active a few seconds ago. He couldn't have had time to read your entire profile. He's just poking you because you're pretty. He only wants one thing...to fuck you. Stay away from him. I'm going to send you a request to chat."

A picture of Damien popped up on the screen. It was taken in his bathroom. It was a shockingly good selfie where the light happened to be shining at just the right angle into his eyes, making them appear like they were glowing. He was beautiful.

"I just accepted your request."

Damien: Hi.
Chelsea: Hi.
Damien: You're very pretty.
Chelsea: You're not so bad yourself.

He peeked over my computer. "Don't return his compliment so quickly. You already have the upper hand. You don't need to kiss his ass, especially with someone who starts off so corny."

Chelsea: I take that back. You're hideous.
Damien: This chat thing is kind of annoying, isn't it? Can I have your phone number so that we can talk?
Chelsea: Sure. It's 95-

He stopped me. "Don't give him your number yet. He could be a psychopath. You don't want him having your personal information."

I chuckled. "I think he *is* a psychopath."

Chelsea: Sorry, my pimp says I can't give you my number just yet.
Damien: Maybe we can meet up, then? I could pick you up.
Chelsea: Actually I'd prefer to meet you somewhere.

"Good girl. You didn't fall for my trap."

Damien: Sure. How about the restaurant inside the Westerly Hotel?
Chelsea: That would be okay.

He put his iPad down in frustration. "No. You choose the place to meet. You don't know what his motives are in getting you inside a hotel. He could plan to slip something in your drink and take you upstairs or some shit. Always choose the location."

Chelsea: On second thought, I'd prefer a different place.
Damien: You just tell me where.
Chelsea: How about the Starbucks on Powell Street downtown?

"Good. Coffee's very non-committal."

Damien: Okay. How about Saturday afternoon at 3?
Chelsea: Sounds good.
Damien: Looking forward to it. See you then.

"Well, that wass pretty easy," I said.

"You'll get used to it. Just always keep in control. You make the decisions."

"Can I ask you a question?"

"Does it matter?"

"Probably not."

"What?"

"How am I going to *know* that the guy isn't a bad person?"

"You can't really know a hundred percent. Use your instinct the best you can. And get his full name. I pay for this background check service. I'll run the same one I do on all the tenants to make sure any guy you date is legit."

"You'd do that for me?"

"What are friends for?"

"Oh...are we friends?" I joked.

"Yeah. Why not?"

And there it was: final confirmation of the fact that Damien wasn't interested in anything more with me.

Handing him back the laptop, I said, "I'd better get back. It's late."

"Oh, hey. Before you go." He walked over to the kitchen and unplugged the toaster oven before reaching it out to me. "Here."

"You're *giving me* your toaster oven?"

"I don't use it much. I get the impression it might be all you use to cook. Am I right?"

"Mostly, yes."

"So, here."

I took it. "Thank you. I'll give it back."

"No need. If I ever need to toast something, I'll just knock. *Loudly.* In case you're holed up with a ménage book in the bathroom."

I rolled my eyes. "Thanks again for dinner."

"Sweet dreams, Chelsea."

As I walked back to my smoky apartment, I couldn't help the smile on my face. I also couldn't help wishing the Saturday coffee date with Damien was real.

CHAPTER **SEVEN**

Change the Story

A couple of weeks later, it was Arts Night at the youth center, and I'd found myself in a major pickle.

The event was our biggest art-themed function of the year and the only one I was held fully responsible for organizing.

Many of the center sponsors would be showing up to view some performances put on by the kids. There were also various workshops that featured a few local celebrities. I'd lined up a jazz musician, an actress from a Bay Area theater group and an oil painter. The idea was to have one person from each category: music, theater, and visual arts.

At the last minute, the painter, Marcus Dubois, called to say his flight home from London was cancelled and that he wouldn't be able to make it. While the event would still have to go on without him, I knew that this wasn't going to look good in front of the donors and wouldn't bode well for center management or me.

Feeling desperate, I wracked my brain for a solution and immediately thought of Damien. I wondered if he would be willing to be my fill-in, if he'd be willing to demonstrate some of his talent. It would also include talking to the kids, which I wasn't sure he'd be comfortable with.

Damien and I had only casually hung out a couple of more times since the night he made me pizza. Both times I had initiated it, knocking on his door and inviting myself in. At no point had he ever really spoken about his art, so I wasn't sure how he would feel about running a workshop, especially on such late notice. But with two hours to go until people would be arriving, I was feeling desperate when I picked up the phone.

My heart was pounding when his voicemail kicked in.

My voice was shaky. "Hey, Damien." I cleared my throat. "It's Chelsea. I have sort of a huge favor to ask, but I'm not sure if it's something you would even consider. Basically, it's Arts Night here at the youth center. It's a huge event, and the biggest artist I had lined up, Marcus Dubois—you might have heard of him—bailed on me. We have all of these sponsors here and are trying to make a good impression and well, this just looks really bad. I'm kind of desperate and freaking out, so—"

BEEP.

His damn answering machine cut me off.

Shit!

Now, I would sound like a total desperado if I called back. Deciding to try to forget about it, I did my best to suck up my embarrassment about having no visual arts presenter. I would explain what happened as best I could and cut my losses.

Feeling completely defeated, I went through the motions, letting the caterer in, helping to set up and eventually greeting the arriving guests with a fake smile on my face.

An entire section of the room that had been set up for Marcus Dubois sat blatantly empty.

Just as I was in the middle of explaining the Dubois situation to another sponsor for what felt like the hundredth time, I heard a deep voice behind me.

"Sorry I'm late."

When I turned around, Damien was standing there in his classic gray beanie, dressed in all black and smelling like leather and cologne. He was carrying a massive bag around his shoulder. My weak knees felt like they were ready to snap from under me. So shocked, I stood there speechless until I finally found the words to introduce him. "This is—"

"Damien Hennessey," he interrupted, offering his hand to the woman along with a flash of his perfect teeth that I wanted to run my tongue along. "Chelsea called me to fill in after Dubois cancelled." He looked at me. "Where do you need me?"

"You can set up right here in this corner."

Damien followed me and dropped his stuff. Once we were alone, I turned to him. "I can't believe you came. I didn't even get to actually ask you to come on the message."

"It was obvious where you were going with it. And Jesus, you sounded like you were afraid or something. Why were you so nervous to ask me?"

Because I have a major crush on you.

After getting lost in his eyes for a few seconds, I shrugged. "I don't know."

"Anyway, I got here as fast as I could."

"You have no idea how much this means to me."

"I think I do. You look like you're about to cry. You don't hide your feelings very well."

He was right. I could barely contain the tears of relief.

"It really means a lot."

Damien looked around. "So, what do I do?"

"Okay...did you bring all the supplies you need to paint?"

"Yeah. I have everything."

"Your workshop starts in a half-hour. All you need to do is create something of your choosing, maybe explain a little bit about how you do what you do, your technique, and then they'll just ask you some questions at the end. You know, stuff like how you got into this... advice if they want to become an artist...things like that."

"I can handle that."

"Seriously, I owe you so much for this."

"You don't owe me anything."

"I owe you a toaster, and now I owe you more."

My director suddenly pulled me away to mingle with some more of the donors, leaving Damien alone to set up and causing me to miss a majority of his workshop. Eyeing him from time to time, I snuck glances as he wore his mask and spray-painted the canvas he'd set up on an easel.

Finally able to break away, I snuck into his workshop in progress. I was standing behind him and unable to see what he'd actually spray-painted, since the easel was now facing out toward his audience during the question and answer portion.

"How did you get into this?" one of the boys asked.

"Well, when I was a teenager, I was going through a particularly tough time after my father died. It started out as graffiti on property that wasn't mine." He held out his palms. "Not condoning that or anything." They all laughed as he continued, "I accidentally discovered I had a real knack for it and found new places to practice, hoping not to get in trouble. I used it as an escape then. But over the years, it's become so much more than that. Now, I live for creating images and bringing them to life."

One of the adults raised her hand then asked, "What do you say to young people who want to become artists themselves?"

Damien addressed his answer to the kids. "You have to find a balance. Most people aren't lucky enough to make a living doing what they love. So, you have to stay in school, find a practical career at first, get some skills to fall back on but always keep doing what you're passionate about. I made some smart decisions early on that allow me to spend my days creating art now, but that's only because I worked hard in school. Now, I'm reaping the benefits."

One of the teenagers, Lucas, raised his hand and said, "I draw, but I don't show anyone. I guess I'm afraid because once my brother found my drawings and laughed at them. So, I feel like I can't share that part of myself now."

"If you're telling yourself you can't do something, change the story in your head. Visualize a different outcome. Change the story. That's beauty of art, too. You can create your own interpretation of anything. Take a sad or awkward memory, for example, and rewrite the ending. I actually did that with this painting. The real story behind it didn't go as smoothly."

Since I had missed his painting segment, I had no idea what he was talking about. Then, I heard one of the teenagers ask, "So, Chelsea didn't really like your dogs?"

What?

He continued, "Actually, when I first met her, we got off to a rough start. She gave me a bit of an attitude, so I dished it right back. She had this impression that I was this mean person. She came over one day smelling like bacon..."

When everyone started to laugh, Damien said, "I know. Who does that, right? Anyway, the dogs go absolutely nuts over that smell. They got excited and trampled her. She didn't like it. They're harmless, but they're pretty big. So, I couldn't blame her." Our eyes met, and he smiled when he realized I was listening to every word. "Anyway, she didn't realize it, but I was mortified that day."

My heart clenched. *He was?*

He faced his audience again. "So, anyway, in a perfect world, maybe she would have been laughing like in the picture instead of almost in tears."

When I finally got a good look at the canvas, I covered my mouth, not knowing whether I wanted to laugh or cry.

It was the spitting image of me.

My wavy blonde hair was spread out all over the floor as Dudley and Drewfus lay on top of me licking my face. It was a lot like what actually happened, except he'd depicted me with the hugest smile, as if I were laughing hysterically, unable to get enough of the big goofy animals.

He changed the story.

I couldn't take my eyes off of it, and now I was wearing a similar smile that matched the one in the painting.

The kids were flocking to Damien for the better part of an hour after the presentation ended, asking more questions and trying their hands at spraying on some blank canvases that he'd brought. Damien had invited them all to the building to look at his mural in progress whenever they wanted. I never dreamt that his filling in at the last minute would leave such an impression on them, but his words were truly inspirational.

When the crowd had dissipated, Damien was packing up his things when I approached him.

"That was amazing."

"It was nothing."

"No. It wasn't nothing." I touched his shoulder as he glanced briefly down at my hand on his arm. I looked him in the eyes. "You're amazing."

I didn't know why I was feeling so emotional in that moment. He'd just awakened a part of me that realized it was craving so much more out of life.

"It was one of the best presentations we've ever had. Seriously, I owe you dinner tonight."

His mouth curved into a smile. "You're gonna burn me dinner?"

"Hell, no. I'm gonna buy it, and I'm not taking no for an answer. Do you have plans tonight?"

His eyes momentarily closed. "Actually, I do. I'm sorry."

Trying not to let my disappointment show, I nodded. "Oh. Maybe tomorrow." Quickly realizing that tomorrow was Friday night, I said, "Oh, shit. I just remembered. I have a date."

"Really…"

"You sound surprised. You're the one who set me up on that website."

"I'm actually not surprised at all, Chelsea. Where are you meeting him?"

"The Starbucks on Powell. Same place that Damien guy stood me up."

"Good ol' Damien." He grinned. "Are you headed back home now? You want a ride?"

"Sure. I usually walk. But today was exhausting."

Damien opened the passenger side door to his black pickup truck and let me in before he packed his supplies into the back. The car smelled like his cologne mixed with air freshener. Closing my eyes, I took a deep breath in. I looked at the backseat and smiled at the towel he'd put down for the dogs.

The ride to our building took all of three minutes. Damien pulled the truck into the special spot reserved for him. Once he put it in park, he didn't move.

It was quiet for several seconds before I asked, "You mentioned your father passed away. What happened to him?"

"He died of a heart attack when I was thirteen. He was only thirty-five."

"Wow. I'm so sorry."

"Thanks."

"Where does your family live?"

"I grew up in San Jose. My mother still lives there. I have one brother, two years younger than me. He lives in San Francisco, a couple miles from here."

"What's his name?"

"Tyler."

"That's a nice name. Your mom has good taste... Damien and Tyler. What nationality are you?"

"My mother is half Greek, half Italian. My father was Irish."

"Thus, Hennessey."

"Yup." He smiled.

"Your father...dying so young. I would imagine that's had a big impact on your decisions in life."

"You mean why I'm living like a retiree at almost twenty-seven?"

"Kind of, yeah. I mean, that's not to say you didn't earn it."

"You're not off base. My father's death definitely motivated me a lot. He was a workhorse, never got to enjoy his life, never had the financial means to. He just lived the daily grind, and then he died. So yes, because of that, I want to enjoy my life unapologetically, and I don't take anything for granted."

We sat in his car for over an hour talking about anything and everything. He'd asked me about my family and how I came to work at the youth center. He also talked about the four years he lived in Massachusetts before moving back to work in the Silicon Valley. I wanted to stay in that truck talking forever. It was a weird feeling because my mind was so engaged, yet my body was flustered, unable to ignore the physical pull it felt toward him. Honestly, I hadn't felt that way toward any man before—not even Elec.

"I have to get going," he finally said.

"Okay."

We walked together back to our second floor apartments.

"If I don't see you again, be careful tomorrow night."

"What do you mean?"

"On your date."

I'd almost forgotten my coffee date with a guy named Brian.

"Oh. Right. Well, I still owe you dinner."

"Okay."

"Have a good night, Damien."

"You, too."

As I watched him open the door to his apartment, I felt flush. I was developing a massive crush on this man. It felt like there should have been a warning alarm going off at the same time, though. He'd told me he had no interest in a future with anyone who wanted to get married or have kids. His last relationship ended because of that issue. I still couldn't figure out the root of why he felt that way. He was so good with the kids at the center today and had such a naturally protective nature about him.

Inside, I walked over to the wall and replaced my artwork with the canvas that Damien had painted of me and the dogs. With a massive smile on my face, I stood there staring at it for a while.

Change the story.

I hadn't thought of Elec once tonight. And that felt damn good.

Restless for the remainder of that evening, I wanted to do something I'd been planning to for a while. Taking a box of baking mix out of the cupboard, I decided to make those blueberry muffins we'd once joked about. It seemed like the perfect gesture to offer my thanks for his help.

My apartment smelled so good when I took the hot muffins out of the oven. After they cooled, I dug up a basket from my room that had been used to hold magazines. I placed a cloth down in the middle and arranged the muffins before covering them.

Originally planning to bring them by in the morning, when I heard what I assumed was his front door close shortly before midnight, I decided to just walk the basket over while the muffins were still fresh.

I took a deep breath and knocked three times. When he opened the door, I noticed his hair was rumpled.

Damien certainly didn't look happy to see me, and his expression was awkward. "What's going on?"

My heart fell when I looked beyond his shoulders to find a woman with long auburn hair sitting on the couch and straightening her shirt.

The words wouldn't come to me. Still holding onto the muffin basket, I just stood there, feeling like my eardrums were beating. I had no right to be insanely jealous, but God, I was.

"I'm sorry. I didn't mean to interrupt. I just wanted to give you these," I said, practically shoving the basket at him. "Enjoy them."

Before he could even respond, I rushed back to my apartment and slammed the door.

CHAPTER **EIGHT**

Friday Night Lights

The next morning, the sound of the dogs barking was oddly comforting. It meant they were disrupting whatever was going on between Damien and his little fling. I wondered if she'd had one of my muffins.

Bitch.

I hadn't even thought to take one for myself before I dumped the basket in his hands.

Was I being ridiculous? After all, I had a date tonight myself! The reality was, I was forcing myself to go on that date.

A knock on the door interrupted my thoughts. Not expecting anyone this early, I wasn't even dressed. My hair was knotted, and I was sure there were bags under my eyes.

Damien didn't look much better when I opened the door.

Still wearing the same clothes from yesterday, he lifted his hand. "Hi."

"Hey."

"Can I come in?"

"Sure."

Looking tense, he placed his hands slowly into his pockets as he looked at me. "What exactly happened last night?"

"What are you talking about?"

Nice try dodging the question.

He moved in closer to me. "What am I talking about? You leaving me with a giant fucking basket of muffins and running off before I could even say anything? Ring a bell?"

"I thought you'd be alone. It caught me off guard."

His eyes softened. "You were upset..."

"No, I wasn't."

"You're a terrible liar, Chelsea. Fucking horrible at it. You don't hide your feelings very well."

"You think you know just about everything there is to know about me, don't you?"

"Not everything. But it doesn't take a rocket scientist to read you. It's one of the things I like about you, though. You're one of the least fake people I've ever met."

"Then, tell me. Why do *you* think I was upset?"

"Honestly? I think you're confused about me."

"Confused..."

"Yes. I think you're wondering why I opted not to have dinner with you and instead ended up with a woman I'd literally just met, someone who isn't as sweet as you and sure as fuck isn't as pretty as you. So, you're wondering what the hell I was thinking. Am I right?"

That's exactly what I was thinking.

He continued, "I know we haven't known each other for very long, but I do feel a connection with you, okay? If you've sensed something, you're not imagining it."

"Well, if I wasn't confused before…now I definitely am."

"I feel like I need to say this now, because I can't stand the thought of you thinking that I somehow find you undesirable when it's exactly the opposite."

I crossed my arms. "Again. Not following you."

He closed his eyes as if to try to find the right words. "It's just that I know for sure that I can't ever be what someone like you needs in a boyfriend, in a partner. It's not that we wouldn't have fun or be great together at first. I'm just not good for you in the long-term—not marriage material. And the reasons are too complex to get into, except to say that it has nothing to do with you and everything to do with me. I can't, in good conscience, start something with a girl like you."

"A girl like me…"

"Yes. You're not the kind of girl a guy takes home for a quick fuck. You're the girl he keeps."

Right. Just like Elec did.

"You didn't have to explain all of this. You don't owe me an explanation."

"Well, if you hadn't clearly been upset, I might not have said anything. I just don't believe in beating around the bush with people or leading them on. I'm not like your ex. But I also need you to understand that there's a difference between not *wanting* to be with someone and not being *able* to. I know more than anything, you're scared to get hurt again. And while I know I would really enjoy crossing the line with you, if I did, I *would* end up hurting you. I'm not gonna be *that* guy."

Feeling a weight on my chest, I said, "Well, I appreciate your honesty. This was a little deeper of a conversation than I expected this early."

"I know. I'm sorry. I felt like something needed to be said after the way you left. I couldn't sleep all night, thinking you were upset."

I swallowed, feeling a numb mixture of sadness and disappointment. Unsure of what to say, I smiled. "Is being friends off-limits, too?"

"Of course not. I feel better about the friends thing now that I explained myself to you. I just don't want things to be awkward between us, you know, if—"

"If you're with a girl..." I interrupted.

He nodded. "Or if you're with a guy."

Damien had said he felt better, but he didn't look it. He didn't look relieved. He looked upset and tense.

And I was more confused than ever.

♦ ♦ ♦

Brian Steinway was a great all-American guy.

Having relocated from Iowa to the Silicon Valley to take a job at Hewlett Packard, he was fairly new to the Bay Area.

During our coffee date, he listened intently to every word that came out of my mouth and kept telling me how much more beautiful I was in person. He had blond hair and blue eyes and, quite frankly, looked like the brother I never had. Brian was sweet and self-deprecating and everything a girl should want on paper.

In our corner couch at the Starbucks on Powell Street, I sipped my latte as we carried on a comfortable conversation amidst the sounds of frothing milk and grinding coffee beans. I pretended to be truly interested in what he was saying, even though thoughts of Damien were ever-present, clouding my head when I should have been giving this sweet man in front of me all of my attention.

I couldn't help thinking about the fake coffee date that was supposed to be here with Online Damien. Then, I'd quickly remind myself of the conversation we'd had this morning, and it would snap me back to reality. The past twenty-four hours had been like an awkward dream.

As we got up after a full two hours of sitting, Brian took my cup to throw it away. "I'd love to give you a ride home."

"Sure," I said without thinking.

Damien would've told me that was a bad idea. But he didn't really have a say. Anyway, I was pretty sure Brian was harmless.

When we made it to my neighborhood, Brian parked a block down from my place. He came around to let me out of the passenger side before walking me toward the building. I didn't want to invite him upstairs, so I intentionally stopped in the courtyard.

Before I even had a chance to say goodnight, a massive amount of light lit up the night sky. Both blinking, Brian and I looked around at what seemed like stadium lighting that illuminated the courtyard as if we were in the middle of a Friday night football game.

What was going on?

When I looked up, Damien was staring down at us from his second floor window. His arms were crossed.

Then, he casually moved out of the way when he saw me glaring up at him.

"What's up with the lights?" Brian asked.

"My landlord is a little bit cuckoo. He must have installed them to fend off burglars."

"Are they on a sensor or something?"

"Something like that," I said, knowing full well Damien was controlling this.

"Can I take you out again? Maybe dinner instead of coffee?"

"Sure. That would be nice."

"I'll call you soon, then." Brian leaned in and gave me a peck on the cheek. He stood in the courtyard watching until I was safely inside.

My first instinct was to storm over to Damien's and demand he tell me why he turned on those lights at the exact moment I'd shown up with Brian. Then, I realized that was probably the reaction he expected from me. After the conversation this morning, I needed to take a step back, have some pride, and just let things be.

Settling into my couch, I tried to focus my mind on a magazine. Mindlessly flipping through the pages, I was bored. It was just past eight, and the night was young.

A few minutes later, I could hear music coming from next door.

Damien suddenly blasted the volume. It took a bit to realize the song was, *Two Is Better Than One.*

My phone chimed.

Damien: Hear that? They wrote a song about you and your ménage fantasies.

Chelsea: Don't you have anything better to do on a Friday night?

Damien: How was the date?

Chelsea: He was nice. How was yours?

Damien: I didn't have one.

Chelsea: Too busy spying on mine? Seriously, what was with the lights?

Damien: I had them installed a while back when some kids were fucking with my mural. I can control them from here.

Chelsea: That was really intrusive.

Damien: Just looking out for you.

Chelsea: By nearly blinding me?

Damien: LOL. Did you get his full name? I can do the background check.

Chelsea: I do have his name, but he's harmless. Trust me.

Damien: You shouldn't have let him know where you live so soon.

Chelsea: I knew you'd say that.

Damien: Then why did you do it?

Chelsea: It's fine.

Damien: Are you seeing him again?

Chelsea: Probably.

Damien: I'm checking him out. What's his full name?

Chelsea: Brian Steinway

Damien: Like the piano.

Chelsea: Yes. LOL.

Damien: Any other info?

Chelsea: Born in Iowa, works at Hewlett Packard, lives in Sunnyvale.

Damien: Alright.

Damien went quiet after that. I didn't hear from him again until there was a knock at the door about twenty minutes later.

I opened. "What's up?"

"I came to tell you the news in person."

"What news?"

"I looked up the guy you're dating."

"And?"

"Well...I'm afraid..." He scratched his chin.

"What? Tell me!"

"Nothing. Completely legit." He grinned.

"You scared me," I said, smacking him playfully.

Damien bent down to lift something off the ground. It was my basket, sans muffins. "Here's your basket back." He'd thrown in a bottle of white along with some cookies that smelled like they'd just been baked.

"What's this for?"

"It's a thank you for the muffins. I've eaten like three of them today. They're delicious."

"You didn't have to do anything. The muffins were to thank you for helping at Arts Night."

"Well, that was nothing. So, I consider the muffins a gift. I don't accept anything without reciprocating. It's just how my mother brought me up."

I took a bite into one of the gooey chocolate chip cookies and spoke with my mouth full. "These are so good. I think you might have unintentionally started a bake off. I can't cook, but I can make desserts."

"Oh, it's on!" he joked. "I try to eat healthy, but pastries, cookies, cake...all baked goods...they're my weakness." He stole one of the cookies and took a bite. "Well, I just wanted to give you the info and the cookies."

"Thanks again."

Don't go.

As he started to walk away, I stopped him. "Damien?"

He turned around. "Yeah?"

"Do you have plans right now?"

"No."

"Would you want to watch a movie?"

He bit his bottom lip to ponder my question then smirked. "Only if I can pick the movie."

"Sure."

"You have a DVD player?"

"Yes."

"I'll come back in a half-hour."

♦ ♦ ♦

The exaggerated banging on the door was rhythmic. "Knock. Knock."

After I let him in, Damien looked down at my outfit. "You're still dressed up."

He'd changed into gray sweatpants that clung to his junk in a way that now ruled out absolutely any chance that he wasn't blessed in that department. The top of his boxer briefs was sticking out a bit.

Damn.

Prying my eyes up, I said, "I didn't realize this was a slumber party."

He moved past me, leaving me with a whiff of his arousing smell. "Well, we're watching a movie. I figured I'd get comfortable. But feel free to stay in a *dress*. Yeah, that makes perfect sense."

After our talk, why did I even bother to look good around him anymore?

He was right.

"Okay, wiseass, I'm going to change into my sleep clothes."

He lifted a microwavable packet that he'd brought and shook it. "I'll make popcorn and set up the DVD player." He looked around. "Bowls are where?"

I pointed to one of the cabinets. "In there."

"Sweet."

"You'll have to change the TV mode to composite two. It's the Sony remote," I said as I walked to the bedroom.

"Got it," he yelled after me.

Even though my mind knew that Damien had closed the door on the possibility of anything romantic happening between us, my nerves certainly hadn't gotten the message. Slipping out of my dress, I still felt like a giddy fool. My heart was beating just a bit faster than normal as I threw on some black leggings along with Elec's old Bruins shirt that I often slept in. Feeling a slight rumbling in my stomach, I decided I should probably take this opportunity to use the bathroom.

Shitting yourself in more ways than one, eh, Chelsea?

My bathroom trip took longer than expected. It surprised me that Damien wasn't giving me hell for it.

When I finally finished, I felt so much better. That is, until I reentered the living area.

My stomach sank at the sound of his voice. Blood started to rush to my head.

His voice.

A voice I hadn't heard in so long. A voice I'd tried to block from my brain on a daily basis.

Elec.

It took me a few seconds to realize that it wasn't really him. It was the DVD I'd left in the player a long time ago, one that I'd watched over and over when we'd first broken up. I hadn't used the DVD player in months, but the disc was still in there.

Damien hadn't realized that I was behind him. He was standing there frozen, intently watching the home-made video. I didn't know what to say or do, so I just stood there feeling ashamed.

When we'd recorded that video, Elec and I were supposed to have been filming a presentation for the youth center and ended up goofing around at the park instead with the loaned camera. At the time, I thought the little movie would make a cute private keepsake. I had no clue it would merely be used instead as a means of self-torture right after our breakup as part of my constant research into what went wrong.

Listening to it was like slowly getting stabbed in the heart with Damien as a witness to my being massacred. I cringed at the sound of my own voice in the video.

"Aren't you supposed to be interviewing me, Elec?"

"I got distracted for a minute."

"By what?"

"By how beautiful you look right now under the sun like this. I just love looking at you through this lens."

"Thank you."

"You're so fucking adorable. I can't believe you still blush when I compliment you."

"Do I?"

"You do. And I'm just warning you, keep batting your eyelashes at me like that, and this will turn into an unintentional adult film in about two seconds."

Giggles.

"Maybe we can try that later at home, Mr. Cameraman."

"Seriously, though, the camera loves you. So do I, actually."

"You do, huh?"

"I do, Chels. I really do."

"How much?"

"Let me show you."

Elec drops the camera.

Kissing sounds.

Laughing.

"It's true, baby, you make me so happy. I'm the luckiest guy in the world."

When Damien finally turned and noticed me standing beside him, he shut the video off and just looked at me.

Silence.

The expression on his face was a mix of sympathy, anger, and understanding. I think he finally realized why I was so fucked-up.

When a teardrop started to fall, he caught it halfway down my cheek and said, "He's a fucking idiot. He's not worthy of the way you were looking at him in that video, and he's certainly not worthy of these tears." He rubbed his thumb along my cheek. "No one is."

"I can't help it."

"But you know...I get it now. Watching that. Listening to that. I get why it's so hard for you. I know I joke about you being crazy and all that...but you have every right to be upset and confused. The things he said to you...the way he said them...I would have fucking believed it, too. And I'm a perceptive motherfucker. You just don't do that to someone. More than that...*you* deserve so much better."

"That was only three weeks before he went to Boston and reconnected with her, when everything changed. When he was away, I found a ring in his drawer. He was going to ask me to marry him."

Damien shut his eyes momentarily and let out a series of profanities under his breath.

"He'd better not ever set foot in our building. I swear to God, if I ever see him, I'm gonna fuck him up."

Our building.

A small laugh escaped me at the thought. "Thanks for wanting to do that for me."

"You shouldn't be watching that video."

"I wasn't watching it recently. I swear. I never use the DVD player now because I have Netflix. That disc has been in there for several months."

He ejected the disc and held it in his hand in front of me. "You don't need to hear this shit ever again. With your permission, I'm going to destroy it. Can I?"

What was I supposed to say? I had to let him do it.

Somewhat reluctant, I nodded anyway. "Okay."

With one hard bend of the disc, Damien snapped it in half before walking over to the trash and discarding it.

He wiped his hands clean exaggeratedly. "What's next?"

"What do you mean?"

"That shirt you're wearing. It was his, wasn't it?"

"Yes."

"Are you wearing a bra?"

"Yes. Why?"

"Turn around."

Expecting him to try to take the shirt off of me, my heart started to beat profusely. I closed my eyes when I felt Damien bunch up the material at my back and tug on it. The closeness of his body behind me made my skin heat up.

"Stay still," he said before I felt him cutting through the shirt with what I assumed were my kitchen scissors. A draft of cold air replaced the warmth of the shirt as he ripped it off of me.

"Go put a new shirt on."

Wrapping my arms around my chest, I disappeared to my room, taking a minute to grab my bearings as I leaned my back against the door. His cutting the shirt off of me ignited an odd mix of emotions. On one hand, it was a symbol of finality. That shirt was the last item of Elec's in my possession. More than that, I was caught off guard by how much his ripping my shirt off had turned me on.

Forcing myself to remember what I'd even come in here for, I grabbed the perfect shirt for the occasion and returned to the living room.

Damien grinned as he looked down at my chest. *"You Bacon Me Crazy.* Good choice."

"Well, it's true. You drive me crazy sometimes, but in a good way. Thank you for pushing me to do something I really needed to do." I leaned in and gave him a friendly hug. I refused to allow myself to acknowledge how fast his heart was beating and how fast mine was trying to catch up to it. Or how he smelled so good that I could practically taste him.

Damien was the first to pull away. "Ready for the movie?"

"Yes. What did you bring?"

He smirked as he walked over to the counter and handed me the DVD that was still in plastic packaging. "It's your autobiography."

"*Firestarter*. I should have known."

"Have you ever seen it?" He smiled.

"Can't say I have."

"Neither have I. But it's about a blonde who starts fires. So, I feel like I know her already."

"Interesting."

"Isn't it?"

"Did you buy it?"

"Ordered it online the night we had pizza. I've been waiting for the perfect moment to break it out."

"You *would* do that."

"I like messing with you. But it's all in good fun. You know that, right? I have fun with you, Chelsea."

"The feeling is mutual...when you're not scolding me," I joked.

"Even when I'm scolding you, it's for your own good."

"I know." I smiled.

As we sat down for the movie, Damien made himself comfortable on my couch, kicking his big feet up on the coffee table and laying his head back. I relaxed my body into my own side of the sofa, careful not to get too close.

Even though I'd always heard of this movie, I had no clue what it was about and was surprised to find it starred a young Drew Barrymore. The main character had the ability to start fires with her mind. It wasn't my type of story at all, so I found myself daydreaming through a lot of it, sneaking glances at Damien as he ate his popcorn. He seemed into it. Was he serious? He appeared to be really enjoying this.

At one point, he turned and noticed me staring at him. "What's the matter? You're not into it?"

"This movie is not really my taste."

"Why didn't you say something?"

"You were taking too much pleasure in the whole idea of watching it. I didn't want to hurt your feelings."

He lowered the volume. "Want to watch something on Netflix instead? What do you feel like?"

I feel like making out with you.

God, that's the only thing I feel like doing right now.

"It's getting too late to start a new movie. It's fine."

"Well, I'm not keeping it on if you're not into it." He grabbed the remote and pressed stop.

It was suddenly quiet.

"Can I ask you something, Damien?"

"The answer is always yes, so stop prefacing everything with that question."

"What was it exactly that you invented that allowed you to buy this building?"

"It was a type of headphone technology. Myself and a co-worker sold the patent for ten million."

Say what?

"That is so amazing."

"After taxes and divvying it up, it wasn't that much money. I used my half to buy this building at auction and fix it up."

"So, you invested all of it here."

"Yup. And it pays off."

"You were very smart to do that and not waste it."

"I love that I can keep a few good people employed. That's honestly the best part."

"Murray had nothing but good things to say about you as a boss."

"My job is easy. What you do at that youth center on a daily basis, shaping kids' views of life and the world, opening their eyes to new things...that's way harder than anything I've ever done."

"It's funny. There's this teenage girl who's been coming to *me* for relationship advice...*me* of all people."

"Just tell her all the answers can be found in the unicorn," he said, rolling his eyes facetiously.

That caused me to erupt in laughter. "I should have *you* go in and set her straight. Although, she might not care about Kai anymore once she became lost in your blue eyes as you were yelling at her to get over it."

I immediately regretted the eyes comment. He simply smiled at me, looking like he didn't know how to respond.

"Do I yell?" he asked.

"Only sometimes."

We stayed making comfortable conversation on the couch for a while until he finally said, "Alright...so we've ruled out another movie?"

"Right. No movie. I think I'm gonna turn in."

He lifted himself off of the couch. "That's my cue, then."

Damien bent down, ejecting the DVD from the player.

I walked him to the door. "Thank you for everything."

He lingered before he said, "Your eyes ain't so bad, either."

I smiled and felt flush from the compliment.

He continued, "Your douchebag ex was right about one thing."

"What?"

"You *do* blush every single damn time someone compliments you." He paused. "Every single time."

I was sure I was blushing even more when I said, "Goodnight."

"Goodnight."

CHAPTER **NINE**

Pandora's Box

Rubbing my eyes, I said, "Seriously? They are extra loud today."

Damien's phone voice was way too bright and cheery for so early in the morning. "Why don't you come have breakfast with us? If you can't beat 'em, join 'em."

"So, the only way I can get The Double Ds to stop barking is to come over there? Seriously, there has to be a better solution."

"What could be better than breakfast with us? They miss you."

"I seriously doubt that."

Over the past several weeks, Damien and I had started to figure out that for some reason, the dogs stopped barking whenever I came over to complain in the morning. As soon as I'd return to my apartment, the barking would start up again. It was almost like they were messing with me.

"Come on, I'll make you some coffee and eggs. If you want toast, you'll have to bring the toaster oven."

"I'll toast some slices and bring them," I said, throwing some clothes on with a smile on my face.

"We'll skip the bacon." He laughed.

"Um...yeah. No bacon, please."

Damien had left his door cracked open and was emptying a frying pan full of scrambled eggs onto two plates when I let myself in.

Carrying a dish of toast, I said, "Look, they're not even burned."

"You must've not been reading and toasting."

Dudley and Drewfus were circling around me, but as expected, they'd stopped barking with me here.

Hoping for some scraps, the animals sat by our feet as Damien and I ate at the kitchen table.

"It's amazing how quiet they are now."

Taking a bite of toast, he said, "They're quiet when they're content."

"So, you're saying they're happier when I'm here?"

"Maybe they like having a female around when they wake up, or maybe they just sense something that other people don't."

"Like sense something about me?"

"You know how strong their sense of smell is."

"Yes, I do." I laughed. "Between your supersonic hearing and their sensitive noses, I'm pretty much screwed around here.

"Maybe they like the way you smell."

"Are you saying I'm like a piece of smoked meat to them?"

"No. You smell better than bacon."

"You've smelled me?"

"Yes."

"What exactly do I smell like?"

"You smell really nice. It's a sweet smell."

"You're *bacon* me paranoid."

He chuckled. "Okay...so either they like your smell, or they just sense that you're a friendly person, and they calm down when you're around."

Damien was giving me a funny look that prompted me to ask, "Are we talking about them or you?"

"Maybe both."

My heart fluttered, and I wanted to stomp on it.

He broke up a piece of toast and threw the remnants on the ground. The dogs scurried to beat each other to it.

When Damien got up to pour more coffee, I said, "So, I'm going out with Brian Steinway again this week-end."

He was stirring in sugar, and his hand stilled for a moment when I'd said it.

"I didn't realize you were still seeing him. You hadn't mentioned him in a while."

Brian and I had only gone out a few times in a span of a month. While he didn't give me the same butterflies Damien did, I'd yet to find a legitimate reason to stop casually dating him. We hadn't done more than kiss; that was mostly because of my own hesitation.

"Yeah...I figure why not? He's nice enough."

Damien slammed his mug down. "Nice *enough*?"

"Yes."

"You do realize you just basically wrote him off, right? So why bother spending any more time with him if you're not crazy about him?"

Because I need a distraction from you.

At the same time, I love being around you.

"What's the harm in spending time with someone?"

"The harm is that while you're passing the time, he's getting more and more smitten with you. And I'm gonna have to kick him off the property when he becomes disgruntled."

"I think you're jumping too far ahead."

"Okay. We'll see about that. Anyway, you shouldn't be wasting your time with him if he's not exactly what you want."

"You can't always get what you want." I was sure Damien had no clue that I was thinking of him when I'd said it. I thought I'd been doing a pretty good job of hiding my true feelings for him lately, going along with us just being friends. But if there was one thing I'd learned from this, it was that you can't control your attraction to someone. If it's there, it's there. It can either be ignored or acted upon but not controlled. But I was grateful for Damien, even if things couldn't progress past friendship. At the very least, he'd helped take the focus off of Elec.

"Where's he taking you anyway?"

"Fondue."

"At least he'll be dipping his stick into *something*."

"You are bad."

"Did you tell him you like to be double-dipped?"

"Excuse me?"

"You know...two guys...double dipped."

"I don't like that at all...nor would I ever do it in real life."

"I'm just messing with you."

"You like to do that."

"Double dip?"

"No! Mess with me."

"I love it, Chels. Especially when you blush."

"You've never called me Chels before."

"Do you not like it?"

"Elec used to call me Chels, so no, I'm not really crazy about it."

"Well, then we need to come up with a new nickname."

"What?"

"I'll think about it." He grinned.

"Oh, boy."

Damien rested his chin in his hand. "Any other names banned?"

"Leeches."

"Leeches? Why would I call you leeches?"

"Elec used to like to scramble the letters of words, to make new words. He once figured out that if you scramble the letters of Chelsea, you get leaches. But then we both later realized that leeches is actually spelled with two E's and no A, but the nickname stuck."

"Hmm. Elec is not that bright. What do you get if you scramble the letters of dumb fuck?"

"Now you have me thinking about that." I laughed.

"Bum fuck?" He chuckled. "No, wait...that's missing the D. I can see how that shit would be addicting, though."

"Bum fucking or anagrams?" I joked.

Damien spit out his coffee in laughter. "Yes and yes."

Staring at Damien, I thought about how at the very least, I was grateful to have found a friend and protector in him.

"You're a good egg, Damien. And you *make* good eggs, too."

"My mother taught me how to make scrambled eggs fluffy but not runny."

"How is your mother? You don't talk about her much."

"She's alright. I'm due to visit her soon. Tyler and I have tried to get her to move closer to us. She's about an hour from here down 101."

"She doesn't want to move?"

"She still lives in the house we grew up in. I think it would be hard for her to leave, since there are so many memories of my father there. She's never really gotten over his death, hasn't even dated anyone since he died."

"That's got to be hard."

"We both keep telling her she needs to move on."

"What does she say to that?"

"She says when you really love someone as much as she loved my dad, it's irreplaceable. She says she'd rather just spend her time alone, trying to seek out and connect to his spiritual presence."

"Wow. God, that makes me want to cry," I said as a lone teardrop travelled down my cheek.

"You *are* crying."

"Well, see? There you go."

He reached over and swiped my teardrop. "Yeah. It's pretty fucking sad to see her so depressed."

"You know, it makes me wonder."

"Wonder what?"

"Wonder if there *are* different levels of love."

"I definitely think there are," he said.

"I think the level of love that is irreplaceable is the highest level. I mean, even after Elec broke my heart, I never once felt that he was totally irreplaceable. But that could just be because he hurt me. I don't know whether it would have been different if he'd died. And I mean... plenty of people remarry after loss. So, clearly, those people were able to move on."

"Well, I wish Mom would move on, because that's no way to live."

"Yeah, but she can't."

"I know," he whispered, swirling his coffee around mindlessly as he gazed into his mug.

"Anyway, I hope to meet her someday."

"She'll come visit at some point."

"Why doesn't she visit more often?"

"She doesn't like to leave her dog by himself. She has a small terrier that's scared of my dogs. Since I have Dudley and Drewfus every other weekend, it makes it tough to get them together."

"That sucks."

"Speaking of sucks, I have to figure out what to do with these monsters next week."

"Why?"

"I have to go to Los Angeles."

"What's there?"

"Just some business I have to take care of. It's too complicated to get into."

Hmm.

"Oh."

"Yeah, so Jenna obviously handles them at night, but I'm trying to figure out a situation for them in the mornings and during the day while she's at work. They're not the type of dogs that can be left alone all day."

"I can watch them," I offered.

What am I, crazy?

"Chelsea, I wasn't hinting at that. I would never ask that of you. You're sweet to even offer, but you and the dogs...not a smart combo."

"Maybe...but I thought they supposedly liked me."

"They do, but you'd have to pick up their shit and all that. We're not talking about little pebbles, either."

"Oh, I know. I've seen you cleaning up their turds."

"Some days, if they eat the wrong crap, it's like Montezuma's revenge. Seriously, I couldn't subject you to that if you're the least bit queasy."

"I can totally handle it, Damien. I can tell you're stressed about finding someone to look after them. I'm right next door. I can take them for two walks before I head to work in the afternoon then be here at night when she comes to pick them up."

"You serious about this?"

The dogs were looking back and forth between us in unison as if they were interested in the outcome of this conversation.

"Totally."

"Alright. But I insist on lining up a backup in case you bail out mid-week."

"I won't. I'm not a quitter."

"I really appreciate it."

"It'll be good exercise. I see your ex running after them sometimes when she drops them off. They're basically walking her."

"Yeah, you just need to hold on and go with the flow."

"I can handle it."

I couldn't figure out whether those would be my famous last words.

◆ ◆ ◆

The following week with Damien gone, I needed to be up early to collect the dogs from Jenna.

That first day, I had to admit that I was a little nervous to meet her up close and in person. At the same time, even though she'd been intimate with the guy I was obsessed with, he'd dumped her. So, I felt an equal sense of sympathy and kinship, seeing as though Damien made it clear that things weren't going anywhere between him and me, either.

Damien told me he always fed the dogs as soon as they were dropped off then took them for a walk an hour or two later. I figured I could try to nap in between their breakfast and the walk then take them out again before heading to work. In the evenings, I would give them one more meal and walk them one last time before she picked them up for the night.

He'd given me the key to his apartment, so I made myself some coffee while I waited for the dogs to arrive.

The door opened, prompting me to straighten in my seat. Dudley and Drewfus ran into the room ahead of her.

Wiping my hands on my pants, I said, "Hi, I'm Chelsea."

"Yes. I know."

Damien had told me that Jenna worked as a hair stylist downtown. She was wearing black pants that hugged her wide hips and a black shirt with the name of the salon written in sequins. Her physique made me wonder if Damien preferred curvier bodies to more athletic figures like mine. Her hair was cut into a straight brown bob. She was definitely attractive, although not someone I would characterize as a bombshell. Jenna was naturally pretty with big brown eyes and a funky style as exhibited by her multi-colored fingernails and fitted retro leather half-jacket.

"It's nice to meet you," I said.

"Is it?"

"Yes."

"I'm sorry. I can be a little snarky. He told me to be nice to you."

"He did?"

"Yeah. He didn't want me to scare you away, maybe." She gave me a quick once-over that made me wish I had dressed up a bit. "You're probably so into him, that wouldn't happen, though, right?"

Great.

"Damien and I...we're just friends."

"Oh, I'm sure that's the official label. But you probably like him, right?"

"Why do you say that?"

"Because I've been there, and I can tell by your face. You're blushing."

"Everything makes me blush. It doesn't mean anything," I lied. "Well, regardless, it doesn't matter. He's already closed the door on that."

"Right. He's not gonna let you get too close, especially after what happened with me. You're probably kidding yourself, though, and still holding out hope, thinking maybe you can change his mind?"

"No," I lied.

Her mouth curved into a somewhat empathetic smile. "I wouldn't blame you at all, by the way. I just pity your situation because it reminds me of a time when I didn't get it. But thankfully, I've moved on."

"Well, I'm glad to hear that." Sadly, I wanted to ask her how she'd managed to get over him—if she were even telling the truth. Ironically, the only thing that'd helped me get over Elec somewhat had been Damien.

"Do you have any questions about the dogs?"

"No. He briefed me on their routine."

"Okay...well, here's my number if you need to reach me." She placed a small piece of paper on the counter.

"Thanks."

After the door shut behind Jenna, I let out a long sigh and looked over at the Double Ds. They were still trying to catch their breaths as they stared at me excitedly with their long tongues hanging out. They were truly beautiful dogs with smooth black hair and copper fur accenting their paws and faces.

"Your mama is either very bitter or very smart. I haven't figured out which yet." I made my way to the cabinet where Damien stored the dog food. "Are you guys hungry?" When they started to jump up and down around me, I joked, "No bacon, though, okay?"

Big mistake.

At the mere mention of it, they started to flip out.

Shit.

The B word had to be banned altogether.

◆ ◆ ◆

By the second day, it was clear that there was only one way I was going to catch up on sleep after the dogs' breakfast. I picked up my phone and sent a text to Damien.

> **Hey. Would it be okay if I napped over at your apartment in the mornings? It's the only way the dogs will stop barking.**

> **Damien: You shouldn't even have to ask. Make yourself at home.**

> **Chelsea: Thanks. I really appreciate it.**

> **Damien: Thank you again for looking after them. Is everything going okay?**

> **Chelsea: Yes. Perfect.**

> **Damien: Cool.**

It wasn't necessary to divulge that I'd nearly lost my grip on them during our first morning walk or that it took me five minutes to calm them down after that first and last mention of bacon. Overall, though, it was going pretty well.

As expected, the barking ceased once I made my way into Damien's apartment and then to his bedroom. I didn't, however, expect the dogs to climb into bed with me.

Thankfully, Dudley and Drewfus were clean animals. Jenna must have washed them often because they never smelled bad even when they were sweaty.

Sandwiched between them, I closed my eyes and relished Damien's smell, which saturated the sheets. Sinking my nails into the goose down pillow, I took a deep breath in and imagined for a moment that it was him.

My heart started to beat faster. That made me realize how badly I'd been craving being close to him, even though I'd been trying to suppress my feelings to avoid getting hurt. He wasn't even with us, but here in this bed, in his most intimate place, I could feel his presence strongly

Allowing myself to release all of the pent up desire, I tightened my grip on the pillow and grinded my body into the mattress, imagining that it was Damien's hard body under me. It was a dance of arousal and frustration enhanced by burying my face in his intoxicating smell.

When I eventually opened my eyes, Dudley was staring at me funny, and it brought me back to reality.

I finally dozed off.

♦ ♦ ♦

By the end of the week, I was getting used to sleeping with the dogs. Dare I say, I was starting to enjoy napping while sandwiched between them.

Things were pretty uneventful until Thursday. That was when Drewfus thought it would be funny to squeeze himself under Damien's bed. The Double Ds were due to go for their walk before I had to go to work. We were running late, and I couldn't get him to come out.

There was a flat, black shoebox underneath that I needed to move out of the way in order to get to him.

After I finally got Drewfus to come out from under, my hand stilled as I went to slide the box back under the bed. Written on the lid in silver Sharpie were the words, *Pandora's Box.*

So incredibly tempted to open it, I quickly shoved it under the bed and forced myself not to think about it as I took the dogs out for their walk.

That entire day at work, it was impossible to stop theorizing about what might have been inside of that box. The only sure thing was that it was something he wanted to keep hidden.

After Jenna picked up the dogs that night, I was alone in Damien's apartment. Deciding to lie back on his bed, I kept thinking about the box.

A thought occurred to me. Damien had taken it upon himself to barge into my bathroom once, seizing my Kindle. He'd satisfied his curiosity despite my protesting. He'd also pressed play on the DVD of Elec and me without permission, so he'd understand my curiosity, right?

Impulsively, I hopped off the bed, knelt down, and crawled underneath, sliding the box out and opening it.

I was surprised to find a mishmash of things, from old trading cards to coins to a few newspaper articles.

Upon closer examination, it occurred to me that one of the newspapers featured the obituary for his father, Raymond Hennessey. My chest tightened. I felt a bit foolish now for thinking that the box contained something salacious.

My fingers then landed on a DVD that was inside of a plain plastic case. It was simply marked, *Jamaica.*

Feeling an intense need to know more about him, I glanced over at the television that was across from his bed, noticing that there was a DVD player right beside it. Without allowing myself the time to let guilt sink in, I quickly opened the case and popped the DVD inside.

The first image on the screen was a man's bare abs. The lighting was bad. He seemed to be adjusting the camera. When he bent down to look inside the lens, a quick glimpse of his face revealed that it was Damien.

Oh. Fuck.

What was I about to watch?

For a brief moment, I closed my eyes until I heard a female voice in the video.

"Is it recording?" she asked.

"Yeah."

When he turned around toward her, his ass was facing the camera and filled the screen. It was perfectly round, muscular, smooth and unblemished—everything I thought it would be. He had a beauty mark about the size of a pea on his right ass cheek. I covered my mouth and couldn't help laughing at that.

Holy shit. I was staring at Damien's ass.

Beautiful ass.

I needed to shut it off, but I couldn't move.

It was difficult to see what she looked like. His back was blocking her, but it seemed that she was rubbing her hands down the front of his body.

"*God, you're ready,*" *she said.*

"*How ever can you tell?*" *he asked seductively.*

His voice gave me chills.

Then, he reached over to grab something, and I heard what sounded like the crinkle of a condom wrapper. He lowered himself over her. I was grateful that I couldn't make out her face.

She moaned out, "I love that first time you sink into me."

"*Yeah? You're gonna love how hard I fuck you even more."*

After about a minute of sitting there frozen, my eyes were glued to Damien's ass as he thrust his hips and pounded into her. I knew I had to stop. Just listening to the sounds he was making—ones I knew would haunt me for many nights to come—I'd decided I'd done enough damage to my psyche.

I ejected the DVD, carefully placing it back in the case before returning it to the box, which I slid under the bed.

My heart was pounding uncontrollably. I really had no right to watch that. It was likely several years old and a part of Damien's past that wasn't meant for anyone else's eyes. I suddenly felt ashamed of myself.

He would never speak to me again if he knew I'd gone through his most personal stuff.

Guilt overtook me.

What had I done?

◆ ◆ ◆

Back at my apartment, the guilt was soon replaced by the sweetest kind of torture. The vision of Damien's ass, the deep, throaty sounds of his pleasure had been etched into my brain, replaying over and over as I brought myself to climax several times that night.

I'd replaced all memories of the woman in the video with myself, imagining what he would feel like as he filled me, that husky voice in my ear telling me how good he was going to fuck me while I inhaled the smell of him all over my naked body.

This was my punishment for snooping, and it came in the form of realizing even more clearly what I was missing.

Later that night, I confessed everything to Jade in a phone call after her performance.

"Block it out of your mind. Seriously. Just try to pretend you never saw it."

"The more I try not to think about it, the worse it is. Sort of like my entire experience with the guy."

"Here's an interesting question," she said. "Would you rather have the friendship you have with him now or a purely sexual relationship you knew would never turn into more? In either scenario, there's no commitment."

"Depends on my mood when you ask me. Earlier tonight, I might have said I'd take the sex."

"But that's not you, Chelsea. It's not me, either. I don't think we know how to not get attached. Some people are really good at compartmentalizing, but we suck at it."

"You're right. I would always want more with him. And because he and I have this friendship, I've already fallen for him as a person. If it could be just sex with no emotional connection, then maybe that would be different. But it's too late for that. There already *is* a connection."

"You know, I used to joke about you boning him and all that, but I'm almost sorry about that now, because I never knew that this thing would turn into a serious dilemma for you."

"Maybe I should move."

"Don't be silly. You don't want to move."

"No, I don't. That's the problem. I'd miss him like crazy...and the damn dogs."

"You and the dogs! *That* I definitely wouldn't have predicted!"

"Yes. They're totally growing on me. As long as I don't mention bacon."

"When does he come back?"

"Sometime Saturday afternoon, I think."

"Does the ex take the dogs on weekends?"

"They alternate. The dogs are staying here this weekend because I guess Jenna is going away. So, she won't pick them up Friday night. They'll just stay over."

"These dogs are like kids!"

"Kids that are practically the size of full-grown men, yeah. You should see how much room they take up in the bed. But I have to say, it's been nice sleeping next to a warm body or two."

"Not exactly the kind of double teaming we read about."

I snorted. "Definitely not."

"Sweet, though."

"Yeah, it really is."

♦ ♦ ♦

I'd decided to sleep over at Damien's on the last night. That way, I wouldn't have to leave my bed so early Saturday morning. If I was already there, the Double Ds might let me sleep in a little longer.

Friday night, I curled up next to both dogs on Damien's couch and watched a documentary.

When I retreated to the bedroom shortly before midnight, they both followed me into the bed. With two snoring dogs flanking me, I fell into a deep sleep.

The next morning, it felt like one of them was wrapped around me. It smelled like Damien in the bed more than usual. When a hand moved across my abdomen, my eyes flashed open. I jumped, then flipped around, only to be met by the most beautiful blue eyes I'd ever seen.

"Damien! What are you doing here?"

He placed his hand on my hip and playfully nudged me. "This is *my* bed."

God, I loved it when he touched me. He rarely did.

Painfully aware of his hand still resting on my hip, I cleared my throat and said, "I know, but what are you doing here so early?"

He slid his hand off of my hip, causing me to ache for its return.

"We drove through the night."

We?

My stomach sank. "Who's we?"

"Tyler and I."

"Your brother went with you to L.A?"

"Yes."

"How long have you been back, and where are the dogs?"

"I came home about five in the morning. When they saw me, they bolted to the living room."

"Why?"

"They know they're not allowed in my bed."

My jaw dropped. "They're not?"

"No. They were taking full advantage of you. They know to stay out of my bed when I'm in it."

The dogs were standing outside of the door looking guilty when I glanced over at them. It was kind of cute.

"I had no idea."

"It's not your fault. I never specified. I guess I trusted that they would follow the rules. They must have been loving you."

"Actually, I enjoyed sleeping next to them. I guess you could say we bonded."

Looking amused, Damien rested his head on his hand as he continued to lie across from me. "Look at you...warming up to the dogs."

"I just assumed they slept with you."

He shook his head. "You're tiny compared to me. If I shared a bed with them, there would be no room. I'd never get any sleep."

"They *are* cover hogs."

"I can't thank you enough for watching them. Let me take you out to dinner tonight."

Disappointment filled me when I remembered my date. "Actually, I can't. I have those plans with Brian."

"Shit. That's right. Well, maybe tomorrow instead."

"Okay. I'd like that."

"Actually, there's this new burger place that opened up in Sunnyvale. Apparently, there's like a mile-long line to get in no matter what time of the day you go, but they're supposed to have the best burgers in the world. They have crazy desserts, too. Wanna try it for lunch tomorrow instead of dinner?"

"That sounds great, yeah."

"Cool." He glanced down at my legs then back up at me. "Where's The Piano Man taking you?"

"Piano Man?"

"Steinway. Pianos."

"Oh." I smiled. "I forgot about that. Actually, fondue, remember? Dipping his stick?"

"Ah, yes. Well, don't let him divert to Bad Boy Burger. That's where we're going."

"Okay." I grinned, becoming lost in his eyes for a few moments before asking, "Was your trip successful?"

"Yeah...saw some friends."

"I thought you said it was business."

He paused then said, "Tyler and I went to meet with some people about some stuff that may happen in the future, yeah, but we also have some friends in that area."

Hmm.

"Well, I'm glad you're home."

He smirked. "Was Jenna nice to you?"

"Nice enough."

"That's Chelsea code for she was a total bitch."

"No. She wasn't overly friendly but not a bitch."

"I'm sure she hates you."

"Why?"

"Isn't it obvious?"

"Actually, I made it clear that there was nothing going on between us, so why should she hate me?"

"Because I doubt she believes that I'm just friends with someone who looks like you."

"Well, it's the truth."

Guilt was starting to creep in as I thought about my snooping.

I suddenly got up. "I'd better get going."

He followed me off the bed. "Stay and have breakfast."

Between my fantasizing about him yesterday and his touching me, I needed relief—not breakfast.

"No, I think I'm gonna go back to my place. I have a lot to do today."

"Okay. I'll come by at noon tomorrow, pick you up to go to the burger place."

"Sounds good."

The dogs started to follow me out the door.

"No, no no. We're not going for a walk," I told them.

Damien was laughing as he watched me try to set them straight. "I'm sorry, but this is the funniest thing I've ever seen."

I knelt down and let the Double Ds lick my face. "We had fun, didn't we?"

Damien just stood there watching us with his arms crossed, massively amused.

"Your daddy's home now. You don't need me anymore. I'll see you soon, though."

Back at my apartment, I plopped down on my bed and couldn't stop thinking about how Damien's hand had felt on my hip.

Needing release, I slid down my pants, readying to masturbate, when right on cue, the barking commenced.

Of course.

CHAPTER **TEN**

Exes and Ohs

Who changes outfits ten times when they're just going out for a burger?

This girl.

I didn't care that Damien was my *friend*. When he looked at me, I wanted him to regret the decision he'd made when he labeled me just that.

I couldn't help how I felt.

Last night, throughout the fondue date with Brian, I kept thinking about Damien: Damien's ass, Damien's hand on my hip, my impending Sunday lunch with Damien. It was pathetic. I would chuckle to myself every time Brian would dip something into the sauce because I could hear Damien joking about that being the only thing he'd be dipping into. I couldn't shake my *friend* from my mind, and I didn't really want to.

Donning a fitted Betsey Johnson mini-dress that had a faux leather top and flared purple bottom, I went to answer the door.

Damien's eyes widened when he got a look at me. "I didn't realize we were going clubbing on a Sunday afternoon."

"I felt like dressing up. Do you have a problem with that?"

"No. You look nice," he said as he brushed past me into the apartment.

"Thank you."

Damien didn't look so bad himself, wearing a brown leather jacket and distressed jeans that hugged his ass.

He looked down at my five-inch heels. "You sure you want to wait in a long-ass line in those shoes, though?"

"How long are we talking?"

"There's a half-hour wait on average just to get in the door. That's how good these burgers supposedly are. The long wait is part of the experience."

"Jeez. Maybe I will change my shoes, then."

After heading to my room to swap my heels for some black ballet flats, I returned to the living room.

"There's my shortie," he said.

"How come I don't hear the dogs?"

"Jenna came back early from wherever she was, so I asked her if she'd take them. I dropped them off at her place after the morning walk. It works out better, since we could be gone for a while today. There's some place else I want to go if we have time after lunch."

"Where?"

"It's a surprise."

The thought of getting to spend the whole day with him filled me with excitement.

It was a sunny Sunday with virtually no traffic on the 101. Damien had the windows to his truck rolled down, and my hair was blowing all over the place.

He looked over at me and spoke loudly through the wind. "You want me to roll up the windows?"

"No. I love this," I shouted.

"Me, too."

"You love the breeze in your hair? You're wearing a beanie."

"No. I love *your* hair all crazy like that. I love that you don't give a shit that it's a wild mess. You don't have a prissy bone in your body."

Throughout the entire ride, I had the urge to reach over and put my hand on his knee, but of course, I restrained myself.

When we arrived at Bad Boy Burger, the line was out the door and around the corner.

"You weren't kidding. This place is mobbed."

"The burgers better be worth it."

After forty minutes, we finally made it to the part of the line that was inside the restaurant. It was cafeteria style, so once the order was placed, you either found a seat inside, took it to go, or sat on one of the benches outside.

We were just about ten people from the cashier when I glanced out to the seating area. My throat felt like it was closing up, and I felt dizzy.

I blinked.

No.

I blinked again.

It couldn't be.

He's in New York.

No, he's here.

Elec.

My ex was sitting with his mother and the woman he left me for—Greta.

He didn't see me.

Oh my God.

I had to get out of here.

"Chelsea, what's wrong? You're turning white."

I grabbed his arm for support. "It's Elec."

"What about him?"

"He's here."

"What?"

"Behind me and a little to the right."

Damien's head whipped toward Elec's direction. "What the fuck is he doing here?"

"His mother lives here in Sunnyvale." I blew out a nervous breath. "He must be visiting."

"What are the fucking chances, seriously?"

"With my luck? Pretty good, apparently."

He glared at them. "That's her?"

"Yes."

"She ain't got nothing on you."

Too nervous to appreciate those words, I said, "I don't want him to see me."

"Then I probably shouldn't tell you he's looking over in this direction."

"Do you think he knows it's me?"

"I can't tell. Do you want to just leave?"

"I do. But I also don't want to turn around."

"You think he'll say something?"

"I don't know. But I guarantee you his mother will. She loves me."

Damien glanced in their direction again before placing his hands on my shoulders. "Okay. Don't freak out, but he's definitely looking over here."

"Shit."

Damien looked like he was pondering something. "You trust me?"

"Yes."

"Just go with it, okay?"

Not having a clue what he meant, I nodded. "Okay."

Before I could question anything further, Damien's hands were on my face, bringing me into him. He pressed his lips into mine and began to kiss me harder than I'd ever been kissed in my entire life.

My heart was pounding so fast, and I didn't know whether it was because I knew Elec was watching or because of the sheer shock of it all or simply because I knew this was going to ruin me.

It's all for show.

Even though I kept telling myself it wasn't real, it sure as heck didn't feel fake as Damien pushed his tongue in and out of my mouth. His hot, wet lips on mine were without a doubt the best I'd ever felt.

Upon the recognition of his taste, all of my senses weakened. My legs felt like they were ready to collapse, like the only thing holding me up were his hands still wrapped around my cheeks.

I opened my mouth wider taking in every one of his breaths as if they were my only oxygen. I kept expecting him to pull away, but instead he only kissed me harder, pressing his entire body into mine. I didn't care where we were anymore or that we were still in a crowded line.

He moved his hands from my cheeks and began threading his fingers through my hair, slightly pulling it. We were making a scene. Even though putting on a performance for Elec was his initial intent, I wasn't sure it was just for show anymore.

The low moan that escaped into my mouth was proof that he'd gotten carried away and lost in it, too. The kiss that started out calculated, calm and collected was no longer that as I felt his heart pound against mine. It was the most beautiful feeling because it was proof that I wasn't crazy, that this chemistry I'd been experiencing wasn't all in my head.

I was sure the people behind us in line were cutting right in front by now, but I was too immersed in the kiss to notice. I sure as hell wasn't going to be the first to break it, because I knew once that happened, I would have to face the fact that my life would never be the same. Because I couldn't erase this. I could never undo knowing how this felt.

He slowed the pace before reluctantly pulling away. I leaned in, trying to continue the kiss, but he turned his cheek and muttered, "Fuck" as if the realization of what he'd done finally hit him. He didn't have to explain. I knew exactly why he was angry with himself. That was exactly how I felt.

Totally fucked.

Dazed and confused, I asked, "Are they still here?" I wasn't sure I even cared anymore to be honest. I just needed to say *something.*

Damien looked behind me. "No. He's gone."

"Good."

We'd totally lost our place in line. People were just bypassing us completely.

I no longer had an appetite, and the smell of fried ground beef was making me nauseous.

"Would it be okay if we didn't go back in line? I'm suddenly really not in the mood for a burger."

"Of course. Let's get out of here."

Once back in the truck, the ride was quiet and tense. Damien wouldn't look at me as he kept his eyes straight ahead. My body was in a confused state. My nerves were shot, but at the same time, I was so painfully aroused. My panties were wet. My nipples were hard. My brain and my body wanted two different things.

My body wanted nothing more than for him to pull over and fuck me into oblivion on the side of the road.

But my brain wanted an explanation as to why he kept fighting his feelings for me, why he couldn't just take a chance and see where things went. It kept wondering why I didn't matter enough to him to take that risk, when he was all that mattered to me.

I wanted to cry for the sheer reason that my heart was still beating just as fast as it had when I first spotted Elec. Except now I knew that it had nothing to do with my ex. My heart was no longer hurting for Elec; it was hurting for Damien. I was afraid Damien was going to hurt me far worse than Elec ever did.

"Where are we going?"

"Someplace where we can both blow off steam. It was where I'd planned to take you after lunch anyway."

"You're not gonna tell me?"

"It's a surprise."

"You're just full of surprises today, aren't you?"

While he didn't respond, his face turned uncharacteristically red in reaction to my attempt to address the kiss. He just kept driving.

Forty-five minutes later, we were in Santa Cruz, and I'd figured out where he was taking me.

I grinned. "We're going to the boardwalk."

"I haven't actually been back here in years. You?"

"Not since I was a teenager."

"My dad used to take Tyler and me here all the time. Many of the best memories from my childhood took place here."

"What made you want to come here today?"

"I don't know exactly. I just knew I wanted to come here with you." His admission gave me butterflies.

After we found a parking spot, I vowed to try to shake off what happened back at the burger joint.

"What do you want to do first?" he asked.

"Well, I'm starting to get my appetite back."

"Let's go get you fed, then."

Damien let me choose the food, and I picked one of the concession places right on the boardwalk. He ordered pizza while I opted for a giant corn dog on a stick that looked obscene. Some angel of perversity must have been laughing down on me because this thing even had a sprouted tip that looked like a crown. It was unfortunately not the best choice for today, given the sexual awkwardness that was still lingering in the air around us.

After we carried our food over to an empty bench that overlooked the Pacific Ocean, I was hesitant to even put the thing in my mouth with Damien watching me. It just seemed wrong. Way to go, Chelsea.

"I don't know whether to lick this or bite it." I laughed.

"Out of everything you could have chosen, you had to order a giant dick?"

"This would only happen to me. Can you like look away or something while I take a bite?"

"No fucking way. I want a front row seat to this."

"Seriously, this has got to be up there as one of the strangest days of my life."

"Whatever are you talking about?" he joked.

"Thank you again for that diversion at the burger place."

"The pleasure was all mine," he said sincerely.

"It brings me great satisfaction to know that instead of making a fool out of myself in front of him, I had the upper hand today. He left believing that I was happy and had moved on, even if that's not the case. It was the best possible scenario." As Damien just continued to stare at me, letting his pizza get cold, I had an epiphany when I said, "You changed the story."

His mouth curved into a grin. "Yeah. I guess so."

"Seriously. This could have been the most devastating day. I could've humiliated myself or lost my words in front of them, but instead, I didn't have to deal with all of that. I'm at an amusement park instead."

"About to eat a giant dick," he added.

"Like this?"

When I exaggeratedly flicked my tongue slowly along my corn dog's obscene crusted tip, Damien looked away. "Okay...um, fuck. That's too much."

"Sorry."

"The fuck you are, you evil bitch." He laughed.

Holy shit.

When I looked down, his erection was apparent.

"Wow, it doesn't take much, huh?"

"Not today, it doesn't."

I reached my corn dog out to him. "Corn dog, meet Horn Dog."

He handed me his pizza, took the corn dog and ate it.

♦ ♦ ♦

After lunch, we hit the amusement park, and every effort was made to combat the remaining sexual tension between us as we rode nearly every single ride in the place. Well, we went on every ride that didn't involve heights; I couldn't handle those.

It had felt so cathartic to intentionally crash into Damien on the bumper cars. I would mentally shout at him with every collision.

"This is for saying you only want to be friends."

"This is for bringing that redheaded whore back to your apartment."

"This is for kissing me today."

Each crash into him felt better than the last.

"We can't leave without going on the Giant Dipper," he said.

"No way. I don't do roller coasters."

"Come on, Chelsea. I'll hold your hand."

Was it sick that I was considering it just so I could touch him again?

"I really don't want to."

He stopped walking and faced me. "Can I tell you a secret?"

"Yes."

"One of the last memories I have of my father was riding that coaster with him. We came here the week before he died. That's part of the reason why I wanted to come back. I hadn't been able to return here since. I felt it was time. Coming back here was on my bucket list, but I didn't want to do it alone. I wanted *you* with me, because you comfort me, Chelsea." He pointed up to the giant coaster. "Tackling that thing is sort of the final step today. I really don't want to go up there without you next to me. So, see...I might need you to hold my hand just as much as you need me."

How was I possibly going to say no to that?

On the verge of tears, I said, "Okay."

He was beaming. "Yeah?"

"Yeah. Let's go before I change my mind."

Just like many things in life, the anticipation was far worse than the actual fall. I chose not to take Damien's hand, instead opting to hold on tightly with both of mine. The anxiety that escalated on the way up unraveled when we plunged down for the first time. It turned out to be exhilarating, and I was really glad that I'd experienced it. I guess the ride was sort of like Damien: I knew it was probably going to end, that it wasn't really going anywhere, but I was still enjoying the ups and downs of knowing him.

A little dizzy when we stepped off, I said, "Wow. That was actually really fun."

"Thank you for going with me."

"I guess we're even today. We helped each other out in different ways."

He moved a piece of hair away from my face. "The sun is setting. I used to love watching all of these lights from a distance on the beach. Wanna take a walk before we head home?"

A walk on the beach with Damien sounded exactly like how I wanted to end the day. "Sure."

We grabbed some cotton candy and made our way to the beach, which had emptied out. It was a cool evening. Damien took off his jacket and threw it over my shoulders. The wind was blowing my hair into my face and into the cotton candy. He surprised me when he took off his beanie, too, and placed it over my head.

"That should hold it back so you can eat."

I loved the warm feel of the knit fabric on my head. "Thanks."

He looked even more handsome with his hair flattened from the hat. I was having a hard time preventing myself from looking over at him instead of the magnificent amusement park lights in the distance.

The beauty of this night was making me emotional. It was quiet aside from the sound of the waves crashing. With each step, the realization of everything that happened today was starting to hit me. At one point, I suddenly stopped walking and just stared out into the lights in the distance.

His voice from behind startled me. "Say it, Chelsea."

I turned around to face him. "What?"

"I can sense all of the thoughts spinning around in that pretty little head. I could feel them for the past several minutes. You need to get something off your chest. Do it."

"Why did you have to kiss me like that today?" I finally spit out.

"I thought it was clear why I kissed you."

"I know *why* you did it...but why did you have to make it feel so...real?"

His chest was rising and falling as his breathing quickened. He was struggling before he whispered, "It *was* real."

"I'm confused."

"Every part of that kiss was real, but it still shouldn't have happened."

"There's supposedly nothing more than a friendship going on between us, right? So, why does being around you hurt so badly sometimes? I think I might've figured it out tonight. It's because you tell me one thing, but your eyes tell me another, your *heart* tells me another. Your heart was beating faster than mine today. Why won't you open it up to me?"

His eyes looked pained when he raised his voice. "My heart is broken, Chelsea. Alright?"

"Who broke your heart? Did she hurt you?"

The girl in that video?

"Who are you referring to?"

"Did *someone* hurt you? Is that why you're so afraid of commitment? What happened to you to make you this way?"

He looked up at the starry sky before speaking. "It's just who I am, how God made me. I can't be what you need for the long term."

"I don't even *care* about the long term."

"You say that, but you don't mean it."

"You're what I need—what I need *today*."

"And you *have* me...as a friend...always. I failed today, though. I wasn't being a very good friend when I let that kiss get out of control. I got carried away, and I'm so sorry. But it won't happen again."

No, it won't.

God, that hurt. It was like he'd closed the door on us and threw away the key. He might as well have just thrown a pile of sand in my eyes, too.

But I finally heard his message loud and clear.

CHAPTER **ELEVEN**

Ducking Drunk

Things changed after the night in Santa Cruz.

Damien tried to pretend it didn't happen, but I just couldn't.

Angry at myself for my inability to control my feelings, I'd decided that avoiding him would be better than trying to deal with things. I didn't want him to witness my weakness anymore.

When he'd call me over for breakfast, I'd make up an excuse. When he'd come by, I'd act cold until he gave up and left.

The dogs were barking more than ever. I knew they were trying to get me to come over, and it pained me because I missed them. And I missed *him*. I just didn't know how to be around him without feeling the sadness of his rejection.

Continuing to be his friend seemed impossible because I was pretty sure I was falling in love with him.

My phone chimed one morning.

The dogs miss you.

Chelsea: I miss them, too.

Damien: It's not fair to them what you're doing. You can't just come see them for five minutes?

Chelsea: I can't.

Damien: It's not just them. I miss you, too.

Chelsea: I'm sorry.

With each day, the pain only got worse. It was the same kind of despair one experiences after a breakup, but in this case, there had been no romantic relationship, of course.

After a couple of weeks, I'd basically hit rock bottom.

It was late on a Friday night, and I'd decided that I was going to make myself this cocktail that I'd read about in one of my romance novels. It was called a Weeping Orgasm. The ingredients were blueberry vodka, Sprite, and fresh berries.

After downing three of them, I was basically off of my ass. Feeling the effects of my liquid courage, I opened the dating site that Damien had set me up on when we first met and decided to play around on it.

For shits and giggles, I looked up Online Damien's profile and saw it was active. That meant that even though the free trial had run out, he'd paid to continue the subscription. That also meant that while he was choosing not to date me, he was using the site to meet other women.

My blood was boiling. My head had already been messed up from the alcohol, but now it felt like it was full-on spinning. While he'd continuously rejected me, he was basically on here, trolling for sex. I'd show him.

I clicked on the option to send him a message and typed.

Wanna fuck?

My heart was pounding. He probably wouldn't even see it tonight. The little dot that would have been green if he was online remained unlit.

I immediately went back to try to delete what I'd written but there was no option to do that once a message was sent.

I looked closer at what I'd messaged him and realized it hadn't come through the way I'd intended. The auto correct had actually changed the message to:

Wanna duck?

Great. That was smooth. Not only had I made a drunken fool of myself to try to prove a point, but the message actually made no sense at all.

I shut my laptop in defeat and nearly passed out.

Some time later, the sound of my front door slamming shut caused me to hop up from the bed.

Damien was slowly walking toward me as I moved backwards away from him.

My heart was racing. "How did you get in here?"

Damien lifted his key in answer to my question. I guess that was a dumb inquiry given he owned the building.

He backed me up against wall. "Did you just message me to come over and fuck you?"

"Technically, it said duck."

"Technically, you're drunk."

"Technically, you might be right." I snorted.

"You reek of alcohol, Chelsea. You think this is funny? Getting sloshed alone like this? Saying shit like that to me?"

"No, I don't."

"You think it's all a joke, that you can just say stuff like that, that you don't have an effect on me? It's taking every bit of strength in my body not to accept your offer right now, take you against this wall and fuck you so hard for being a bitch these past two weeks."

"I wish you would."

"If I had a condom and you weren't drunk as hell, I just might have. And that scares the shit out of me. That's how little control I have around you."

"Do it."

"I wouldn't touch you like this."

"You wouldn't touch me, period," I said bitterly.

"That's what you think? You have no idea how close I've come to losing it with you so many times. No clue."

"Really. When?"

"That day you came over smelling like bacon for one. Don't think I can't tell exactly what you're thinking when you look at me. You are so transparent, and it drives me crazy."

"What do you mean?"

"I was half-naked when I opened the door that day, remember? You were fucking me with your eyes. I wanted to rip your shirt off faster than the dogs did."

"What else?"

"That night we were hanging out when I cut that douchebag's shirt off of you. I wanted to cut everything else off you too and fuck every memory of him out of you right then and there on the kitchen counter. Then, I wanted to wrap you in my own shirt and fuck you all over again. You want me to continue, don't you?"

"Yes."

God, he was turning me on.

"When we kissed, I didn't think I was ever going to be able to stop. It was by no means the first kiss I'd ever had, but it was the *best* kiss, Chelsea. The best. Ever. I never wanted it to end."

I breathed out, "I know."

"And this next thing...I'm only going to admit because you're drunk as shit and won't remember it tomorrow."

"What?"

"When you were licking the tip of that fucking corn dog...I wanted it to be my cock in your mouth. So fucking badly. I'm so hard right now just thinking about your lips wrapped around my dick. Remember how I went to find a bathroom after lunch that day? I went to jerk off because I couldn't stop thinking about you taking my cock down your throat."

"Wow."

"So, yeah. You think I don't want you. That couldn't be further from the truth. I'm always one second away from losing it."

Don't ask me what compelled me to say what came out of my mouth next. We would just have to blame it on the alcohol.

"I dream about the mole on your ass."

He backed away a bit, and his eyes widened. "What?"

Realizing the mistake I'd made, I tried to save myself. "You have an amazing ass."

"That's not what you said. How do you know I have that birthmark?"

"Um..."

"What the fuck, Chelsea?"

"I've seen your ass."

"Okay...I'm missing something, because I've never *shown* you my ass."

"I know."

"So, then how did you see it?" When I didn't respond, he simply said, "Chelsea..."

Having backed myself into a corner both literally and figuratively, I had no choice but to tell the truth. "Okay. So, you know how I was watching the dogs. Well, Drewfus went under your bed. I was trying to get him out. There was this box." Swallowing, I said, "I opened it. I just wanted to know more about you. It was wrong. I shouldn't have been snooping, but I was curious. This disc said *Jamaica* on it. I never dreamt it was a sex tape. I watched a little of it. I'm sorry. It was a mistake."

A long, very uncomfortable silence ensued. He seriously looked stunned, and it made me feel so much worse.

Say something.

He finally inched his face close to mine and whispered, "You little fucking perv."

I kept waiting for him to say something else. My breathing was erratic as I stayed backed up against the wall with his face in mine.

After several seconds of silence, he simply backed away and left, slamming the door behind him.

♦ ♦ ♦

"You haven't heard from him at all?"

"No. The last thing he did was call me a 'little fucking perv' before going back to his apartment that night. It's been a week and nothing."

"Ouch."

"Yeah. Remind me never to drink like that again. Nothing good ever comes from it."

"So weird that he would admit all of that stuff—that he wanted to stick his dick in your mouth and what not—then be so quick to call *you* a perv for accidentally stumbling upon that video."

"I didn't accidentally watch it for five whole minutes, Jade. I don't blame him. It was an invasion of his privacy. There's no excuse."

"So, what now?"

"Try to move on from this. Try to move on from *him* once and for all. What choice do I have?"

"Are you still seeing that guy, Brian?"

"No. He gave up on me. Just as well. He was a nice guy, but I just wasn't that into him."

"You're not into anyone but Damien."

"Well, that has to change. I'm going out with someone new this Friday, in fact."

"Oh, really? Someone from the site?"

"Yes. His name is Mark."

Dudley and Drewfus were barking up a storm next door, prompting Jade to laugh. "Wow, you weren't kidding about those dogs. I can hear them."

"It kills me that I haven't seen them in so long."

She sighed. "This is really proof, you know."

"What do you mean?"

"That men and women really can't be friends, not if one of them is attracted to the other."

"I feel guilty, like I failed him as a friend because I couldn't control my feelings. He's been nothing but good to me and up front."

"Maybe you'll hit it off with this Mark guy or someone else, and that will make it so that you can handle being friends with Damien again someday."

"Anytime I think about moving on from these feelings for Damien, it just makes me sad. It doesn't feel natural to me. I can't explain it. It feels like even though a part of him is forcing himself away from me, there's still this pull that is ever-present. I can't imagine my feelings going away as long as that contradiction exists."

"Well, you can't run in circles forever. He's told you in every which way that he doesn't feel like there's a future there. At some point, regardless of his reasons, you just have to listen to him."

"Those are his words, yes. But his heart...you should have heard the way it was beating when we kissed. I think that's the main reason I can't accept what he's telling me."

"I don't want to see you wasting this precious time in your life pining over someone who's not going to be there for you in the end. He's told you his piece. I guess I just don't understand why you're not listening at this point."

That was hard to hear, and I didn't really have an answer. Matters of the heart weren't always logical or easy to explain.

That afternoon after Jade and I got off the phone, I made some coffee and sat at my window. Damien was painting in the courtyard. I knew this was the time of day when the sun was just right when he usually worked on his art. I wasn't normally at home at this time but had taken a personal day.

I sat and watched him for almost two hours as he painted a mountain with a sunset behind it. It was amazing how something that started out as a series of sprayed lines could be transformed into an image so realistic with the right blend of colors.

I wondered what he was thinking about and what made him decide to draw a mountain and a sunset. The dogs were sitting down watching him with their tongues hanging out, and that made me smile. It took everything in me to stop myself from going out there and joining them, but I didn't want to disrupt him or worse—upset him.

My phone rang, interrupting the stalking session. It was Ariel from the youth center.

"Hey, Ariel. What's up?"

"I was looking for you, but you're not in today. You said I could call you anytime if I needed you, right?"

"Yes. Of course. What's wrong?"

"Promise you won't get mad at me?"

"I promise."

"I had sex with Kai."

Shit.

"Wow. Alright. Are you okay?"

"I think so. I mean, it wasn't that great."

I laughed inwardly. "Yeah, first times usually aren't."

"I see that now."

"What made you decide to take that step?"

"I was curious. I wanted to see if it brings us closer. And I love him."

"Well, as long as you're okay with it and didn't feel forced into doing something you weren't ready for."

"It's too late now anyway, right?"

"It's not too late to stop having sex moving forward."

"I just thought I'd feel different...better about things...and I don't."

"Sex sometimes only complicates things even further."

God, look who's talking. It was like I needed my own advice.

"I almost feel more afraid than I was before," she said.

"Since you're being so honest with me, I'm going to tell you something very personal."

"Okay."

"You asked me a while back if I'd met anyone since Elec. At the time, there wasn't anyone, but since then, I have met someone. He became my really good friend, but the problem is, I ended up developing strong feelings for him."

"Did you have sex with him?"

"Well, that's the thing. Even though we're adults, which makes it less risky than it is at your age, he doesn't want to take that step with me. It's not because he's not attracted to me. The temptation is there. But for some reason, he doesn't feel that he can commit to me in the long term. So, he made the decision to not let things go any further, because he understands that sex does complicate things, and he's trying to protect my feelings. He's right, because a sexual relationship is not a step that anyone should take unless they're sure. Even though I wish things were different, deep down, I respect his decision. I respect him so much for not using me or taking advantage of my vulnerability and for not wanting to hurt me."

In an odd way, it made me love him even more, which was so fucked-up.

"Are you crying?" Ariel asked.

Wiping my eyes, I chuckled through my tears. "I'm sorry."

"It's okay."

"See...sometimes, adults need to talk, too."

♦ ♦ ♦

Everyday I would tell myself that today was the day I would go over to Damien's and apologize, and each day, I would let the opportunity pass me by. It never felt like the right time.

Sometimes, life doesn't wait for the right time. Sometimes, a sudden situation brings people together whether they are ready for it or not.

One Wednesday, upon arriving home from work, the building super was standing outside with one of the dogs—but not both—which seemed odd. Upon closer look, I realized he was with Dudley.

"Hey, Murray. What's going on? Where's Damien?"

The look on his face worried me. "Drewfus was hit by a car today."

My stomach sank. "What? Is he okay?"

"I'm not sure. He took him to the animal hospital. Boss was pretty shaken up."

Dudley would normally be jumping up and down around me, but instead, he was quiet and didn't seem himself.

"Did Dudley see it happen?"

"I think so. I wasn't here. I guess Drewfus just took off suddenly, and it all happened so fast."

My heart was aching for Damien. The dogs were his life. Filled with dread, I took out my phone and sent him a text.

Is Drewfus okay?

It was several minutes before he responded.

Damien: He's in surgery. Some broken limbs and internal damage. I won't know more until he's out.

Breathing out a sigh of relief that the dog was alive, I typed.

Chelsea: I'm with Murray. Can I take Dudley to your apartment? What can I do?

Damien: That would be great.

Chelsea: Okay. I still have my key from last time.

Damien: Thank you.

Chelsea: Of course.

Once inside Damien's apartment, it broke my heart to see how flustered Dudley was as he frantically searched all of the rooms for his best friend. The Double Ds were like right arms to each other. If he'd seen the accident happen, that had to have been traumatic.

He also refused to eat, which was very unlike him. I didn't know what else to do. When I sat down on the couch, he hopped up to join me and rested his chin on my stomach. I began to slowly massage his smooth scalp to calm him. I couldn't think of any better purpose for myself today than to be comforting this animal. My fingers continued to stroke his forehead until his lazy eyelids fluttered closed. He'd fallen asleep.

Since I hadn't peed since coming home from work, I carefully slid my body from under Dudley to use Damien's bathroom.

Upon returning, I noticed a notepad on the kitchen counter that seemed to have a number of different things scribbled on it from telephone numbers to grocery items to doodles. But it was the word written randomly in the corner of the notepad in an elaborate graffiti-like font that really stood out: *Chelsea.*

In the midst of such a sad day, that made me smile and filled me with hope. I vowed not to read into it and just to appreciate it for what it was: verification that he'd been thinking of me, whether as a friend or otherwise.

Even though I was dying for an update on Drewfus, I opted not to bother Damien. He'd contact me when he was ready. So, I returned to my spot on the couch next to Dudley. He'd now woken up but was sullen and lethargic.

The door opened shortly after 11PM. Dudley started to pant as he ran to it in search of his best friend. Damien was alone and knelt down, rubbing his fingers along Dudley's head.

Speaking softly, he said, "It's okay, buddy. It's okay. He's not here, but he's gonna be fine. He's gonna be okay."

With my hand on my pounding heart, I let out the breath I'd been holding. Still kneeling down, Damien smiled up at me, and suddenly everything seemed right in the world. I'd longed to see that smile directed toward me again.

He stayed crouched down for a while, trying as best as he could to reassure Dudley.

Damien finally stood up and walked toward me while Dudley stayed by the door waiting in the hopes that Drewfus would be coming through any minute.

Not knowing what to say or do, my body stiffened. Damien shocked me when he pulled me into him and held me tightly as he let out a long breath into my neck. My body relaxed into him as we just continued to hold each other.

"He's really gonna be okay?"

He took a step back to look at me. "Yeah. The vet thinks so. They have to keep him there for a couple of days. He's gonna have a bit of a recovery, but he's gonna make it."

"God, you have no idea how scared I was for you."

"Me, too."

"I've been praying so hard."

"Thank you. It worked."

"Is Jenna okay?"

"She's still at the hospital, actually. We got into it a little, though. She was being a pain in the ass. I'm fucking exhausted."

"Got into it about the accident?"

"Yeah. She accused me of not watching him closely enough."

"That's bullshit. You'd give your life for those dogs."

"I almost did when I ran after him, Chelsea."

The thought of something happening to Damien made me ill.

"How did the accident happen?"

"He saw a little dog on the opposite side of the road. Drewfus goes crazy over little dogs. Anyway, I tried to stop him, but he'd bolted faster than I could catch him. The Corolla didn't have the chance to stop. He's lucky the woman wasn't going any faster."

"You do look exhausted."

"You sayin' I look like shit, woman?"

He plopped down on the couch and rubbed his eyes. "I should go and let you get some rest."

"No."

"No?"

"Can you stay?" When I didn't respond, he said, "Please."

I nodded. "I can stay."

He patted the spot next to him. "Come sit next to me."

"Alright."

He laid his head back in silence until he finally turned to me. "Nice try."

"What do you mean?"

"You were trying to get out of talking to me about what happened between us."

"Tonight isn't the right time to bring that stuff up."

"You were never going to bring it up. If it weren't for what happened with Drewfus, you'd still be avoiding me."

"I'm sorry. But you're right. I would rather forget that night. Everything about it is mortifying."

"Why is it mortifying? You were drunk. We had a moment. Shit happens."

"You called me a little perv."

"You *are* a little perv."

"Thanks for confirming that."

"It's not a bad thing. I love that you're a sexually curious person."

"You love that I watched your sex tape?"

"No. That I don't love. But I'm not faulting you for your curiosity. You're human." We continued to stare at each other until he said, "You're wanting to ask me something. Go ahead. Ask me."

"Who is she?"

"An ex-girlfriend named Everly. We had taken a trip to Jamaica. That video is over five years old. She's married now with a baby. It's fucking old news, Chelsea."

"Is she the reason you're so fucked-up?"

"Whoa...I didn't realize I was fucked-up. And you accuse *me* of name calling?" He chuckled. "No. She has nothing to do with anything. She was just a small chapter of my life. Everly thought it would be fun to record us that day. I threw that disc in a box where I'd always kept random shit. Never even watched it once. Forgot I even *had* it until you reminded me. End of story."

"I thought my admission about the video was why you were mad, why you left."

"God, no. It was never about the video. I don't give a shit about that. I was pissed because of the message you sent me."

"I was just messing around. It upset me a little that you still had an active profile. I got jealous." I shook my head. "Why am I even admitting this?"

"Because you're honest. I respect that. Since we're being honest...speaking of the site...I don't want you going out with that guy Mark until I have a chance to check him out."

"You can't dictate who I date." I paused to ponder how he even knew about that. "How do you know about Mark?"

"You're not the only one who knows how to snoop, Sherlock."

"I'm not following. Are you a hacker or something?"

"I created that account. Remember, genius? For Christ's sake, you never changed the damn user name and password. All I need to do is type in your name and fire3, and I see everything you're doing."

"You have no right to spy on me like that."

"I wasn't spying on you. I was trying to keep you safe."

"How is that your business?"

"Because you're my fucking best friend. That makes you my business."

His admission made me speechless for a moment.

His best friend?

"I am?"

"Well, you *were*...until the night you asked me to duck, then stopped talking to me."

"I didn't know you felt that strongly about our friendship."

"Well, now you know."

"Yeah. I guess I do."

"Anyway...about that Mark dude. I have a bad feeling about him. Get his last name and let me check him out before you go out with him. Okay?"

"Okay."

"Have you eaten?"

"No."

"I'm not going to be able to sleep. Need to get my mind off of Drewfus. Why don't I make us a pizza?" He got up from the couch before I could answer.

"Okay. Only if I can help, though."

"There's not much to do. You can entertain me while I make it. How about that?"

Leaning my arms against the counter, I watched as he took out the dough from the refrigerator.

"When did you start making your own pizza?"

"Actually, I used to work in a pizza and sub shop with my brother when we were younger."

"That explains it."

"Ty and I used to compete for the affections of this one girl who'd come in. One day, she challenged us. Ordered two pizzas and told each of us to make one. She wanted to see which one she liked better. The maker of the winning pizza got a date with her."

"Who won?"

"It never got that far. We got into a fight before we even started. Fucking flour and pepperoni everywhere. The owner fired us for making a scene."

"Wow."

"Years later, we concluded that the girl was a bitch for ever pinning us against each other. It was a good lesson."

"So, you and your brother were competitive growing up?"

"Somewhat. After my father passed, we both became the men of the house and had more responsibility than many of the kids we knew. My mother's depression was pretty bad—still is to this day—although the worst years were the first few after my father died. The stress brought out the worst in us. I love the guy, but we definitely have the same competitive streak."

"What does he do for a living?"

"He's a restaurant manager, but he's thinking of moving to L.A. to pursue acting full-time. He's had some acting gigs here in the Bay Area. Tyler's not as practical as me when it comes to building his nest egg. I do what I want with my painting and all, but that's because I also have this building to fall back on."

"I can't believe you never told me your brother is an actor. You know my sister, Jade, is an actress on Broadway."

"Yeah...you mentioned that. What does your other sister do?"

"Claire. She's a teacher. The three of us couldn't be more different."

"In what way?"

"Well, Claire is the oldest. She's the sensible one. Never got into any real trouble. Married her high school sweetheart. Jade is the youngest. Tall, model looks, overachiever, outgoing—complete show off. She's funny as hell, and I'm closest to her. Then, there's me. I'm the short, crazy one in the middle and neither sensible nor outgoing. Just..." I hesitated.

Damien answered, "Quirky and sweet...adorable."

"I wasn't going to say that."

"Well, that's my take."

"I suppose you'd also say a little perverted."

"No." He winked. "I'd say *a lot* perverted."

We ate the pizza on the living room floor while Dudley sat between us. He was finally getting his appetite back and ate some of our scraps. The television was on, but we weren't really paying attention as we chatted, making easy conversation about our families and the latest happenings with the tenants in the building.

Everything was kosher until our attention turned to a graphic sex scene that was part of the movie that we supposedly weren't paying attention to. Things started to get really awkward fast. Damien grabbed the remote and changed the channel as quickly as he could.

I got up off the floor. "I think it's time for me to head next door."

"You sure?"

"Yeah."

Dudley had other plans. As I made my way to the door, he started to whimper.

I scooted down. "I'm sorry. I have to go, buddy."

He began to lick my face as I scratched his head.

"I know you don't want me to leave."

I snuck out fast, but as soon as I returned to my apartment, the howling started. Dudley wasn't letting me off easy.

My phone rang. It was Damien.

"He started to really freak out after you left. Do you think you can come back? Just for tonight. He's all fucked-up."

"It's really late."

"You can sleep in my bed with him."

"Where are you going to sleep?"

"On the couch."

"I guess neither one of us will get any sleep if I don't come over, huh?"

"I'd say that's a safe bet."

"Okay, let me just change into my pajamas."

Damien let out a breath into the phone. "Thank you."

The idea of sleeping over there didn't sit well with me. Here I was trying to get over my feelings for him, and I was about to spend the night at his apartment for the first time with him there. It was for Dudley's sake, but still.

After brushing my teeth and changing into my pajama shorts and long-sleeved cotton sleep-shirt, I returned to Damien's door.

"You look comfy." He smiled. "Thanks for coming back."

"I'm gonna go straight to bed," I said, walking past him and toward the bedroom.

Dudley followed me, seeming to understand exactly why I'd returned. Damien had folded down his sheets just right for us and turned on the small lamp. So much had happened between us since the last time I'd slept in this bed. We'd had that amazing kiss, but he'd also managed to destroy most of my hope.

I really wanted to go back to my apartment but couldn't do that to Dudley.

I slept on my stomach while the dog nestled himself at my side. Damien's smell was all over the pillowcase just like I remembered, but it no longer gave me pleasure to inhale him. It made me feel nothing but sadness and painful longing.

I hated myself for being unable to shake this, for my inability to just appreciate him as a friend. Maybe I was too vulnerable for a friendship with a man because the wounds from my breakup with Elec were still fresh. Maybe if this were another time in my life, I could've handled the situation with Damien better.

Damien had gotten up to use the bathroom that was right outside his bedroom. Listening to him pee, I tossed and turned.

He must have heard me because he stopped in the doorway. I could barely make out the silhouette of his bare, sculpted chest in the darkness.

His voice was low. "You need anything?"

"No, I'm good."

"Dudley's out, huh?"

"Yes." My answers were short to match my odd temperament tonight.

"Are you alright?" he asked.

I didn't answer.

Rather than returning to the couch, Damien approached the bed and sat down at the edge. He placed his hand on my head and ran his fingers slowly through my hair. That simple gesture was my undoing.

"Please don't touch me."

Seeming shocked at my abrupt reaction, his hand stilled. "I'm sorry. I wasn't going to do anything Chelsea. I was jus—"

"Oh, I *know* you weren't. Believe me, I know that." He went quiet, and I continued, "You keep sending me mixed messages, Damien. For the record, I *love* it when you touch me, but it's better for me if you don't. You've been very upfront with me. You've made it clear that there's no future. I appreciate your honesty so much. But I can't handle it when you touch me. I just don't understand why I can't ignore these feelings despite everything you've said. Sometimes, I honestly think it would be better if..."

"What? Better if what?"

I shut my eyes tightly, willing the words to come out. "Better if I moved."

"Don't fucking say that, Chelsea."

"Not right away. Maybe I just start looking casually. I don't really see another solution. I don't want to see you with other women. Our walls are thin."

"What if I promise not to bring anyone home?"

"That's unrealistic, and you shouldn't have to do that to protect my feelings."

"I'll do anything to keep you from moving."

"No."

"That's it? You really want that? We'd never see each other. That would make you happy?"

"No. It really wouldn't. But we could still be friends. I want you in my life. I just don't want to know every single thing you do—or person you do—under the circumstances."

"I need you next door. Don't leave. We'll figure this out."

"You can't have it both ways, Damien. You can't look at me the way you do. You can't call me over in the middle of the night to sleep in your bed with your dog. You can't keep me close and treat me as if I'm a huge part of your life and expect me not to get attached to you. It's unnatural and unhealthy, and whether it's your intention or not, you're hurting me." Fuck. My eyes were starting to fill with tears. Since I had already made a fool of myself, I went on. "I'll never forget that kiss. I can't ever undo knowing what that felt like. Sometimes, I wish I could."

He exhaled. "I won't ever forget it, either."

"I know you have the best of intentions. I know you don't mean to hurt me. But to use your own words...this has nothing to do with you and everything to do with me. That's why I have to leave. It's something I've been thinking about for a while."

Still at the edge of the bed, Damien put his head in his hands. "I'm so sorry," he whispered. "So fucking sorry."

My heart had never felt heavier than this moment. Still so confused, I was only sure of two things.

One: I had to move.

Two: I was desperately in love with him.

CHAPTER **TWELVE**

Oh, Brother

"I can't believe you're really going through with it," Jade said.

I was gathering things I wouldn't be keeping into a garbage bag while chatting with my sister before one of her performances.

"A huge part of me doesn't want to. I feel so safe here. But for my sanity, it's necessary."

"He's letting you out of your lease?"

"He is."

"That's good, because he could've totally been a dick about it."

"He knows why I'm leaving. He wouldn't be a dick under these circumstances. We've been cordial since the night in his bed when I lost it with the poor dog sleeping next to me. Damien isn't happy about this, but I think he understands. He knows he can't stop me."

"How's the injured dog doing by the way?"

"Drewfus is good. I've been going over there and visiting. He's still recovering, limping around. But thank God, he's gonna be okay."

"Good. When do you actually move?"

"In a couple of weeks. The new place isn't vacant yet. I'm slowly packing all of my small things. Mom and Dad are coming to help me with the big stuff on moving day."

"I wish I could fly out and help, but I won't get any breaks from the show for a while."

After a brief pause, I asked, "Do you think I'm being ridiculous?"

"In what way?"

"Moving because I can't control my emotions. In an ideal world, I would learn to just deal with it, wouldn't I?"

"Well, it doesn't sound like your feelings for him are easily controlled. You're removing yourself from a situation that you know would be painful for you long-term. And you're being upfront about it instead of making up excuses for leaving. That's brave. So, no, I don't think you're being ridiculous, Sis. I think he's the ridiculous one."

Letting out a relieved breath, I said, "Thank you."

"More people should be open about their feelings even if it hurts." Someone's voice rang over an intercom in the background. "Shit. I have to go," she said.

"Thanks for listening, as always. I have to run out and take some of this crap to the dumpster out back anyway."

"Catch you later, sista."

On my way back from taking out the trash, a voice stopped me in my tracks just as I was opening the door to my apartment.

"You must be Chelsea."

It sounded like Damien.

When I turned to him, for a split second, I thought it *was* Damien. The guy standing in the hallway looked like him. I had to blink a few times before it sank in that this was his brother.

"Yes. Hi. And you're Tyler."

Flashing a megawatt smile, he said, "Call me Ty."

Holy hotness.

There are more of them.

"Ty." I grinned. "Nice to meet you."

"Same here."

Upon closer look, he wasn't exactly the spitting image of his brother. Tyler was stunning in more of a movie star way while Damien was more rough around the edges. But he had the same beautiful blue eyes as Damien, the same tanned skin (minus the arm tat), the same bone structure, the same strong build, and the same flirtatious smile. *God.* I wanted to swim in their gene pool.

The door opened. Damien came out holding one of those lighters for the barbecue grill. "I forgot to give you the—"

Damien's expression darkened as he looked at me suspiciously then over at his brother. He swallowed. "I see you've met Chelsea."

"I have. You've been holding out, D. You told me she was pretty. You didn't say she was a knockout."

"Pipe down, or I'll have to knock *you* out."

Whoa.

My cheeks burned.

Ty smirked, seeming unaffected by Damien's threat as he took the lighter from his brother. He looked over at me. "I made you blush."

Damien was quick to say, "Everything makes her blush."

I cleared my throat and turned to him. "Are the dogs with Jenna?"

"Yes."

"I figured. It's quiet in there." Damien's gaze lingered on mine for a bit before Tyler interrupted our tense staring contest.

"We were just about to barbecue steak out back. You should join us for dinner."

"I'm sure Chelsea has better things to do...with the move and all," Damien bit out.

Seeming truly confused, his brother looked between us. "What move?"

"She's moving to another apartment."

"In this building?"

"No. Across town," Damien answered.

Ty looked shocked. "Why?"

I finally spoke. "It's sort of a long story. I needed a change of pace."

"Damien didn't mention it."

Damien was still looking at me when he said, "I didn't have a chance."

"Well, then you definitely have to have dinner with us if you're moving soon."

I was curious.

I wanted to have dinner with them.

"You know…it's been a long day of purging and packing. I didn't have time to think about supper, so maybe I'll take you up on that."

Ty playfully flicked the lighter. "Cool. I make a mean barbecued corn on the cob."

"He likes to eat it the long way," Damien quipped.

Shaking my head at their comical sparring, I asked, "Can I bring something?"

"Just your pretty little self," Ty answered before adding, "You're blushing again."

"Actually, I think I'll bring some alcohol." I was definitely going to need it.

After stopping back at my apartment for the bottle of wine and to change into something other than my housework garb, I met Damien and Ty outside.

I followed the plumes of smoke to the back of the building where they'd set up a chiminea and three plastic Adirondack chairs. It was the perfect night for a fire—cool and dry with the sun setting.

Add chivalry to Tyler's list of attractive qualities. "Hey, Chelsea. Let me take that bottle and open it for you." He was super charming. It was no wonder Damien had daggers in his eyes while he looked over at his brother opening my wine and pouring some into the glass I'd brought.

"Why don't you sit over here so the smoke doesn't blow in your face." Ty directed me to the chair he'd been sitting in.

"Thanks." I smiled then looked over at Damien in an attempt to make conversation. "You missed an opportunity to make a joke about me and smoke, Damien. You're slacking."

He still seemed pissed as he looked up from the grill. "What's that?"

"Never mind."

Ty took a sip of his beer then gestured with the bottle. "Oh, that's right. He told me you almost burned the building down."

I nodded. "Yes. It's a running joke between us now."

"You mean when Damien manages to find his sense of humor. Clearly, it's up his ass this evening." He lifted his index finger. "Oh. Speaking of smoke, I brought some Cubans tonight."

"They're joining us?"

Ty laughed. "God, you're cute."

Damien cracked a reluctant smile. "Cigars, Chelsea."

"Oh."

Ty took a baggie containing the long cigars out of the inner pocket of his jacket. "They're for after dinner." He turned to me. "Want to smoke one with me later?"

"I've never smoked a cigar."

"These are the best—Montecristo. You've got to try one."

"Okay, maybe."

"By the way, Damien is cooking two different sets of steak tonight. One was marinated and seasoned by me and the other by him. You'll have to let us know which one you like better. I won't tell you which is which."

The dirty thoughts in my head were aplenty. Taste testing their meat. Great.

Get your mind out of the gutter, Chelsea!

"Is this the pizza shop competition all over again or something?" I laughed.

"D told you about that?"

Damien finally came around from the grill to join us. "Yes, I told her how I beat the shit out of you that day, and I'm not above doing it again if I have to."

"You're *very* moody today, Damien," Tyler said tauntingly before turning to me. "So, when do you move?"

"Two weeks."

"That's set in stone?"

"Yes. The other occupant in the new place is supposed to be out by then. I rented a U-Haul, and my parents are coming to help."

Damien cracked open a beer and said, "Tell them to cancel."

"Why?"

"I'm moving you."

"That's really not necessary."

Ty interrupted, "We can both help. Your parents shouldn't have to do it."

Damien gave him a dirty look that implied he was annoyed at Tyler for offering his services.

"Well, I really appreciate that. My folks will probably still come, but we could use the manpower for the heavy lifting."

"Why exactly are you moving again?" Ty asked.

I simply didn't respond. There was no way I was going to embarrass myself in front of him.

He sensed my apprehension. "That's okay. You don't have to explain. It's none of my business."

"No, it's not," Damien said before he suddenly got up. "I think the food might be ready." You could cut the tension in the air with a steak knife.

"Make sure you give her some of each kind of meat," Ty called out.

Damien arranged the medley of steak tips, sliced steak, grilled corn and grilled vegetables onto three paper plates.

I got up to retrieve mine. "Smells amazing. I can't believe we've never barbecued out here before."

"Well, technically, I don't allow barbecuing on the premises."

"Oh, that's right. Well, thankfully, I have an *in* with the landlord." I smiled. "This is nice. Thank you for including me."

The expression on his face lightened and eventually transformed into a full-on smile. "Well, you didn't let my crappy mood scare you away. I'm glad you're here."

"Me, too."

The three of us ate in silence for a while until Tyler put me on the spot. "Okay, so which of the meat tasted better to you? The tips or the flank steak?"

Looking between the two gorgeous, dark-haired brothers with the matching smiles, I couldn't help but laugh at their little competition. Taking a sip of my wine, I crossed my legs and leaned back into the chair, pretending to ponder it as if it were a tough decision. Truthfully, the flavor of the flank steak was phenomenal compared to the tips.

"The flank wins. It tasted amazing."

The smug look on Damien's face gave away whose seasoning recipe it was. Ty shook his head and downed the rest of his beer while Damien broke out in laughter. It just figured that my taste buds gravitated toward his concoction. Every part of me was attracted to this man apparently.

I listened for a while as Damien and Tyler told me some stories about growing up in San Jose.

The mood darkened a bit when Tyler asked, "Have you talked to Mom lately?"

"Not in a few days, why?"

"The doctor put her on a new med. She said it's making her sick." He hesitated. "Is it okay if I talk about this in front of Chelsea?"

"Yeah. She knows Mom is depressed." Damien rubbed his eyes and exhaled. "I really need to pick her up and bring her here whether she likes it or not. Maybe this weekend." He looked at me. "My mother doesn't drive."

"I didn't realize that."

"She used to, but then she started to get panicky whenever she'd drive on the freeway. One of us goes to get her when she comes to visit."

"Our mother was never the same after our dad died," Tyler added.

"I know. Damien's told me a lot about that."

Damien changed the subject. "How about those cigars?"

Tyler took out the clear plastic bag. "You gonna smoke one, Chelsea?"

I shrugged my shoulders. "Sure."

He cut the long, tightly rolled cigars and gave one to both Damien and me. Rubbing it in between my fingers, I took it to my nose and breathed in the spicy yet earthy scent. He then came around with the barbecue igniter and lit it for me.

Sucking in the smoke, I immediately coughed.

"You didn't inhale it, did you?"

"I did a little."

"Don't." Ty took it from me and brought it to his mouth, drawing in the smoke, slowly blowing it out into my face. "Just taste it for a few seconds then let it go."

I was suddenly massively flushed. There was something about those words that seemed sexual. When I looked over at Damien, I saw that the death stare from earlier had returned in full force.

"You know, the longer and wider the cigar, the more intense it is," Ty said.

"That goes for a lot of things, which is unfortunate for you, little brother," Damien said before taking a long drag of his own cigar.

Ty spoke through his laugh, "Shut the fuck up."

As I started to get the hang of cigar smoking, I leaned back and looked up at the night sky as I practiced blowing smoke rings into the air.

It was quiet, and I could feel both of their eyes on me.

Ty was the first to break the silence when he said, "There's something so goddamn sexy about a woman smoking a cigar."

"Really? A woman? Or *that* woman?" Damien snapped.

"You're right. It does depend on the girl."

An uncomfortable silence lingered in the air.

Ty's next question threw me for a loop. "Do you have plans for the rest of the night, Chelsea?"

"Um...no."

"Would you want to head to Diamondback's?"

I knew that was a bar and club not far from our building that often featured live music and dancing.

I immediately looked over at Damien for guidance. Was his brother asking me to go out with him alone? Was he trying to take me out on an impromptu date? Was Damien going to *let him*? Did he even truly care, or was his anger tonight just a matter of their competitive natures?

I suppose a part of me wanted to find out when I said, "That sounds fun. Yeah."

"Cool."

Damien didn't utter a word. He just continued to stare at me as he blew smoke rings.

I got up, straightening my shirt and gave my cigar to Ty. "I should shower and get changed, then."

"Sounds good." He smiled.

Jitters followed me all the way back to my apartment. What was I doing? I wasn't even going to lie; it hurt me that Damien didn't say anything when Ty asked me to go out. Not knowing exactly what I'd agreed to, I was left with an unsettled feeling.

I took a shower and slipped on a fitted, blue minidress. I blew out my normally wavy hair and put on a full face of makeup.

Letting out a slow nervous breath, I knocked on Damien's door.

Ty opened and was dressed in the same jeans and black shirt he'd had on outside. He'd wet his hair down and must have sprayed on a fresh coating of cologne, because it was pungent.

The air was filled with tension and testosterone.

Damien was leaning against the kitchen counter. He was wearing the same dark jeans but had changed into a gray shirt that hugged his muscular chest. He was also wearing his beanie. I loved when he wore that hat in a way that his hair peeked out from the front. His sleeves were rolled up, showcasing his forearm tattoo. His angry glare was really working for me. It made me think back to his threat about angrily fucking me against the wall the night of my drunk messaging. He just looked so freaking good right now, and I caught myself forgetting why I was even here as I continued to stare at him.

Ty came up from behind me. "Ready to go?"

"Yes."

Just when I thought Damien was going to let us leave, he began to follow us out the door.

I turned around. "I didn't think you were coming."

"I wasn't going to, but I changed my mind."

The three of us walked in silence to Diamondback's, which was about three blocks away.

It was eighties and nineties music night. There was no band on duty tonight, just a DJ. *2 Become 1* by the Spice Girls was playing, and it totally brought me back to memories of singing that song in front of the bathroom mirror with my sisters.

Ty leaned in. "What are you having to drink?"

"You already know she likes white wine." Damien huffed.

"Maybe she feels like something else."

Were they being serious?

"A glass of Chardonnay would be fantastic."

Ty went to get drinks, leaving me alone with Damien. It was a long and awkward three minutes until the DJ started playing *Burning Down the House* by The Talking Heads.

"If you weren't standing here, I would've thought you told him to play that song, Damien."

"Just a funny coincidence."

I playfully nudged on his shirt. "I'm glad you decided to come out with us. I wasn't sure if you were coming."

"Well, someone's got to keep tabs on him."

"Tabs on him or tabs on *me*?" When he didn't say anything, I added, "Your brother's a really nice guy. You two are almost too much alike."

"Neither of us is that nice. Ty's my brother, and I love him, but I trust him with you about as much as I trust myself. And that's not saying much."

Ty returned with our drinks and handed me my wine before giving Damien his beer. "Did I hear my name?"

"I was just saying how similar you two are."

After a few minutes, *Diamonds and Pearls* by Prince came on. Ty took the wine glass out of my hand. "I love this fucking song. Dance with me, Chelsea." When I didn't move, he said, "Come on."

What the hell. Why not?

I let him lead me to the platform. His hand was on my lower back. Lights on the dance floor flashed around us. He wrapped his arms around me, and I placed mine around his neck.

As we swayed to the music, it became clear as day: even though this younger, debatably hotter version of Damien was expressing interest in me, I wasn't feeling anything more than the cheap thrill of his body pressed against mine. It proved once and for all that my obsession with Damien was so much more than physical. He essentially had a clone who was actually showing romantic interest in me, and all I wanted was to be with the grumpy dude sulking in the corner—the one who repeatedly rejected me. I was somehow connected to Damien in a way that I didn't even understand, connected to the way he made me feel, the way I knew he understood me, the way his heart beat for me.

The dance was getting to be too much. When the song finally ended, I excused myself and headed to the bathroom for a breather. I was alone drying my hands when the door opened behind me. My body froze when I felt his low, penetrating voice vibrating against the nape of my neck.

"Do you fucking like him?"

Turning around slowly to meet Damien's incendiary stare, I whispered, "I wish I did."

"You're not acting like you don't. Or maybe you're living out some little twisted ménage fantasy?"

Now, he was making me angry.

"Are you jealous?"

"Yes. I'm fucking jealous," he said through gritted teeth.

"Get over it."

"Look who's talking. You're not over *me*."

My voice was strained. "I'm trying."

"You've been trying to get over me...or under me?"

I wanted to slap him. "Fuck you. Now all of a sudden you want me because you think I like your brother?"

"No, Chelsea. I've *always* wanted you, from the moment you knocked on my door and called me the devil. But tonight...it's finally making me insane. I'm not thinking straight. Right now...I just need to taste your lips, feel you moan over my tongue again.

He suddenly pulled me into him.

"Oh, God," I muttered over his mouth as he gripped my waist, his mouth enveloping mine. He kissed me so hard, and his breath tasted of cigar and beer as he ravaged my mouth with his tongue. I couldn't move my tongue around fast enough, couldn't taste him enough. Feeling the heat of his erection pressed against me, the heat between my own legs was overpowering; I was so wet and throbbing. My entire body was buzzing, ready to explode.

He suddenly stopped kissing me. Panting, we just stared at each other with lust-filled eyes. Bunching my hair in his fist, he pulled it back as he lowered his mouth to my neck. Damien kissed me softly and traced his teeth along my skin. He then started to suck on the skin at the base of my neck. The pain was euphoric. I knew he was trying to mark me, staking his claim on me so that Tyler would clearly see which one of them I truly belonged to. And the truth was, only one man did own me—heart, body, and soul—and that was Damien.

Fuck me.

Please.

Just fuck me right here.

A woman's voice startled us. "Excuse me! You're not allowed in here. You need to leave right now."

Shit.

Damien moved away from me and blinked a few times, seeming to come out of the trance-like state he'd been in.

"I'm sorry."

That was all he said before exiting the ladies' room.

And that was that.

Five minutes later, I rejoined them over at the bar. Damien was back to his angry, guarded self. It was as if the bathroom incident hadn't happened. Everything was back to *normal*—until a knock on my apartment door later that night.

It wasn't whom I might have expected.

CHAPTER **THIRTEEN**

So Fucked

The view through my peephole revealed a distorted version of Tyler.

What was he doing here in the middle of the night?

My stomach was in knots. The guys had left me at my door a half-hour ago. I'd changed into my pajamas and washed off my make up. He knew I was in here, so it wasn't like I could pretend I wasn't home. Sucking a deep breath in, I opened the door.

"Tyler. What are you doing here?"

"Can I come in?"

"Um...sure."

As he brushed by me, he said, "Damien just jumped in the shower, so I figured it was safe to knock on your door without him hearing me. He fucking hears every-thing."

"Yeah," I chuckled nervously. "Supersonic hearing."

"For real."

His eyes landed on the large hickey at the base of my neck. "Jesus Christ. Is that what I think it is?"

There was no sense in denying it. "Yes."

Damien's sucking on my neck in the club bathroom had left a humongous bruise.

His eyes widened. "Did Damien do that to you?"

"Yes."

"How did I miss that?"

"Well, it was dark. You couldn't really see until now."

"No, I mean, how did it happen?"

"You don't know how it happened?"

He laughed. "Okay, wiseass...*when* did it happen?" He shut his eyes and then snapped his fingers when he seemed to realize the answer. "The bathroom. You went, and he followed. I feel like a dumbass now."

"What brings you by, Tyler?"

"This is the first opportunity I've had to get you alone tonight."

Swallowing the lump in my throat, I said, "It's late."

"I know."

Ty's demeanor seemed more serious compared to earlier tonight and markedly less flirtatious.

Not knowing what to say, I asked, "Can I get you some water or something?"

"No. I'm good."

"Okay."

He walked into the living room. "Can I sit?"

"Sure."

Making himself comfortable on the couch, he asked, "Why are you really leaving?" When I didn't immediately answer, he said, "Maybe I should rephrase that. You're moving because of Damien, correct?"

I hesitated then said, "Yes."

He nodded in silence. What he said next floored me.

"I've never betrayed my brother's trust, but I'm about to for his own good."

"What are you—"

"My brother is in love with you."

My heart started to beat faster as I processed his words.

Did he really just say what I think he said?

I shook my head. "No, he's not."

"He is."

"Why would you say that? He doesn't even want to date me."

He leaned his arms into his legs as he looked up at me. "He's crazy about you. I've known about it for a while, but I really saw it with my own eyes tonight."

My heart continued to pound, wanting so badly for him to be right. "If you really believe that, then why were you, you know..."

He lifted his brow. "Flirting like hell with you all night?"

"Yes."

"It was an act. I was trying to prove a point. Don't get me wrong. You're a beautiful girl. But I would never go after someone my brother has true feelings for. *Never*. Deep down, he knows that, too."

"Why did he seem so threatened by you, then?"

"He knew what I was up to. What upset him was that he was afraid you might actually like me and that he'd have to witness it."

Wracking my brain to make sense of this conversation, I needed him to back up. "You said you were trying to prove a point. I'm sorry, but I don't get it. Can you please explain?"

"I was trying to show him that he's not actually able to handle letting you go. He's been trying to push you away. That's not what he really wants."

"Why?" I cried out. "Why is he trying to push me away?"

"Damien thinks you'd be better off without him."

"I don't understand."

Tyler paused and looked up at the ceiling for a while in an attempt to gather his thoughts. "There's something you don't know, Chelsea. But I can't be the one to tell you. It's not my place. He needs to explain it to you. All I can say is that it's nothing to be afraid of, and it's nothing that would make you see him in a negative light. You would not be putting yourself in any kind of danger in being with him. It's nothing like that. He just truly feels that he can't get involved with you, even though that pains him."

The wheels were turning in my head. What could it possibly be?

"I'm confused."

"I know. There is still a lot that is unknown, even to us. But please be patient with him. He'll tell you when he's ready. I know he will. Don't give up on him. Wait for him if you can. That is...if you really *want* to be with him."

"I have wanted to be with him from almost the very beginning—from the night of the toaster oven fire. I felt a connection stronger than anything I'd ever felt before."

Ty's mouth curved into a smile. "That was the night he set you up on that dating site, right?"

"Yes. He told you about that?"

"I'm so gonna go to hell for this."

"What?"

He took his phone out. "I'm gonna show you a text he sent me that night. Give me a minute because I have to go through my messages. At the time, I remember thinking it was funny as hell and so unlike him to be saying the shit he was. Let me find it."

As Ty scrolled through his phone, my heart was palpitating. This felt like an invasion of Damien's privacy, but Lord knows I wasn't a newbie in that arena. I was dying to know what he'd said about me.

"Okay." He faced the screen toward me. "Here. Look."

I took the phone from him and read their exchange.

Damien: I'm so fucked.

Ty: What's up?

Damien: I'm SO fucked.

Ty: What the hell is going on?

Damien: The blonde I told you about next door.

Ty: You sleep with her?

Damien: No.

Ty: What happened?

Damien: SO fucked.

Ty: Bad? Or good?

Damien: SO fucked.

Ty: Yeah, I got that.

Damien: She almost burned down the building.

Ty: WTF?

Damien: Toaster fire. I put it out. Everything's fine. She came over after.

Ty: And now there's a fire in your pants? LMAO.

Damien: Basically. Yeah. She's gorgeous. But it's not just that. She's amazing. Sweet as hell. Honest. No bullshit. What you see is what you get.

Ty: So this is good!

Damien: No. I can't mess around with her.

Ty: Why not?

Damien: She's a good girl, already had her heart broken once by some asswipe.

Ty: Why can't you date her?

Damien: How many times have we talked about this?

Ty: It's bullshit.

Damien: I set her up on a dating site.

Ty: That's fucked up. You're crazy about her and you set her up to date other men?

Damien: I had to do something. She scares the shit out of me.

Ty: I've never heard you say that before.

Damien: You probably never will again.

Ty: Well, damn.

That was the end of the exchange.

My hand was shaking as I held his phone. While I felt a little guilty for prying into his personal messages, my heart felt like it was going to burst. It overwhelmed me to know that Damien had experienced all the same things I'd felt that night. Our chemistry had been off the charts. That confirmed it wasn't my imagination. Even though he'd left me feeling so rejected at the time, there was apparently more to it than simple disinterest.

Ty took the phone from me. "You never saw that, okay? And we never had this conversation, either. It's just...when I found out you were moving, I knew I really needed to say something to you. I love my brother more than anything. I don't like going behind his back like this, but ultimately, I feel it's for his own good."

"What do you suggest I do?"

"I think you should continue with your plans. If I know Damien, he'll come to realize the mistake he's made some time after you're gone. Just continue to be his friend. I can't guarantee he'll come to his senses, but I suspect it will really hit him once you're not around anymore."

"I can't say I necessarily agree that he'll come around if he hasn't already, but I won't stop being his friend. Ever. I never planned to. Living practically on top of each other, though, is just too much for me under the circumstances. So, that's why I'm moving."

"I get that. You know, even though we're a lot alike... deep down, Damien is more like our mother—complex and emotional, like how he expresses himself through his art. Those images. What do they even all mean, you know? I guarantee you there is meaning to each and every one of them. I'm more like our dad was, laid back and easier to read." He looked down to check the time on his phone. "I'd better go before he hears me. Remember, this visit never happened."

"What visit?" I joked.

It was difficult to get to sleep after Tyler left. Even though his revelation filled me with newfound hope, it wasn't enough to totally convince me that things with Damien would ever change.

I had no choice but to trust Ty's word that whatever was going on with Damien was nothing to be afraid of and to trust that fate would work things out.

♦ ♦ ♦

The two weeks flew by, and before I knew it, I found myself sitting in my emptied out apartment, looking at dozens of boxes and once again second-guessing my decision to leave.

My parents were scheduled to be here in the morning, and the plan was still for Damien to help us move. Even though Tyler also offered, Damien had told him not to bother, that he wanted to handle it himself.

It was Saturday night, and I wasn't sure what Damien was up to. The dogs were with him this weekend, and all I knew was that I wanted to spend my last night here with the three of them.

I picked up my phone and dialed him.

He answered facetiously, "Damien's Moving Service and Dog Grooming."

Laughing, I said, "Dog grooming, too, huh?"

"We're a full service establishment."

"What other services do you provide?"

God, that sounded suggestive.

"For you? I can negotiate."

I cleared my throat. "How are the Double Ds?"

"They're good. I actually just gave them a bath, thus the dog grooming. I swear these dogs have the cleanest asses on the face of the Earth."

"I have no doubt."

"How are you?"

"I'm okay...kind of sad, looking around at all of these boxes. The place is so empty, I can hear an echo."

"You should shout out a bunch of obscenities. I bet that would feel good. Just don't gear them toward me."

"My landlord doesn't like it when I disturb the peace."

"I don't think he'd care today. He's a little down that he's losing his favorite tenant."

"Well, he's raising the rent on me. I have to leave."

"He fucking wishes that were the reason you were leaving."

Several seconds of awkward silence ensued before I spoke up again.

"You think the landlord would want to hang out with me on my last night? Unless you have other plans?"

"If I did, I'd break them."

That gave me butterflies.

"Okay. That's a good thing, because everything is packed away, so if you didn't take me in, I'd just be starving and staring at the wall."

"Ironic. Isn't that how our friendship started? Because of a wall?"

"Yes, sort of. Technically, it started with you eavesdropping on me."

"You're right. It did."

"Oh, you're admitting to that now?"

"It was accidental eavesdropping, maybe. I sure as hell learned a lot about you really fast."

"Tell me again what you learned?"

"That you were a lot more than the bitchy dog complainer next door. I figured out that you were a sensitive, caring person who'd had her heart broken, a person who loves and trusts with her whole heart...a person who needs to be handled with care, even though you'd deny that. Basically, I knew you were amazing long before we ever became friends."

I closed my eyes to stop myself from crying. Taking a deep breath, I let his words sink in.

This was really happening. I was really moving.

"Well...*friend*...how about you make me a pizza tonight. I'll bring a movie. Should I come by around six?"

"Alright. We'll be waiting."

With a heavy heart, I killed some time cleaning the empty living space before it was time to head to Damien's. The Lysol smell was giving me a headache.

When six o'clock finally rolled around, I grabbed a bottle of wine and the DVD and headed over to his apartment.

Damien opened the door, and a waft of marinara sauce greeted me, along with the scent of his cologne. I concluded that those two smells were basically like home to me. *This* was home—not the empty apartment next door but right here with him and these dogs.

Dudley and Drewfus immediately ran to me. Poor Drewfus still had a limp.

"You guys are so clean and soft! Your daddy takes really good care of you."

"I'm not saying anything to them about you know what," Damien said. "I swear they can understand English. They'd probably freak out."

It made me sad that the dogs would soon realize I wasn't right next door anymore. Out of everything, thinking about their reaction made me feel the most guilty.

"I think that's better, even though they'll figure it out soon enough."

"I'll deal with it when I have to."

Handing him the DVD, I smirked. "I brought a movie."

He examined the case. "*The Omen.* I should have known you'd get me back at some point."

"It's only fair. You made me watch my autobiography, so tonight we get to watch yours."

He rolled his eyes. "Can't wait." Walking over to the counter, he said, "Pizza's ready. You want mushroom and olive or pepperoni?"

"I'll take both, one of each."

He flashed me a mischievous smile. "One of each, huh? Going back to your ménage roots?"

"I'll never live that down, will I? Why does being here tonight seem like déjà vu? You making pizza...and teasing me about wanting to be double teamed?"

He rolled the pizza cutter over the pie. "So, pervy girl, why did you tell your parents you're moving?"

"I haven't said anything about you if that's what you're wondering. I just told them I found a better apartment."

"But it's *not* a better apartment."

My eyes widened. "You've seen it?"

"Yeah. I went to check it out, make sure it was safe over there."

"You didn't have to do that."

"How are you gonna explain to them why you're moving to a crappier place?"

"They're not going to question it. I'll just tell them I have my reasons."

"Right before your dad looks me in the eye, sees through this, and kicks my ass," he said before placing my two slices of pizza in front of me.

"It'll be fine. My parents are really nice. You'll like them." I took a bite then asked, "Do you have people coming to look at my apartment?"

"Not yet. I'm gonna throw a fresh coat of paint on the walls after you leave and air out all the Chelsea cooties before I list it." He winked.

"Very funny. Well, whoever it is, they'll be lucky to be living here. You really do make this a nice, clean and safe environment."

"Right. Great place...just don't get emotionally involved with the landlord and everything is cool, right?" When I remained silent, he said, "I'm sorry. Enough about the move."

I changed the subject. "How is your mother?"

"She's good, actually. I'm picking her up next weekend to spend the day here. The dogs will be with Jenna, so that will work out. Ty and I will take her out for lunch."

"Oh, good. I'm glad to hear that." I'd always wondered what Damien's mother was like. "Do you have a picture of her?"

"My mom?"

"Yes. I would love to know what she looks like."

"Yeah. I do. Hang on."

Damien pulled out his phone and began flipping through the camera roll. He smiled then turned it toward me. "This was last summer."

Damien's mother was standing between her two sons in front of a massive water fountain. She had shoulder-length, chestnut brown hair, and aside from some wrinkles around her eyes, looked quite young. I could see a lot of Damien in her.

"You look just like her."

"Yeah. People say that."

"How old is she?"

"Well, she was twenty when she had me, so she's forty-seven."

"She's beautiful. What's her name?"

"Monica."

"Pretty."

"She'd like you."

"How do you know?"

"You have a pulse."

"What?"

"Just kidding. I said that because I don't bring girls home."

"Ah."

"Well, seriously, she'd like you because she can read people really well, and she'd think you were sweet."

"Did she ever meet Jenna?"

"Yes. She did meet her a few times, wasn't crazy about her, thought she was too loud."

I laughed. "Too loud?"

"Yes. My mother is kind of a quiet person, very introspective. She's more of a listener than a talker."

"Well, she's lucky to have two good sons looking after her."

Damien and I talked for a while and finished off both pizzas. I sipped my wine and tried to enjoy these moments with him, unsure if anything would be the same between us after tomorrow.

After dinner, the Double Ds joined us on the couch. There was one dog on each side of me, serving as a welcome buffer between Damien and me. We started watching *The Omen*, which was seriously one of the freakiest films I had ever seen. I'd always remembered hearing about the character of Damien but never actually sat through the movie.

It was dark in the living room, except for the lights coming from the television. I turned to him. "I'm sorry. Your autobiography is way more terrifying than mine ever was."

"You think?"

The weirdest part about the movie was the inclusion of Hellhounds, dogs that assisted Damien in his acts of evil. They were the same exact breed as The Double Ds.

Unable to keep from laughing, I said, "I swear to God, I had no clue that there were rottweilers in this movie."

He pretended to be angry. "You planned this, didn't you?"

"Yup. I was around in the seventies orchestrating a movie to haunt you with years later."

"How freaky is this shit, though?" He looked over at the dogs. "Look at them. They don't seem amused by their cameo, either."

"I don't blame them. I'm definitely going to have nightmares tonight."

His phone chimed, and he looked down to check it. I wondered if it was a woman but curbed my temptation to ask. My reaction served as a reminder of exactly why I was moving.

We stuck it out until the end of *The Omen*. The dogs had given up on the movie and were hiding out in the other room. It was getting late.

"So, what next?" Damien asked. "Want to watch something else?"

"I should probably go back. We have a long day tomorrow."

"This is it? Your last night here, and we ended it watching that crazy shit? That's what you're gonna remember me by? Damien and his Hellhounds?"

"You act like you won't see me anymore."

"Honestly, I kind of do feel like that. When you live right next door to someone, it's effortless. But you'll be across town, and realistically, it's only a matter of time before things change. You'll meet someone. He's not gonna want you hanging out with me."

Whenever he would pawn me off to other men with his words, it stung. I noticed how quiet it was all of a sudden with the dogs in the other room and the television off. I also noticed Damien staring at the bruise he'd given me on my neck. Shivers ran through me when he briefly grazed the area with his fingertip.

"You should really cover this up tomorrow."

It was the first time he'd acknowledged it.

"Why?"

"Your parents are gonna wonder where it came from."

"I'll just tell them you attacked my neck in a women's bathroom."

Damien didn't seem amused. "No, you won't."

"I was just joking."

"Seriously, you should cover it up."

"You don't like looking at it?"

When he ran his thumb over it, my breathing quickened. The brief touch ignited awareness throughout my body. What he said next totally undid me.

"I *love* looking at it. Too much."

We just stared at each other for a bit. His ears were red, and I could just sense that he was burning up inside as much as I was. I wanted so badly for him to kiss me, to touch me, to suck on every inch of my body. I had never wanted him more than I'd wanted him in that moment. The fact that I was moving tomorrow did nothing to curb the fire inside of me.

"What if that woman hadn't walked in on us, Damien?" I whispered.

That question had been haunting me.

It took him a while to answer before he said, "I don't know, Chelsea. I would've been fucked."

"Technically, *I* would have been fucked."

He cracked a smile and looked at me like he didn't know whether he wanted to kiss me or strangle me.

I wanted to scream out that I knew he was hiding something. I wanted to scream out that whatever it was, it didn't matter to me because there was nothing worse than losing him. But I couldn't betray his brother, who'd shared that information with me in confidence. Feeling like I was going to burst, I needed to get it off my chest.

"I have to say something, because I don't think we're gonna have much time alone tomorrow, and I just want to set the record straight. And I swear, Damien, this is the last you're gonna hear me speak of it."

He backed away from me a bit. "Alright."

"You say that I'll forget you once I leave, but I can guarantee you that won't be true. I might move on, yes, because you've left me no choice. But that doesn't change how I feel about you. You're in my heart, and I can't get you out. I don't know if I want to. Being with you is the only thing that *feels* right. It would be one thing if you just didn't have feelings for me, but if you're telling yourself that I am better off without you, then you're just wrong. If the emptiness I'm feeling tonight is any indication, I am definitely *not* better off."

"Chel—"

"Let me finish. When I first met you, I was in the worst place. The *worst*. The ironic thing is, even if you choose to disappear from my life after tomorrow, you are the reason that I now have the strength to handle it—to handle anything. I will always be indebted to you for bringing me out of that funk, for showing me that I deserved better, for being a friend and for being honest with me even when it hurt. I'm stronger now than I was, and I'm stronger than you think. Anything you ever have to say...I can handle the truth, Damien. That's it. I've said *my* truth."

My statement was a bit risky. It sort of implied that I knew he was hiding something when technically, that conversation with Tyler "never happened," but I needed to say it.

"I hear you," he simply said.

"On that note, I should try to get some sleep." I hopped up from the couch. "Big day tomorrow."

He followed close behind me as I walked toward the door. It seemed like either he didn't want me to leave or that he was readying to say something. He never did. He just stood at the doorway with a look in his eyes that seemed to carry the weight of a thousand unsaid words. I didn't know if he'd ever allow himself to set them free. In the meantime, I needed to move on with my life.

I guess you could say I was throwing in the towel. But in a sense, it felt more like I was giving it to him, hoping he'd hand it back someday.

CHAPTER **FOURTEEN**

Moving On

Sleep was impossible that night.

Somehow, now that moving day was here, it seemed more and more like leaving was the wrong decision. There was no going back. My belongings were boxed away, and I was trying to mentally pack away my feelings along with my possessions. I had to keep reminding myself that, ultimately, Damien wasn't fighting for me to stay. A part of him wanted this scenario, too, because it somehow made his life easier if I were gone.

The toaster oven that he had given me sat unplugged on the counter. I decided to take it next door to return it.

With disheveled hair and red eyes, Damien looked like he'd also had a rough night. His muscles were busting through a form-fitting, blue t-shirt. "What are you doing?" he said, his voice raspy from sleep.

"Returning this."

"Are you kidding?"

"No, it's yours."

"Keep it, Chelsea."

"What if you need to toast something? It won't be right next door anymore."

"I'll live."

"I really would prefer you take it back."

"Are we seriously arguing about a fucking toaster right now? Keep it, alright? Kind of like a memento."

Adjusting my grip on it, I conceded. "Alright. Since you put it that way."

"Go put it back, then get your ass back here for some breakfast with us."

We ate quietly, neither of us bringing up the subject of what was happening today. Damien would be dropping the dogs off at Jenna's after we ate, so that he could spend the day helping me move. We had agreed that I wouldn't actually say goodbye to the animals, that I would simply treat it like any other day. Well, that was ideal in theory, but when I got up to leave, they followed me to the door, and I could have sworn it was like they knew. They usually didn't let me leave without a lick fest, but this time it lasted longer. They also let me hug them, whereas normally they were too jumpy for an embrace. The Double Ds definitely sensed something.

Wiping the tears from my eyes, I refused to look at Damien as I made my way back to my apartment to wait for my parents. I also refused to look out the window at Damien walking the dogs through the courtyard because it would make me cry all over again. I had to pull myself together before my parents got here.

♦ ♦ ♦

It was a cloudy day, and that seemed fitting. The fact that it was cooler out also helped justify my wearing a turtle-neck to hide my hickey.

My parents had just arrived. Since Damien went to pick up the U-Haul truck, they hadn't met him yet.

My mother wrapped a vase in some bubble wrap. "You know we love seeing you, but why exactly are we doing all of this today? This apartment is absolutely beautiful. Why would you leave?"

There was no way I was going to get into everything with them, so I lied, "I just needed a change of scenery."

Dad chuckled. "Seems like a lot of effort for a change of scenery."

"I realize that. Thank you again for coming to help me."

My mother examined my face. "Are you okay? You don't look right."

"I'm good. I'm just a little tired, didn't get much sleep last night."

She placed her hand on my shoulder. "Were you nervous about the move?"

"Maybe a little, yeah."

"Well, hopefully when your friend gets here, we can get you settled, so you can have it behind you. Dad's gonna take us out to dinner to celebrate."

"That sounds nice." I smiled.

"What is your friend's name again?" my father asked.

"Damien. He's actually the landlord, and he lives next door."

"Oh. That's interesting," he said.

My mother smiled. "Damien...where do I know that name?"

Dad laughed. "Reminds me of that movie, *The Omen*."

"Speaking of the devil," Damien said as he entered the room.

"I apologize for my husband's rudeness."

"Like father, like daughter. That was exactly what Chelsea said when we first met." Damien smiled and held out his hand to my mother. "Mrs. Jameson, it's a pleasure to meet you." He turned to Dad. "Mr. Jameson."

"Call me Hal."

"Okay, sir."

Damien looked at me. "I've got the truck parked right outside and a couple of dollies out in the hall. I'm gonna see what heavy stuff I can take myself before I need your dad's help."

"Okay. Sounds good. Thank you."

"No problem."

After he left, my mother said, "He seems nice."

"He is." I just kept taping boxes and wouldn't look her in the eye.

Dad walked toward the door. "I'm gonna go help Damien now. He shouldn't be doing all of the heavy lifting himself."

My father and Damien worked together as Mom and I made numerous trips up and down the elevator with all of the smaller items.

After a couple of hours, the truck was fully packed, and it was time to head over to the new place.

My parents got into their Subaru, and Dad punched my new address into his GPS. "Are you riding with us or with Damien?"

"I'll ride in the truck with him."

"Alright." My mother smiled. "Dad wants a coffee. We're going to stop and get some on our way. You want one?"

"Yeah. I'd love one."

"How about Damien?"

"No, thank you," he quickly said.

After my parents drove off, Damien and I were alone for the first time when he asked, "Ready?"

"I'm just gonna go back upstairs one last time. I can't remember if I checked under the bathroom sink."

Really, I just wanted to see my place one final time.

"Alright."

My shoes echoed against the wood floor. The apartment may have been empty, but it was filled with so many memories. I looked out my window to catch a last glimpse of Damien's mural from this view.

I didn't think he followed me upstairs until his deep voice echoed behind me. "Did you find anything?"

"Huh?"

"Under the sink."

"No." I said, still staring out the window.

"That's not why you came up here, is it?"

Turning around, I told the truth. "I wanted to look around one last time."

Damien walked slowly toward me. "You can come back and visit anytime, you know."

"I know."

His body was close as we just stared at each other. The silence was deafening. I knew in my heart that nothing would be the same after today. As I breathed in his now familiar and comforting smell, it truly felt like I was leaving home, in some ways even more than when I'd first moved out of my parents' house the first time.

"We should go," he whispered. "I don't want your parents to have to wait for us."

Inside I was crying, but in reality, at this point, my actual tears were all dried up. I needed to put on my big girl panties and get this show on the road.

"I'm ready."

The ride was quiet, neither of us saying a word.

When we pulled up to the new building, my parents were waiting outside, sipping their coffees.

My mother handed me a to-go cup. "It might not be as hot as you like it."

As Damien opened the back of the U-Haul, my father joked, "Now we get to do this all over again."

Remembering that I didn't have the key, I said, "I just have to go to the management office. Be right back."

After verifying my identification, the woman at the desk handed me three keys on a chain. "Here are your keys."

"Isn't there just one? Are these duplicates?"

"No. The landlord had some new locks put on your door. So, you'll actually need three keys, one for each. This one is for the deadbolt, this one is for the padlock, and this one is for the bottom lock."

"Does every tenant have three? I don't remember that when I came to see this place."

"No. It was a special request by a third-party."

This had Damien written all over it.

As I returned to the truck, I waved the keys. "Three locks?"

Damien laughed guiltily. "When I came to check this place out, I was able to break into your apartment. I had a little chat with your landlord about all of the other violations I happened to notice—nothing that puts you in danger, only stuff I would notice because I'm a building owner myself. Let's just say, he was happy to add those locks free of charge."

"You're nuts."

"I'm not next door anymore to keep an eye out. I just want you to be safe."

Mom interrupted, "Is this not a safe neighborhood? It doesn't seem as nice as Damien's building."

"It is pretty safe," Damien answered. "But with the locks, it's much safer."

My father placed his hand on Damien's shoulder. "Thank you for looking out."

"No problem. I'm gonna start taking up some of the heavy stuff."

My mother gave me a confused look. She was picking up on my mood and was starting to suspect something in regards to Damien and me. I could tell she really wanted to talk to me, but she likely wouldn't have the chance.

Another two hours passed, and we'd finally moved everything inside. While none of the small stuff was put away, all of the big items were situated in their rightful places.

Dad clapped his hands together. "Well, I don't know about you guys, but I'm starving."

"We were going to go out to dinner, Damien. I hope you'll join us?" my mother said.

"Only if it's okay with Chelsea. She might want to badmouth me in peace for turning her apartment into Fort Knox."

Smacking him playfully, I said, "You'd better be coming."

"Alright, then."

Dinner at Hooligan's Family Style Restaurant started out pretty routine. We each ordered the salad bar, which they were known for, and an entrée. Dad and Damien drank from the same pitcher of Blue Moon beer, while Mom and I shared a bottle of Chardonnay. They listened as I spoke about the latest happenings at the youth center, and Damien told the story of his presentation on Arts Night.

After the waitress cleared our plates, my father decided to start questioning me about the move. That was when things went seriously downhill.

"I have to admit, honey. I was not very impressed with this new place. I love spending time with you, but that was an awful lot of work just to move you to a crappier neighborhood. If there was a legitimate reason, I could see it. It makes me question your judgment a little."

After downing my wine, I glanced over at Damien.

He was staring at me when he suddenly dropped a bomb. "She's moving because of me."

"What are you doing?" I whispered.

"What are you talking about?" my mother asked.

"It has nothing to do with the apartment. She's moving because of me."

"Damien..." I said in an attempt to get him to stop where this was going.

"Let me explain it to them. They're your parents. They love you. And I don't want them questioning your judgment. There is nothing wrong with your judgment."

He turned to my father. "Your daughter is one of the best people I've ever known. She's become a great friend and has opened her heart to me several times. I care for her deeply, and as you probably figured out, I'm very protective of her. That also means protecting her from me. I just can't be the kind of man she deserves as a lifelong partner. I've had too many moments where I've seemed to forget that, because she makes it so damn easy to forget. I was trying so hard not to hurt her like *he* did, but I somehow managed to anyway. She's moving to protect herself from getting hurt any further." He turned to me. "I'm so sorry."

I needed some air. "Excuse me." My chair scratched the floor as I got up and rushed to the bathroom.

Somehow his being so open in front of my parents, apologizing to me in front of them, gave an unwanted finality to the situation. He wasn't even trying to pretend that things were great between us anymore, because they weren't.

This felt like a breakup.

There hadn't been any actual sex involved in our relationship, but my emotions had been all in since day one.

Damien helping me move.

That speech.

I needed to see the situation tonight for what it was.

Damien was ending it.

After I returned to the table, the rest of the dinner was quiet.

When Damien eventually took off in the empty U-Haul truck, I urged my parents not to pry any further and assured them that I would be okay. They hugged me goodbye and left me alone in my new apartment.

Later that night, sitting on my bed and surrounded by boxes, I got an unwanted housewarming present. It came in the form of an email from the last person I ever expected.

Chelsea,

It took me a while to figure out if I should even send this message, mainly because I just don't want to upset you. I needed to let you know how good it was to see you at Bad Boy Burger. I'm pretty sure you saw me, but in case you didn't, it was the day you were sucking face with some dude who had a lower arm tat. I was going to go over and say something, but you seemed a little busy. I've lived with a lot of guilt since our breakup. Seeing that you'd moved on with someone else made me truly happy.
I wish you nothing but happiness.

Elec

I wouldn't write back. The timing of that message was seriously like a sucker punch to the gut.

Shutting my laptop, I closed my eyes and cried myself to sleep for the last time, vowing that tomorrow would be the beginning of a new phase of my life.

CHAPTER **FIFTEEN**

Stalker

My sister liked to call me during her meal in between performances.

Jade spoke with her mouth full, "You haven't heard from him at all in two weeks?"

"No. And I'm telling you, after that speech in front of Mom and Dad, I just knew this was going to happen. It was like he was setting me up perfectly for life without him—apologizing to my parents, putting those locks on the doors. And his mood was just really bizarre and guarded that whole last day. It's out of sight, out of mind now apparently for him."

"So, you don't plan to visit him or call?"

"I'm not going to be the first one to do that, no. It's like what you were telling me a while back. You didn't understand why I wouldn't listen to all of the warnings he gave me. I just kept holding out hope. But the fact that he hasn't contacted me since that night is really disappointing. I seriously feel like I'm never gonna hear from him again." It pained me to say those words.

"I can tell you're trying to be strong about this, but

deep down, I know you're hurting, and I know it's not easy for you to not call him."

"I just can't believe he hasn't called or texted."

"It's probably for the best, you know? I know you wanted to stay friends with the guy. But really...I don't think you were ever capable of keeping your feelings in check. You needed this space he's giving you now. On some level, I think he knows that's really best for you, too."

"So, what's my next step?"

"You need to get back on that dating site."

Even though the thought of that made me cringe, I knew I had to force myself to keep my mind off of Damien. "Actually, there was this guy Mark I was supposed to have gone out with weeks ago. I kept putting it off."

"Then contact him. You definitely need to get out, but more than that, you need a distraction."

"Okay. You're right, even if it's just to get out of the apartment."

"You know, you're not going to get over him overnight."

"I don't know if I'll *ever* get over him. I just have to accept that."

"Accepting the things you can't change...now there's a novel idea."

"I preach that to the kids all the time. It's time I started taking my own advice.

♦ ♦ ♦

"I'm so glad we're finally doing this," Mark said as he opened the car door to let me out. "I was beginning to think you were totally blowing me off."

"No. I was busy with the move and all. I'm sorry if I gave you that impression."

We'd just arrived at the cinema for a nine-forty showing of the new James Bond movie. I figured a crowded theater was a safe place for a first date, although Damien would have scolded me for getting into Mark's car.

Damien doesn't have a say anymore.

The smell of buttery popcorn filled the air. Mark wrapped his arm around my waist as we walked to get in line. He was definitely forward, and I wasn't sure how I felt about that, since the verdict was still out on my level of attraction to him both mentally and physically. There was also the minor detail of the fact that we'd just freaking met.

After we got tickets, we were waiting in the concession line when Mark spoke in my ear, "Were you ever a gymnast?"

That was an odd question.

"No. Why do you ask?"

"Your body looks very limber, like you might have a gymnastics background."

Was he serious?

"No. Can't even do a cartwheel."

After we'd gotten our popcorn and drinks, we stood in the line where the man was collecting tickets to enter the theater. I jumped when I felt Mark's hand on my lower waist. With each second that we waited, his hand slid lower until it was fully planted on my ass. My body stilled. After a minute of dealing with it, I positioned myself to face him so that he could no longer cop a feel.

Once inside, the lights hadn't even dimmed yet, and I was already planning my exit strategy for after the movie. To be honest, I wasn't even sure if I was comfortable getting into this guy's car again.

I was just about to shut my phone off when it started buzzing.

Do you always let guys you've just met grope your ass?

It was Damien.
My heart started to pound.
It beat faster and faster as I frantically looked around the dark theater for him. Was he here?

Chelsea: Are you in this theater?

Damien: Where are you?

Chelsea: Don't you already know the answer to that question, since you're apparently stalking me?

Damien: You were supposed to be going to see the new James Bond movie. That's where I am. Where are you?

Chelsea: We went to see the Will Smith movie. James Bond was sold out by the time we got to the counter.

Damien: Tell him you have to use the bathroom and meet me outside.

When I didn't immediately answer, he texted again.

Damien: I just need five minutes.

Chelsea: Ok.

"I'll be right back," I whispered just as the previews were starting. "Going to the restroom."

Seeing Damien standing there, leaning against a wall as he waited for me nearly took my breath away. It made me realize that my feelings for him hadn't lessened one bit throughout this time apart. Every bit of longing returned instantaneously, and that really sucked for me. My heart wanted to leap into his arms and ask him to take me home, but my brain stopped my legs from moving any farther than a foot away from him.

Wearing his beanie, he looked and smelled so good. He wore a white collared shirt under a fitted black sweater, which was a different look for him. The sweater clung to his muscular chest, and he had the sleeves rolled up, displaying a thick metal watch I'd never seen before. Black jeans and big black cargo boots finished off the look.

He'd gotten all dressed up to stalk me?

"Hi," he finally said. His voice sent shivers throughout my body. I'd missed hearing it so much.

"What are you doing?"

"You never gave me his information to check him out."

"I didn't even realize we were still *speaking*. How did you know I was here and planning to see the James Bond movie?" I snapped my finger. "Oh, that's right. You hack into my account."

"You never changed your password."

"I shouldn't have to. That doesn't give you the right to do this."

"I'm just making sure you're safe."

"You're a stalker."

"I don't give two fucks if that's what you think. I already told you I had a bad feeling about that guy. If I need to swallow my pride and make a fool of myself to make sure you get home safe, I will."

"Why are you getting involved in my life? You dropped off the face of the Earth—not one word since you moved me out."

"That doesn't mean I stopped caring about you. Staying away from you these past few weeks has been the hardest thing I've ever done."

"Why don't you spend Friday night picking up one of your whores and stay out of my business?"

"If you'd choose men who weren't creepy, maybe I wouldn't have to get involved."

"You don't have a right to tell me who to date." Anger and bitterness rose like bile through me as I said,

"I'm only out with him because I didn't matter enough to you."

"You have no idea how much you fucking matter to me," he spat out.

"This time away has taught me a lot. I couldn't ever really be your friend because I couldn't limit my feelings for you. I didn't know how to do that. You were right in keeping your distance. You should have kept it that way."

Just then, a tall brunette seemed to come out of nowhere. Her lips were painted bright red. "There you are," she said. "I thought maybe you ditched me."

I looked her up and down then turned to him. "You're on a date?" Raising my voice, I repeated, "You brought a date to stalk me on mine?"

"No. That's not how it happened."

Jealousy was pumping through my veins. I turned to her. "Do you know you're dating a stalker?"

"Is this your sister or something?" she asked.

"It would seem that way, wouldn't it?" I huffed.

"I'll be there in a minute, okay?" he told her. "Go watch the movie. It's gonna start."

When she was gone, I shook my head. "I can't believe this."

"I didn't mean for you to see her."

"Whatever," I said under my breath.

As he approached me, I backed away, refusing to allow myself any reaction to the nearness of his body.

"Look, I was out to dinner nearby, and I happened to log into the site on my phone. I saw you were gonna be here. I thought maybe I would catch you coming out of that dude's car, so I could run his plate to get info and check him out. You ended up getting here late, fucked up my plan. I don't want you getting in his car again until I've checked him out."

"If I want to get in his car…if I want to let him *fuck me* tonight…that's my decision."

A vein popped out of his neck. "Don't say that."

"You can't handle even a little of your own medicine? You mean to tell me you're not gonna take her back to your apartment tonight?"

"Actually, no. I don't even like her."

"Isn't that the point?"

"It used to be. It doesn't feel right anymore. This was the first time I'd gone out in a very long time. I forced myself because I desperately needed a distraction, since I've been trying like hell to stay away from you."

"You really shouldn't have followed me here."

"I swear to God, it wasn't my intention to let you see me. And it definitely wasn't my intention to let you see me with her."

"I bet," I said, crossing my arms.

"I just wanted to check things out. When I saw the way you let him touch you, I fucking lost it."

"Do you have any idea how badly it hurts me to see you with that fucking bimbo? You didn't need to follow me here with her." I muttered, "Stop hurting me."

Again, he started to move in close to me, prompting me to back away.

"I'm sorry, Chelsea. I know I fucked up. I didn't handle this well, but I don't want you getting in his car again."

"How am I supposed to get home?"

"I'll drive you."

Laughing angrily, I chided, "I'm sure your date would love that."

"I don't give a fuck what she thinks. I just want you home safe."

Now, I was getting in his face intentionally. "You're insane. You've lost your mind, Damien."

"I don't trust him. I'm telling you, he's dangerous."

"I think *you're* the dangerous one tonight. Please stay out of my life. I don't want to ever see you again."

I turned around and never looked back. After entering the theater, I bypassed my seat, instead exiting out an emergency door to the parking lot.

As I passed Damien's parked truck, I noticed he'd added three decals to the rear window: a man and two dogs.

My heart clenched at the sight. I missed him so much, yet I couldn't deal with being in his presence anymore.

Replaying the night repeatedly in my head, I walked a couple of miles then hopped a bus home.

Damien sent me one text sometime after midnight.

I didn't mean for shit to go down like that. I really was just trying to make sure you were safe. I fucked up. I'm sorry. Please just let me know you got home okay.

I never answered.

◆ ◆ ◆

The more I thought about the movie theater incident over the next week, the angrier it made me.

The more I thought about the movie theater incident...the more I missed Damien.

I was still so confused.

I told myself I was going to his apartment that day to give him a final piece of my mind, to have the final say, since I never answered the text. That was a lie. I was going to his apartment because I missed him and the dogs, but I would tell myself otherwise to justify it. The truth was, I was satisfying the intense urge to see him.

An unusual sight greeted me as I approached the building. A crowd was gathered outside. Had the fire alarm gone off?

When I spotted The Double Ds with Murray, it made me wonder where Damien was in the midst of this chaos. Dudley and Drewfus were both chained to a fence.

The dogs had almost no reaction as I bent down to rub their heads. Looking up at Murray, I asked, "What the heck is going on?"

"It's Damien."

"What about Damien?"

"He collapsed. Ambulance just took him to the hospital."

I had to ask the question again, because the answer he gave me wasn't possible.

My heart and head were pounding in synch. "What? What happened?"

"The dogs were banging themselves against the door, scratching against the wood, barking like crazy. When I knocked, he didn't answer. I used my key and found him on the ground unconscious, called 911." He shook his head. "Poor Boss."

If I weren't already crouched down, I might have collapsed myself.

"Is he going to be okay?"

"I don't know."

"Where did they take him?"

"I don't know."

"I need to know!"

"Memorial and General are both equally close. It has to be either one of those."

I felt dizzy because I stood up so fast. "I took the bus here. I need your car."

Murray gave me his keys, and I took off before realizing I didn't even know which car was his.

He followed me and put his hand on my shoulder. Sensing my disoriented state, he said, "You shouldn't drive like this."

"I have to. You need to stay with the dogs."

He pointed to a small older Nissan. "That's my car. Be careful."

"I won't crash."

"I'm not worried about the shit car. I'm worried about you."

Running to the vehicle, I dialed Damien's phone. It went to voicemail. I then punched the address for General into my phone. Ten minutes later, I parked illegally at the emergency room entrance.

Out of breath, I rushed to the front desk. "I need to know if Damien Hennessey is here."

"I'm sorry you'll have to wait in line."

Leaning into the counter, I shouted, "No! You need to tell me if he's here!"

She must have noticed that I was crying, because she decided to check her computer.

"Spell his last name?"

After I obliged, she shook her head. "I'm sorry. No one by that name has checked in here. He must be at Memorial."

Without responding, I ran as fast as I could back to the car, punched the other address into my GPS app, and sped the entire way to Memorial.

While tears streamed down my cheeks, my mind raced with fearful thoughts, namely that if something had happened to Damien, my very last words to him were, *"I don't want to ever see you again."*

I would never forgive myself if something happened to him.

I just needed to see him.

I needed to get to him.

He needed to be okay.

When I finally arrived at Memorial Hospital, my heart felt like it was in my mouth as I made my way to the emergency room.

"I need to see Damien Hennessey. He was brought here about an hour ago."

The receptionist punched some keys and said, "He was admitted."

"Where is he?"

"Are you family?"

"I'm not related, no."

"They may not be able to give you much info or let you see him. He's on the third floor, though. Take those elevators."

Everything seemed to be happening in slow motion: sliding into an elevator at the last second; weaving my way through the halls of the third floor.

Then, I saw him. Or so I thought. In my haze, I had mistaken Tyler for Damien. Tyler was pacing with his hands in his pockets.

He stopped when he saw me and looked a bit panicked. "Chelsea?"

A rush of adrenaline hit me. "Where is he?"

"He's okay. He's okay. He's alive."

Thank God.

Thank you, God.

"I need to see him."

"You can't right now."

"Why not?"

"He's with his doctor."

"I'm going in."

He placed his hands on my arms to stop me. "No, Chelsea."

"Tell me what's going on."

Tyler just stared at me for the longest time. He walked over to the nurses' station and grabbed a tissue before handing it to me.

"Come on. Let's take a walk."

CHAPTER **SIXTEEN**

Broken Hearted

Tyler led me out to a grassy area just outside of the hospital doors. The late afternoon sun was starting to set, and the cool breeze dried my tears a bit.

He was alive.

I reminded myself that whatever Tyler was about to tell me couldn't be that bad because Damien was alive. He was talking to his doctors, right?

"It's gonna be okay," he said.

"What's going on, Tyler? Don't beat around the bush anymore. I can't handle it."

"Come sit." He led me over to a bench. "This is a conversation you were supposed to have had with him. But if he had his way, it never would have happened. I don't care if he kills me. You need to know."

"What? Need to know what?"

"Damien fainted. His blood pressure dropped suddenly. He was probably under a lot of stress lately and not taking good care of himself. That's what brought him here today."

"Okay...that's not that bad."

"It's happened before. Over the past few years, he's been getting more symptoms—symptoms that didn't exist until recently."

"Symptoms of what?"

"Damien has a heart condition, Chelsea. It's called hypertrophic cardiomyopathy."

"What?"

"A long name, I know. It's inherited. It's the same condition that killed our father."

My heart sank, and I swallowed the lump in my throat. "What does it mean?"

"It means a part of his heart muscle is thickened. Sometimes, there are no symptoms and people, like my dad, don't even know they have it. They just go into sudden cardiac arrest. Many of them die. In Damien's case, we found out through genetic testing that he has it. More recently, he's been experiencing some mild symptoms."

"How long has he known?"

"For about five years. My mother wanted us both to get tested for it, because it took my father so young. There was a fifty percent chance that either of us had it. I tested negative. When Damien realized he has the same condition that killed Dad, he became convinced that the same thing would happen to him. That's partly why he bought that building. He decided he didn't want to spend precious time working the daily grind. He preferred to spend his days doing what he loved, making art."

"Is everyone with this disease destined to die young?"

"No, that's the thing. Many live completely normal lives. There is just no way to know."

"But Damien is convinced he'll die young?"

"Yes. And that's why he refuses to get involved with you, because he doesn't want what happened to my mother to happen to you."

"Why couldn't he tell me?"

"Because he knew you would say it didn't matter. He didn't want you to know. He wanted you to move on, find someone else, so that you never had to get hurt. It kills him to push you away, because he's crazy about you."

I had to stop to compose myself. It was an over-whelming a-ha moment. It was like he'd just handed me a gigantic missing puzzle piece. Everything finally made sense.

Damien's words from our conversation on the beach in Santa Cruz rang out in my mind.

"My heart is broken."

It finally made sense!

"He's crazy."

Ty chuckled. "I tell him that all the time."

"What are the doctors discussing with him right now?"

"When Damien's doctor from Stanford found out he was here, he made a special trip to come down here and see him." Ty scratched his chin. "Okay, so there's another part to this story. For some time now, Damien's cardiologists have been trying to convince him to have open-heart surgery."

"Oh, my God." My heart was pounding uncontrol-lably.

"Yeah. He's scared. He thinks the surgery alone might kill him. It absolutely terrifies him, but more and more, it's seeming like something he should consider."

"What will the surgery do to help?"

"They would basically remove part of the overgrown muscle to help blood flow. They think it would improve his quality of life as time goes on and might lengthen his life expectancy. But there are serious risks with that type of surgery. Remember our trip to Los Angeles...when you watched the dogs?"

"Yeah."

"We'd gone to speak to a specialist at Cedar Sinai. He has doctors there and at Stanford."

"Wow."

"That trip to L.A. was when I realized Damien was really falling for you. He wouldn't stop talking about you."

"I love him," I said without hesitation. It was the first time I'd said it out loud, but far from the first time I'd said it.

"I know. I can tell."

"What do I do?"

"Don't listen to the asshole. He's going to continue to try to convince you that it's best not to get involved with him. He will fight you tooth and nail. He thinks every day could be his last. There's good and bad that comes from that attitude. He lives each day like it's his last, yet the one thing that could make him the happiest, he won't allow himself out of fear of hurting you. He's a selfless person, but he should let *you* make the decision. He's trying to make it for you because he thinks he knows what's best for you."

"*He's* what's best for me." I stood up from the bench and started pacing. "I need to see him. Can I tell him you told me everything?"

"Yes. I'll deal with his wrath. It was time, especially after what happened today. If he had his way, you'd still be in the dark. He never had any intention of telling you he was here."

"I believe it."

"He's really stubborn."

"Don't I know it."

"We should go back inside," he said.

"Okay."

When we got back to Damien's floor, Ty said, "I'll let you have some time with him. You'll need it. I'm gonna get some coffee down at the cafeteria."

"Okay. Thank you, Ty."

I slowly approached Damien's room. Through a small, narrow window in the door, I could see he was fully dressed and sitting up at the edge of the bed. Knocking three times, I inhaled deeply then exhaled before entering.

His eyes nearly bulged out of their sockets when he saw me standing there. He said nothing. He didn't ask me what I was doing there. He just stared at me for the longest time, looking straight into my glistening eyes that gave everything away without my even having to say anything.

"You know," he said.

"Yes."

"Ty told you."

"Yes."

He dropped his head. "Fuck."

After allowing him almost a full minute to process, I finally spoke. "I understand."

"No, you don't. You just think you do."

"I do."

"This doesn't change anything, Chelsea. The end result is the same."

My instinct was to argue with him, but the smarter part of me knew that this wasn't the right time. He was recovering, and the last thing I wanted was to upset him. So, I just focused on today.

"Do you remember fainting?"

"No. I only remember waking up with the paramedics there."

"The dogs went to your rescue, you know. They alerted Murray, who called 911."

"Remind me to make them some bacon."

"Remind me to stay far away that day."

The mood lightened a bit when he cracked a slight smile. "How's your boyfriend, Marky Mark? I see you're still in one piece."

"I never went back into the theater that night. I skipped out a side door, never saw him again."

Damien feigned disappointment. "Such a shame." He looked so cute when he puckered his lips.

"How's the whore you were with?"

"She wasn't too happy. She told me I was way too interested in my sister's business, made me drive her straight home."

"Shame." I sat down next to him on the bed. "Nice try changing the subject off of you, by the way."

He let out a deep breath. "Didn't Tattle-Ty tell you everything? What do you want to know?"

"Why didn't you just tell me?"

His stare burned into mine. "You know why."

"It doesn't matter to me."

"That's exactly why I couldn't tell you. It was never that I thought you'd leave. It was that I knew you'd *stay*. You don't realize what getting involved with me could mean. Here today, gone tomorrow, Chelsea. You've already had your heart broken once. Is that what you really want?"

"You don't know what will happen. Any one of us could die tomorrow."

"But only some of us are *wired* to die early. It happened to my father. I have the same exact defect. And I don't want what happened to my mother to happen to you. I care about you far too much. End of story."

A moment of silence ensued.

"Your brother told me that they're trying to convince you to have surgery."

"That comes with its own risks." He paused. "I'm considering it, though. I don't want to get into that right now, okay?"

Respecting his wishes, I asked, "Are they discharging you soon?"

"Yeah. It really was just a fainting spell. Because of my condition, I'm more prone to that. Probably happened because I was dehydrated and under stress."

I hesitated to ask, "Were you stressed about me?"

He chuckled. "I've been stressed about you for months, so that probably wasn't it." He playfully tapped my thigh, causing my skin to prickle. "How did you find out I was here?"

"I'd gone to the apartment to apologize for being so harsh, and because I missed you and the dogs."

"They miss you, too."

"They said so?" I smiled.

"Not in so many words." He smiled. "But they stop at your door all the time."

"I miss the Double Ds. Actually, I miss...the Triple Ds." I cracked myself up. "I can't believe I've never thought of that before."

"That only just now dawned on you? I was waiting for you to figure it out."

"Thank God I went to the building when I did. If I'd waited until tomorrow, I would have never known about this. You would've never told me anything. I just know it."

"You're right. I wouldn't have. But like I said, your knowing doesn't change anything. I'm not good for you."

"Don't tell me what's good for me," I barked.

I stood up and walked toward the door, peeking outside to see if the doctor was coming.

Returning to Damien, I began to massage my fingers slowly through his hair and watched his resolve weaken with each second. He closed his eyes before clutching the material of my shirt and pulling me closer to him.

He leaned his head into my chest. "You're not allowed to come around anymore." Breathing into me, he said, "You make me forget all the shit I'm supposed to be doing right. I can't think straight." He then looked up at me. "You have no idea how much I wanted to kill that guy for touching your ass that night. I realized then more than ever what a lost cause I am when it comes to you. It pissed me the hell off."

"I love your jealousy. And you were totally right about him."

"I'm always right. Haven't you figured that out?"

The door opened, and Tyler walked in, holding a coffee. "Hey. I just talked to your doctor. They said you're free to go."

I turned to Ty. "Are you taking him back to the apartment?"

Knowing I didn't have a car, Damien asked, "How did you get here?"

"I pretty much stole Murray's car."

"That piece of shit? You were probably in more danger than I was."

"Do you want me to come take care of you?"

"Trust me, he wants you to *take care of him* very much," Ty cracked.

Damien shot daggers at him. "Shut the hell up."

◆ ◆ ◆

I ended up letting Damien rest that night, opting to head back to my apartment while Tyler took him home.

The first thing I did was open up my laptop to search the Internet for information on Damien's condition. Some of the stories about hypertrophic cardiomyopathy were terrifying. There were countless reports of young people who'd dropped dead without warning, some of them on athletic fields. Their families had only discovered the condition after the fact. One of the articles indicated that conditions like Damien's were responsible for at least forty percent of all sudden deaths in young athletes.

I also looked up the types of surgeries and the risks associated with them. It was all starting to hit me. It was easy to see how Damien let fear rule his world, especially when his fears weren't totally unfounded. An unbearable heaviness weighed on my chest. While it was all too easy to let my mind wander to that horrible place of "what ifs," I wasn't going to let fear rule *my* world.

I shot Damien out a text.

> *I was going to stop by tomorrow after work.*
> *Will you be home?*

> *Damien: Actually, I'm leaving in the morning.*
> *Going away to San Jose for a few days. I need*
> *some time away from here to think.*

What did that mean? Not knowing how to respond, I texted back the first thing that came to mind.

> *Chelsea: Do you know the way to San Jose?*

> *Damien: I do. And that's a song.*

> *Chelsea: Very good! My grandmother used to*
> *sing it to me. I used to always want to go to San*
> *Jose as a kid, thinking it was some far off place.*
> *Little did I know you were there.*

> *Damien: I would have tugged on your ponytail*
> *and thrown sand at you back then. I was a dick.*

> *Chelsea: So, not much has changed?*

Still making girls cry.

Damien: We'll catch up when I get back.

Chelsea: Actually, when you get back, I'll be gone. I'm leaving for NY to visit my sister. I'll be staying with her for a week.

Damien: Wow. I'm glad you're finally doing that.

He knew that was a big step for me, that I'd always avoided New York because Elec lived there. A few days before Damien's fainting episode, I'd finally bitten the bullet and purchased tickets to see Jade.

Chelsea: I guess I'll see you when I get back.

Damien: Ok. Be careful in the big city.

CHAPTER **SEVENTEEN**

Hit the Floor

It had truly been a dream come true to see Jade perform. She had a lead role in a new off-Broadway musical called *The Siren and The Suit*. The banter between her character, Eloise, and the main male character, Tom, was hysterical. Tom was played by a handsome actor named Jeremy Bright. I later learned Jeremy was very married in real life. Up until that point, I thought maybe something was brewing between Jade and him, but I guess they're just really convincing actors with great chemistry.

After the show, Jade took me to dinner with the cast. We went to a Japanese restaurant and bar called Sake Sake. Between the drinks and the loud conversations, I'd almost forgotten about Damien for a couple of hours. *Almost.*

When we got back to Jade's tiny apartment, though, thoughts of him were back in full force. It was the first time I had an opportunity to tell Jade the news of my discovering his heart condition. Since I knew I was coming to Manhattan, I'd waited to talk to her about it in person.

Jade sat on the floor with her legs crossed. Her face was still in full makeup. "Wow. I'm just...I'm speechless."

"I know."

"It's like everything I thought I knew about this situation just went out the window."

"What changed?"

"Well..." she said, "There was always a part of me that felt despite what he was telling you, that his feelings for you weren't as strong as yours for him. But this news is a game changer. He really *was* trying to protect you from getting hurt. I do think what his brother said was right, that he's in love with you and truly feels like he's protecting you."

"I won't believe that he's in love with me until I hear it from him. As much as I want to be with him, more than anything, I just want him to be okay." I glanced out at the city lights. "Bet you never thought I'd be in New York without a single mention of Elec, huh?"

"Well, that is the only great thing about your Damien woes."

"Seriously."

"Are you gonna call him while you're here?"

"I'm trying not to. I'm supposed to be giving him space. The ball is in his court. I can't force him to be with me. He said he had to go away for a few days to think."

"Where did he go?"

"Home to San Jose. His mother lives there."

"Well, then let's just try to get your mind off of things. I have the day off tomorrow. We'll go shopping, go see a show—one that I'm not in—and have a nice dinner."

"That sounds awesome."

◆ ◆ ◆

The week in New York City flew by. It was my last night, and I was alone while Jade was performing. My flight was scheduled for the next morning. As I waited for her to return so that we could have a late dinner together, I impulsively picked up my phone and decided to text Damien. Something about being so physically far away from him gave me a false sense of courage. My emotions just came pouring out.

> *This is bullshit. Of course I'm terrified to lose you, but I am way more terrified of living without you while you're alive and well. For the record, I would rather have a single day of truly being with you than twenty thousand days of going through the motions with someone who doesn't have my heart. I don't care if I never have the chance to grow old and decrepit with you. I want today. I want to watch creepy movies with you and the dogs, burn toast in your apartment. I want to feel you inside of me. I want to experience everything with you while we're both alive. WE ARE BOTH ALIVE. A good life is about quality, not quantity. I just want to be with you for however long that may be. But I can't force you to see things the way I do.*

When I hit send, I noticed that the message was faded and didn't say delivered. I had no clue whether or not it went through. Maybe it was an omen signifying that I had made a dire mistake.

Not knowing if it was my phone or an external issue, I decided to call him. I really needed to get everything off my chest one way or another while the words were fresh in my mind.

Damien's line rang, and my heart nearly stopped when a sleepy female voice answered, "Damien's phone."

Shock paralyzed me, so I said nothing for several seconds.

She repeated, "Hello?"

Swallowing, I said, "Who's this?"

"It's Jenna. Who's this?"

"Jenna..." I paused, dumbfounded. "It's Chelsea."

"Oh. Well, Damien's in the shower right now."

"What are you doing there?"

"What do you *think* I'm doing here?"

I quickly hung up.

Fuming, I grabbed my coat and ran out of Jade's apartment to get some air. Weaving through crowds of people on the busy streets of Times Square, I was too preoccupied with my thoughts to even realize how far I'd travelled. I didn't even know where I was anymore, both literally and figuratively.

While I was here in New York, still pining over him, he was apparently fucking his ex-girlfriend?

After about an hour of wandering around in a daze, I took my phone out of my purse and texted him.

You're a fool.

I kept waiting for him to respond. The minutes went by, and nothing came back from him.

I was done.

The fact that he hadn't responded was proof of his guilt.

I didn't understand whether he was on some self-destructive binge or whether he truly wanted to be with her. I just knew I wanted nothing to do with him anymore and vowed never to contact him again.

♦ ♦ ♦

The long flight back to San Francisco was torture. I'd actually considered cancelling my return ticket and staying in New York indefinitely with my sister. The only thing keeping me from doing just that was my job at the youth center. The kids needed me, and I couldn't risk losing the only thing that was going right in my life.

When I arrived home to my quiet apartment, I was already missing Jade.

I picked up the phone to call her.

"You made it home?"

"Yes. I'm here, but it doesn't feel like home anymore."

"I was pondering everything while you were up in the air. I really think you should call him."

"No. No way."

"You didn't hear it from him that he's back with her. You'll feel better if you talk to him even if it's not easy to hear what he has to say. At least you'll know. How much worse could the situation get? You're absolutely miserable."

"Are you forgetting he didn't even respond to my text?"

"I know. But I know you. Until you actually speak to him, it's going to be eating away at you."

"I can't call him."

"Don't call him. Just go over there. Check the situation out for yourself."

"I don't know. I'll think about it."

♦ ♦ ♦

The following day, I was leaving the youth center in the evening. We had a function that ran late. I ended up heading in the opposite direction of my apartment, instead venturing toward Damien's building.

A sick feeling stuck with me the entire way because I didn't know what I was going to find. I just knew I needed to see him one last time. My sister was right; it was only going to eat away at me if I didn't face him.

Jitters followed me up the stairs to my old apartment. To my surprise, the door was cracked open. I peeked inside to find that it was still empty. I had assumed that Damien rented it out ages ago.

Slowly creeping inside the doorway, I said, "Hello?" My voice echoed.

Damien emerged out of my old bedroom. Sweat glistened off his chest. Paint was splattered onto various sections of his body. He looked even more jacked than I remembered. His jeans were slightly opened at the top, and his hair was unruly. His feet were bare. He looked hotter than I'd ever seen him. His heady smell was a mix of cologne and sweat.

I *ached* for him.

Swallowing, I asked, "What are you doing?"

"I got your message. Your text fucked me up. So, I'm doing a little painting."

"Well, I meant it. You *are* a fool."

"That's not the message I'm referring to."

I realized he was talking about the text I'd sent right before I called and discovered Jenna at his apartment—the text where I'd poured my heart out. It must have gone through after all.

Shit.

"I didn't think it went through. I was hoping it didn't. It was a mistake."

"No, it wasn't."

"How's Jenna?" I bit out.

His tone was insistent. "Nothing happened between me and Jenna. She'd used her key to enter the apartment when I was in the shower. I didn't even know you called until later."

"She answered the phone sounding like she'd just rolled out of your bed. When I asked her what she was doing there, she told me I should know."

"She's full of shit, Chelsea."

"Why would she lie?"

"Because she can be a bitch when she wants to be. She was messing with you, wanted to hurt you. If you call her and ask her right now, she'll tell you the truth."

"Why didn't you respond to my text, then?"

"Because for a short, slightly insane period of time that night, once I figured out what happened, I got a bright idea. I used it as an opportunity. I actually *wanted* you to believe it. I wanted you to believe it so you would run the other way once and for all. Because at the time, I still truly thought that was what's best for you."

"At the *time*...what changed in a day?"

"Everything." He walked toward me. "Everything fucking changed."

"How?"

"I didn't get your long text until this morning. I'd felt so guilty before that for not responding to your text when you called me a fool. I've been so fucked-up since you found out about my condition. I never intended for you to know. Anyway, last night, I had a dream. It was extremely vivid. I dreamt that your plane..." He hesitated. "I dreamt that it crashed. And you died. It felt so real, Chelsea. All I could think was that I had never told you how I truly felt about you. I was filled with a completely unbearable regret. In the dream, I remember thinking that I would have given anything for just one more day with you. I'd wasted so many. When I woke up, I was soaked with sweat. I went on the Internet just to make sure that there weren't any planes that crashed, because that was how real the dream felt. It totally fucked me up. I'd powered down my phone before bed. When I turned it on, I saw your message. Everything you said was exactly what I experienced in that dream. It was like the two things were connected. And I just saw everything so clearly."

"Why didn't you contact me after that?"

"I've been so overwhelmed, just trying to process what I'm feeling. I wasn't sure how to express it to you. I still really don't know how to put it into words. So, I did what I know how to do best. I painted. I painted all damn day."

"What did you paint?"

"Your room."

"*My* room? How come you haven't rented this apartment out? I assumed you'd done that a long time ago."

"No. I couldn't. This is your place. I think a part of me was always waiting for you to come back."

Walking toward the room, I wanted to see what color he'd chosen for the space.

I stopped short and nearly fell over.

When he'd mentioned he painted my room, he didn't mean a solid color. He'd used my wall as a canvas. He'd used *our* wall to create one of the most beautiful images I'd ever laid eyes on. Spray painted onto the smooth surface using a mixture of white and pastel paints, was a gigantic unicorn that looked like it was flying freely through the sky.

I covered my mouth. "Oh, my God. What did you do?"

"It's you."

"What?"

His mouth curved into a smile. "You're my unicorn..."

I blinked repeatedly. "This is insane."

He stepped toward me slowly. "Mythically beautiful. Unattainable. Remember what your therapist said?

At the time, I thought it was ridiculous. But the more I think about it, the more it makes sense to me. You were a fantasy that I never thought would come true. That's what you have always been to me. I didn't get it then. But you're my unicorn." He placed his hands firmly around my cheeks. "You're my fucking unicorn, Chelsea."

"I am?"

"Yes. And there's something else I need to tell you." Goosebumps peppered my skin from the contact when he pulled me closer and placed his forehead on mine. "When I first woke up in that ambulance, for a split second, I didn't know if I had died. They say your life flashes before your eyes, right? Well, you were the only thing that flashed before mine. Just you."

He just kept looking into my eyes. For the first time, I could feel him surrendering to his feelings. You could literally *feel* the release emanating through his bones. I could feel it in the possessive way he was holding my face, in the way his hand was trembling ever so slightly. He was giving into the need within him—within us. He'd loosened the reins—no longer stopping the invisible pull. It had always been there and had only grown stronger.

"The way you look at me, Chelsea. No one has ever looked at me that way. When I was watching that video of you and him—the one I broke—you were giving him that same look. It killed me. That was the main reason I wanted to break it."

"There's no comparison, Damien."

"You were never able to understand how he could do what he did to you, why things happened that way.

I figured it out. You know why it didn't work out with him?"

"Why?"

"Because God made you for *me*."

Not even "I love you" could have topped those words.

"Then that explains it." I smiled. My fingers raked through his already messy hair. "From the very beginning, even when you were pushing me away, I felt like I belonged to you." Unable to wait a second longer to devour his lips, I reached up to kiss him. This time, I fully relished it, because I knew those lips were mine. His taste was all mine. *He* was mine. Finally.

He broke the kiss and spoke over my swollen lips, "You're perfect for me, baby. I always knew that, never doubted it."

Lifting me up, he wrapped my legs around his torso. He did it so effortlessly as if he'd done it a hundred times before. In his strong arms, I felt weightless. There was so much I wanted to say, but I was too worked up to speak. Things moved fast and furiously.

Grinding my clit against him as he kissed me, I swirled my tongue faster around his as he moaned into my mouth.

"You still on the pill?"

I nodded. "Yes."

I didn't bother to ask how he knew about my birth control situation. Damien just knew everything about me.

"You said you wanted to feel me inside of you. You mean that?"

"Yes."

He unzipped his jeans and adjusted my body over him as he positioned the head of his shaft at my opening. I watched his eyes close in ecstasy as he sunk into me slowly. The girth of his cock was seriously a shock. He was so thick. My opening stretched to conform to him until he was fully inside of me.

"Oh...my...fuck...Chelsea. You're so tight." He filled me so completely as he moved in and out slowly. "You feel that?"

"Yes."

He began to fuck me harder. "You feel me now?"

"Fuck. Yes." I bucked my hips. "I feel you. I feel you."

"I can't believe I'm inside of you. Never thought I would get to feel this. You're so wet for me. It's so fucking incredible."

Tears were pouring from my eyes. I thought I knew what good sex was, but this...this was insane. He'd taken control of my body like no one ever had, playing it like an instrument that only he knew how to operate to perfection. I didn't realize until now that everything I'd always thought was great wasn't perfect after all. *This.* This felt perfect.

"My dick is drenched. Your pussy feels so good wrapped around me."

Still inside of me, he gently lowered us to the ground and began to fuck me against the hardwood floor. He placed his hand around the back of my head to prevent it from slamming against the wood as he rammed into me.

My hands were wrapped around his muscular ass, palming it as he moved in and out. At one point, Damien reached behind himself and grabbed my hands, pinning them over my head as he fucked me harder. I gladly gave up the control, feeling blissfully powerless—drugged—by this man.

"I'll never get enough of this," he whispered in my ear. "You are so fucked, Chelsea Jameson, because I'm gonna want to be inside of you all of the time."

My orgasm caused me to spasm around him. When I screamed out suddenly, I felt his body begin to tremble. "Fuck. Chelsea. Fuck." His groan echoed throughout the empty space as he rocked against my body and came inside of me. I loved hearing him come. Damien was normally so calm and collected. It pleased me to witness him coming apart and knowing it was my doing.

He stayed inside of me and showered my neck with soft kisses until he eventually pulled out. Resting his mouth on my neck, he whispered against my skin, "I love you." He placed his index finger on my mouth. "Before you say anything, I want you to know that I don't use that term lightly. In fact, I've never said it to a woman before."

"You haven't?"

"No. I vowed never to say those words unless I was sure I meant it."

His heart beating against my chest was a bittersweet reminder of the fears I'd been trying to keep at bay.

"I love you so much, Damien. I *have* said it to two other people before. And in both instances, I truly thought I meant it. It's only in retrospect that I realize I have a much greater capacity to love than I ever knew, because nothing has ever compared to how I feel about you. It's made me question everything that ever came before it."

He continued to hover over me. "Are you as scared shitless as I am?"

Grabbing onto the back of his neck, I nodded. "Yes. You scare me so fucking much, Damien."

He kissed me then chuckled. "You scare me more than *The Omen*, Chelsea Jameson."

"Oh, my God. That's bad."

"You really want to do this with me? It's not gonna be pretty." His tone turned serious. "It's gonna be scary at times. I never wanted to have to drag you into my health issue."

"I promise to be strong for you."

"You're gonna be a wreck. Stop lying."

"You know me too well."

"We'll be wrecks together. How about that?"

"It's a deal."

Damien flipped me around so that I was lying on top of his chest. He stared into my eyes for a bit before he said, "We have a lot of serious shit to talk about. But not tonight, alright? Tonight, I have better things to do— things of a more urgent nature."

"Oh, yeah? Like what?"

"Like exploring every inch of the tight little body I've coveted for months. I'm nowhere near done with you. Plan on spending the night."

"When are the dogs coming back?"

"I'm picking them up tomorrow."

"I miss them."

"Better they're not around tonight, though. They might think I'm attacking you. I'm pretty sure their allegiance to me is down the toilet when you're around." He gripped my ass. "I never asked you, did you have a nice time with your sister...aside from the parts where I fucked it all up?"

"It was fun. It went by really fast."

"You looked like you were having *a lot* of fun one of those nights."

"What are you talking about?"

"With your little ginger friend. Your sister tagged you on Facebook."

At dinner one night, a redheaded castmate of Jade's named Craig sat next to me and flirted the whole night. We were photographed in a bunch of pictures together. Someone must have posted them.

"Now, you're using Facebook to spy on me? The dating site wasn't enough?"

"Not really. It's not a good tool. You're never on there unless someone happens to tag you, which is once in a blue moon."

"I didn't even know you had a profile."

He wriggled his brows. "Ah...so you've searched for *me*, then."

"Yes."

"Who's the stalker now?"

"Don't even get me started on stalking, D.H. Hennessey. What's the H stand for anyway?"

"It's a secret."

"You're good at those."

"Ouch," he said, poking me playfully in the rib.

"Are you feeling okay today?"

"Oh, no. Don't tell me you're gonna start asking me if I'm feeling okay every single hour...like my mother does."

"I'll try not to be annoying about it."

"I feel great. In fact, I can't remember the last time I felt this good."

"Me, neither."

"So, who *was* the guy hanging all over you?"

"I was hoping you'd drop it."

"No such luck, baby."

"His name is Craig. He's in the show with my sister."

"I see. Well, he almost made me lose my shit. I was ready to fly across the country."

I decided to mess with him.

"He had asked me to go out with him. But I was too obsessed with someone else who kept rejecting me to entertain it."

"That someone else was a real fucking fool."

"He was, but he had his reasons. He's a good guy."

"He's not that good. He wants to do very bad things to you right now."

"He can do whatever he wants."

"Don't say that if you don't mean it."

"You've already done everything to me in my imagination. It's been a long year."

"Fuck. Really? What the fuck have I been doing to you without my even knowing? Is it possible to be jealous of your imaginary self? I want to beat the shit out of him—nasty fucker."

"He and I...we've had a lot of good times."

"Well, as of today, he's done."

I tugged on his hair. "We should probably get up off this floor at some point, huh?"

"I'll never look at this floor the same."

"Why don't I go home and get some things. I didn't exactly expect to be spending the night here."

"What did you come here for again?" He laughed.

"I came here to give you a piece of my mind."

"I got a *piece* of something, alright. It wasn't your mind."

♦ ♦ ♦

When I returned to my apartment to grab some clothes, my phone buzzed, indicating I'd received an email. It was a notification from the dating site that I'd received a new message.

It was from Online Damien.

Chelsea,

I'm sorry I stood you up at the Powell Street Starbucks that day.

I'm just writing to let you know that I am cancelling my account after today, so you won't see me on here anymore.

I had the best sex of my life tonight. It was with my best friend. And it was fucking awesome.

I should have listened to her weeks ago when she asked me to DUCK her.

CHAPTER **EIGHTEEN**

Bathrooms and Treehouses

To say we were making up for lost time was putting it mildly.

Over the next few weeks, Damien and I were insep-arable. My insatiable man insisted that I spend every night at his apartment. Much to Dudley and Drewfus' dismay, they were still banned from the bed now that I was a permanent fixture in it.

Damien and I still hadn't had any real serious conversations about his heart condition. It remained a constant elephant in the room. I think we just needed to enjoy each other without the stress of thinking about anything else for a while. After all, his worrying about the "what ifs" had kept us apart long enough.

Sex was our distraction. We'd become addicted to it. I'd never had so much sex in my life, and yet I still couldn't get enough of him. I'd count the minutes at work just to be able to get back to his place where he'd already be fully erect and waiting for me.

Damien and I had also developed an affinity for spontaneous fornication in public places. Maybe it stemmed from our near-miss in the bathroom at Diamondback's way back when.

We were driving to San Jose one early Saturday afternoon on our way to visit his mother—my first time meeting her—when Damien flashed me a look from the driver's side—a look I knew all too well.

"I want to fuck that beautiful mouth." He squeezed my thigh. "There's no way I'm gonna be able to keep my hands off you until tonight."

"You're gonna have to. I don't think your mother will appreciate it if we excuse ourselves to sneak into the bedroom for a quickie."

"I need something before we get there."

"I could give you highway head."

He grunted. "I would love that, but no fucking way. You'd have to take off your seatbelt. I'd crash the car. I'd never forgive myself if we got into an accident while you were blowing me unrestrained." He adjusted himself. "Shit. It's not even safe for me to drive while *thinking* about you going down on me."

I rubbed my hand over the erection straining through his jeans. "Don't think and drive."

"No. I definitely can't think about your wet mouth wrapped around my cock when I'm at the wheel. But now that you've also touched me, it's too late." He suddenly pulled into a rest area with a service station.

"What are you doing?"

"I'm suddenly hungry."

"For what?" I joked.

"For your ass."

"You're crazy."

"Just a little snack."

"You don't do anything *little*, Damien."

"You go in first. Then, I'll follow when the cashier isn't paying attention."

Making my way past the aisles of chips and candy, I hoped the attendant didn't notice me enter the single occupancy unisex bathroom.

I looked at myself in the mirror and laughed at my red-faced complexion. A minute later, in my reflection, I could see Damien opening the door behind me. My nipples hardened in anticipation.

With his chest pressed against my back, he immediately began to devour my neck. Placing my hands on the sink for balance, I watched us in the mirror. Damien groaned as he lifted my dress and admired my ass. I loved watching the look of desperation on his face. There was no bigger turn-on than witnessing how much he wanted me.

The buckle of his belt clanked as he undid his pants, letting them fall halfway down his legs. Within seconds, I felt his thick cock pushing inside of me with ease because of how wet I was. All of that talk in the car had really gotten me going.

"Someone was ready," he teased. "Fuck, you're wet." He slowly glided in and out of me.

I nodded silently and pushed my hips back into him. "I'm always ready for you."

"I fucking love it," he rasped.

Damien's eyes were smoldering as he stared at me through the mirror. He cracked a slight smile as he fucked me harder. He loved watching me lose control as much as I loved watching him.

"Look how beautiful you are when I'm inside of you, how pink your cheeks are." He slapped my ass. "These cheeks, too."

"I love when you do that."

"Keep your eyes on me," he demanded. "I like to watch you looking at me when you come." Through the mirror, our eyes remained fixed on each other as he continued to pound into me.

When someone knocked on the door, Damien placed his hand over my mouth and yelled, "Just a minute!"

"Shit," I mouthed.

He whispered in my ear, "Fuck it. Take your time. We're not leaving until you come. I'll wait for you."

Grabbing my hips, he guided me with smooth precision over his cock until I'd completely forgotten that anyone was waiting for us. My muscles pulsated around him. I watched his eyes roll back as his hot cum shot inside of me. I could never get enough of this.

He flipped me around and spoke over my lips, "You slay me, Chelsea."

"We'd better get out of here."

I followed Damien out of the bathroom as we did our mini walk of shame back to his truck. All eyes in the store were on us.

It was worth every shred of embarrassment.

♦ ♦ ♦

We pulled up to a small, gray stucco house.

The street Damien grew up on in San Jose's Willow Glen neighborhood was quiet and residential.

My palms were sweaty as I rubbed them together.

Damien placed his hand on my leg to stop me from bouncing it up and down. "You nervous? Don't be."

"I am. Very."

"She's gonna love you."

"How do you know that?"

"Because *I* love you."

"I love you, too."

"I've already told her a lot about you. So, it's like she already knows you."

"How long has she known about me?"

"I used to talk about you to her before we ever got together."

"Really?"

"Yes."

My heart was racing as we exited the car.

Damien's mother answered the door with a tiny dog yelping at her feet. She was really even more beautiful than I remembered from the one photo that Damien had shown me. Both Damien and Tyler definitely got their dark looks from her.

She smiled at Damien before looking at me.

He spoke first. "Chelsea, this is my mother, Monica."

She gave me her hand. My own hand was trembling a bit as I extended it to her. "I'm sorry. I'm so nervous."

"Me, too." She smiled. The fact that she also seemed nervous comforted me a bit.

"Really?"

"Yes. Of course, I am." She smiled over at Damien. "How was your ride?"

Damien looked at me impishly. "The ride was absolutely perfect."

I felt my face heat up.

"Good," she said. "Well, I made your favorite sausage lasagna for lunch. I hope you're hungry."

"Starving," he said.

"Why don't you show Chelsea around? I'm just gonna go back in the kitchen and check on the oven."

Trying to calm my nerves, Damien traced his fingertips along my arm and kissed my cheek.

The décor was very Bohemian with lots of vibrant patterns. Despite her shy nature, Monica's style seemed to be very adventurous and indicative of a free spirit. Damien had mentioned that while not very religious, his mother was quite spiritual.

Noticing some family pictures on a table, I made my way over to the living room. Damien followed me and snatched a frame out of my hand just as I lifted it.

"You can't look at that."

"Why?"

He reluctantly flipped it around to show me. It was a picture of two boys, assumably Damien and Tyler. Damien looked quite...chubby.

"You were so cute."

"I look like I'm about to eat Tyler."

"You never told me you were heavier as a kid."

"Well, this was before I learned that you should actually stop eating when you're full."

"I think you look adorable."

"You *would* say that."

"I mean it."

Putting the picture down, I picked up another one—his parents' wedding picture. "Wow, your parents are both stunning. It's no wonder where you get your looks." Now that I'd seen Damien's father, I realized he actually looked a lot like him in the face despite having his mother's complexion.

Damien took the picture from me. "They were really in love. There wasn't a day that went by where my father wasn't all over her. Tyler and I had to look the other way a lot."

"That's the way it should be."

"I have no doubt it would have still been that way if he were around."

Monica entered the room. "He *is* still around. I feel his presence every day."

I hadn't realized that she'd been listening to us.

She continued, "It's not the same of course, but he is still very much here."

It warmed my heart when Damien wrapped his arm around his mother and kissed her forehead. I knew he wished that she would move on with her life, but he'd also explained that he no longer argued with her about it, because it only seemed to cause her stress.

We sat down to a quiet lunch out back on the screened-in porch. Monica had made mojitos with fresh mint and strawberries. I had to stop myself after one because the rum was getting to my head. I didn't want to say or do anything stupid in front of her.

Looking out toward the yard, I said, "You have a beautiful garden."

"Thank you. The mint is freshly-picked from it, too."

"Gardening is her thing," Damien said.

"I feel very close to Raymond out there—in nature. I see him in everything; in the wind, in the butterflies that land on me when I'm out there, in the red cardinals that fly overhead."

My heart was breaking for this woman, even though she seemed to be finding solace in her own ways.

"I think it's wonderful how in love you are with your husband."

"You only get one true love, one soulmate. Not everyone is lucky enough to find that person in a lifetime." She turned to Damien. "My greatest wish is that each of my sons is able to find the person who was meant for him. She looked down at Damien's and my intertwined hands. "I strongly believe Damien has."

Looking at him as I spoke, I said, "Thank you. I have no doubt that he's *my* person. I can't explain it. It was just a feeling I had very early on. Even when he was constantly rejecting me, I always still felt a strong connection."

She nodded. "That's what it is. Intuition. I was worried that Damien would never allow himself to experience this. I know you recently found out about his genetic heart condition. My husband never knew he had it. In many ways, that was a blessing. He never had to live in fear. At the same time, he never had the opportunity to do anything to prevent it from killing him. So, the lack of knowledge was a double-edged sword."

Damien looked tense as he let go of my hand. "What my mother is trying to say, Chelsea, is that *she* thinks I should have the surgery my doctors are recommending."

Monica placed her hand on Damien's tattooed forearm. "I think you should do whatever it takes to ensure the longest lifespan, yes."

I suddenly felt nauseated. It hit me then that I'd really been intentionally blocking out anything having to do with Damien's condition for a while now. He'd told me that some days he felt great while others he would become tired quickly. He also occasionally had trouble breathing. But the good days outnumbered the bad ones. Before I knew about his diagnosis, though, not once had I ever suspected something was wrong because he was so active and virile. He hid it very well and never complained; that helped me to live in denial.

Still, even though he took such good care of himself, there was only so much he could do on his own to prevent something bad from happening.

"Chelsea and I haven't really discussed it. We've been trying to enjoy being together for a while without worrying about the serious shit for the time being."

"Well, you'll know when the time is right to have that discussion." She looked over at me. "I'm sorry if I dampened the mood at all. That wasn't my intention. Thank you for making my son happy."

"Thank you. He makes *me* so happy."

Damien chomped on the leftover ice from his drink and promptly changed the topic of conversation. "Wanna go see the treehouse?"

My eyes widened. "Treehouse?"

"Yeah. Tyler and I built it with Dad. It was ninety percent finished when he died. We completed it ourselves a few years later and went all out. It's pretty damn cool."

"It's more like a man cave in the sky." Monica grinned.

"I would love to see it."

Damien led me to the side of the house where a magnificent wooden structure sat amidst a giant tree. The treehouse even had windows. A long ladder made of rope hung beneath it. It literally looked like a little home.

Inside there was a bed with a plaid comforter and a small couch across from it. A lamp was plugged into an electrical outlet. There was a television and DVD player.

"There's electricity?"

"Of course. How else would I sneak in here to watch porn?"

"That's what you did in here?"

"Tyler and I definitely took advantage of this place in our teen years."

"Okay. I don't need to know any more than that."

He laughed. "You know what I think?"

"What?"

"I think I would really like to christen it with you right now."

"I can't do that with your mother right downstairs."

"Well, we're gonna have to figure out a way, because I can't go the entire weekend without having you. Maybe after she goes to sleep, you can sneak up here to visit me."

We were spending the night here in San Jose. The plan was for me to stay in Tyler's old bedroom, and I had assumed Damien would be sleeping in his room at the house.

"You're sleeping in the treehouse?"

"Yeah. It's really peaceful being up here at night. My second favorite place in the world."

"Second favorite?"

"Inside of you is always my number one." He winked, pulling me close.

"I should've known."

♦ ♦ ♦

Later that night, I'd said goodnight to Monica and retreated to the guest room after Damien kissed us both and headed to the treehouse.

An hour later, he texted me.

Get your beautiful ass up here.

Chelsea: What if your mother catches me leaving?

Damien: My mother knows we fuck. She's not stupid. We're adults.

Chelsea: Okay. Is there enough light for me to see where I'm going?

Damien: You're good. I'll make sure you get up okay.

Damien held a lantern at the entrance to the treehouse so that I could safely make my way up without falling.

After I climbed up the ladder, he pulled me into his arms. "It seems like I haven't touched you in forever."

"Well, it's not every day we're under the watchful eyes of your mother."

Damien squeezed my ass cheeks as he kissed me. After he slowly released my bottom lip, he said, "My mother really likes you."

I pulled back to examine his face. "She told you that?"

"She didn't have to. I could tell by the way she was looking at you. She was smiling and engaged while talking to you. That's rare. Basically, she sees all the things I see. You're very real, and she appreciates that."

"I'm so relieved."

His eyes trailed down from my chest to my legs. "And *I* appreciate that you look like a teenage dream right now in these tiny shorts."

"Well, I'm sneaking into a boy's treehouse. I had to look sexy."

"I spent many nights in this very treehouse fantasizing about imaginary women who didn't hold a candle to you."

"You know...I didn't think I was your type when we first met."

He slipped his finger under the strap of my cami. "Why did you think that?"

"I look nothing like Jenna or the other couple of girls I've seen you with, for that matter." Just thinking about that made me cringe. "I don't have huge boobs or a big ass or wear a lot of makeup."

"I never had a type. And honestly? From the first night we hung out, all I fantasized about was the beautiful, lithe blonde next door." He ran his hands through my hair. "I'd wonder what this would feel like between my fingers." He lowered his mouth to my neck. "What it would be like to suck on this…" He gently bit my skin before lifting my shirt off. "What these tits would taste like." Bending down, he took my nipple into his mouth and sucked hard before licking a line slowly down to my belly button. "What the grooves of this tiny navel would feel like against the tip of my tongue." As he continued to kneel, he said, "Don't get me started on this navel. I've *painted* this navel. That's how much I love it."

"You have?"

He caressed it with his fingertips. "Yes. I'll show it to you sometime."

I ran my fingers through his hair as he stayed on his knees. He then slipped my shorts down my legs.

"You know what I love about you, Damien?"

He looked up at me, flashing a crooked grin. "My massive rod?"

"I wasn't going to say that, but honestly you far exceeded my expectations in that area. The first time we had sex, I swore your dick was the width of a Coke can."

Damien bent his head back in laughter. "You mean a twenty-four ounce Coke can, right…the tall one?"

"Of course."

He kissed my stomach. "I interrupted you. You were about to tell me what you love about me."

"Oh." I paused. "Everything. That was what I was going to say."

He looked up at me with a devilish expression, and I just knew I was in for it tonight.

Damien stood up. "What do you want to do tonight?"

"I want you to deny me until I can't take it anymore."

"You seem so innocent when someone first meets you, but you're a little masochist. I fucking love it." He lay back on his bed and pointed to the wall across from it. "Stand over there."

Completely naked, I leaned against it. My nipples were hard as steel as I watched Damien peel off his boxer briefs. His rock hard cock stood fully erect, glistening with precum. My mouth watered as my eyes travelled from his naked abs back down to his cock. I'd seen his body naked so many times now, but it never ceased to amaze me how beautiful he was fully naked.

This was going to be good.

I loved the little games we played.

"Open your legs. I want to see you. Then put your hands by your knees. You're not allowed to touch yourself. I want you to watch me while I jerk off to your sweet little cunt."

Damien fisted his cock and began to stroke himself while he stared at me. The need to rub my clit was enormous. Clenching my inner muscles, I moved my hips around in a feeble attempt to satisfy myself without the use of my hands. I knew I wasn't going to last long before I was begging him. Still, the waiting, the challenge was precisely the point. The longer the wait, the bigger the payoff.

"Fuck, I can see how wet you are from here." He jerked himself harder. "You see what you're doing to me?"

"Yes."

"Come here and lick it off."

I walked over to him and sucked all of the precum dry off his tip. Tasting him only made the muscles between my legs throb harder. I was going to need relief soon. When I started to deep throat him, he stopped me.

"This will end in ten seconds if you keep that up. And I really want to come inside of you. So, no."

"I need to touch myself."

"Not yet. You're not there yet. Go back to the wall."

As much as I needed him, he knew I secretly loved this desperate feeling. More than that, I loved the intensity of the moment he finally gave in.

This time, Damien got up from the bed and stood right in front of me while he masturbated. The up close sight of him jerking himself against the backdrop of his abs only made me crazier. When he finally kissed me hungrily, it ate away some of my frustration. When he stopped the kiss, yet continued the game, my body started to tremble in need for the return of the contact. Whenever I would start to shake, he knew I was done.

"Turn around and touch the wall."

My body buzzed with excitement when I felt the warmness of his chest at my back, a prelude to what I knew was coming soon.

Within seconds, I felt the slow burn of his engorged cock sinking into me. So worked up, I needed release, but held on for as long as I could.

Fucking me so hard to the point of pain, he whispered in my ear, "Come all over my dick. Come on." We were so sexually in sync that he always seemed to know my breaking point.

As soon as I let go, Damien released his load into me. We stayed panting, leaning against the wall until the movement of our hips slowly came to a halt.

My body was completely limp. Damien was still inside of me, his mouth resting on my skin. A bead of sweat ran from his forehead onto the back of my neck. Our breathing and the rustling of the leaves outside were the only sounds left.

It was bliss.

CHAPTER **NINETEEN**

Penthouse

Damien and I lived in sex-filled denial for quite a while. That ended one night when an eventful dinner at my parents' house in Sausalito smacked us back to reality.

Mom and Dad weren't surprised when I'd told them Damien and I were now together. Apparently, after that messy finale to my moving day, they'd long suspected it wasn't the end of the story with him. I'd filled them in on everything that had happened since, and they welcomed Damien with open arms.

My sister, Claire, and her husband, Micah, had also come for dinner that night. At one point during dessert, Micah clinked his fork against a glass and asked everyone at the table for our attention.

Claire cleared her throat and looked straight at me. "So, we kind of have a special announcement."

My jaw dropped because I had a feeling I knew what was coming.

"We're pregnant!" Micah shouted gleefully as he rubbed my sister's back.

Unable to stop myself from breaking out into tears, I immediately got up from my seat to hug them. This was huge. She was the first of us to have a child, and I was going to be an aunt. Visions of chubby legs, blowing raspberries and big toothless grins flashed through my mind. I was so thrilled for them—for all of us. Even still, I was surprised that the news caused me to cry so easily. It was more poignant of a moment than I'd ever imagined.

"I'm so happy for you, Claire Bear. I love you so much. I just know you're gonna be the best mother in the world."

My parents and I took turns hugging Claire and Micah. Everyone immediately started pondering potential baby names. My sister dialed Jade so that we could all FaceTime. Jade also broke out into tears upon hearing the news.

So wrapped up in the excitement, I hadn't even noticed the empty chair.

Damien had disappeared. At first, I didn't think anything of it, but with each minute that passed, his absence became more and more disconcerting.

After confirming that he wasn't in the bathroom, I made my way out to the back of the house and found him standing alone in the yard. It was cold out and drizzly, not a great night to be outside. This was odd.

"Damien? Are you okay?"

He turned around, looking sullen. "Yeah."

My mood had gone from happy a few minutes ago to panicky now. "What are you doing out here?" When he didn't respond, I said, "You're scaring me."

The memory of being sideswiped by Elec's change of heart was never too far. As much as I knew Damien truly cared about me, my own experiences had conditioned me to expect something to go wrong whenever everything seemed perfect.

"We need to get away from here and talk in private."

Swallowing the lump in my throat, I nodded. "Okay. Let's get going, then."

Nervously grabbing my purse and jacket back inside, I said goodbye to my parents and sister as Damien waited outside in the truck. I'd made up a story that he was feeling a little sick to his stomach when in fact it was my own stomach that was turning.

As Damien drove us over the Golden Gate Bridge, I sat in the passenger seat, staring at the beads of drizzle gathering on the window. Feeling nauseous, I turned to him and examined his expression. He seemed troubled and kept his eyes on the road. I wasn't sure where he was taking us until he eventually turned toward our neighborhood.

Once inside his apartment, it was quiet, since the Double Ds were with Jenna.

Damien leaned against his kitchen counter with both hands. "I'm sorry for scaring you, but I don't think this conversation can be put off any longer."

His chest was heaving. It scared me whenever Damien seemed stressed out now that I knew about his heart. I just wanted him to calm down.

"What happened to you tonight?"

He released a long breath. "When I saw the way you reacted to your sister's news, it really hit me, how much you'd be missing by being with me."

"What do you mean?"

After a seemingly endless pause, he said, "I can't have children, Chelsea."

What?

"What do you mean?"

"I mean I can *physically* have them, but I can't in good conscience father a child, knowing there's a fifty percent chance that I could pass along my heart defect." He repeated, "*Fifty percent*. It would be selfish, and if I ignored that and something ever happened to my kid, I could never live with myself."

Although I'd read about the odds, I'd never considered that he wouldn't want to take the risk. To hear him admit how he felt was as sobering as it was heartbreaking.

When I stayed silent, he continued, "We've never discussed this before, and we really should have. It was a big reason I tried to avoid getting involved with you. When I used to say I never wanted to have kids, I meant it. You just didn't understand why at the time."

It felt like the safety cocoon of denial I'd mentally built over the past several weeks was beginning to unravel. This was devastating, but so help me God, I couldn't imagine life without him. Not now. Not anymore.

I didn't know how to express my feelings; the words just wouldn't come to me.

"I'm sorry," he whispered.

"It's okay."

"But see...what I know I should do and what I want, totally contradict each other. I say I don't want to have kids, but there is nothing more that I *really* want than to see your belly swell with my baby growing inside of you someday. I want to hold our baby in my arms so badly. But I just can't do it. And *you* deserve to experience that. I made the selfish decision to give into my feelings for you before having this discussion. I can't say I regret that, but at the same time, I don't think you really understand what you're getting yourself into. I should've initiated this conversation a long time ago."

Would he think I was crazy if I admitted that I'd rather have him?

"I'm not gonna lie. I want children badly, but I don't want them with anyone else. There are a lot of kids who need to be adopted. We could take that route. I feel like I need *you* to breathe. And I understand your reasoning for not wanting to risk it. So, if given a choice between biological children and you...I choose you. And I don't even have to think twice about it."

"How can you possibly mean that?"

"It's not the perfect scenario. It's painful. But the choice is not a tough one for me. I can live without children. I *can't* live without you."

I hoped that didn't make me sound desperate; it was the honest truth.

He pulled me into the longest hug. He was breathing so heavily, as if he seriously didn't expect my answer, like he was both relieved and conflicted at the same time.

Releasing me, he said, "Here's my worry, alright? And hear me out."

"Okay."

"Say we never have kids of our own, and then something happens to me...but it's too late for you to have kids and then you've lost me, too. Then what?"

"Don't think like that."

"It's a very real possibility."

I refused to entertain the thought. "No."

"You want to know the really fucked-up part? I would love to sit here and say that if something happens to me, I want you to meet someone else, move on, fall in love again, but here's the kind of selfish prick I am. One of the reasons I don't want to die is because I don't want anyone else to ever have you. As much as I knock my mother for how devoted she is to my father, I would kill for you to feel that way about me. I only want you to ever have eyes for me. Is that messed up or what? I'm terrified you'd eventually forget about me."

"That will never happen."

"I used to be afraid of the prospect of dying, but I had somehow accepted it, spent my days painting pictures of all the places I believed I'd never get to see. But things are different now. I can't seem to accept it anymore. Now, I just want to live. My will to live is stronger than my fear of death now...because of you. You're the reason I want to live so badly."

My heart filled with so many emotions upon hearing his admission. There was no doubt in my mind that I loved this man more than anything in the world. He'd rendered me speechless, and despite all the things I should have said, I attempted to make a joke instead. "This from the same guy who used to pawn me off to other men."

"I never really wanted that. I subconsciously did everything I could to derail those efforts, which I suppose was counter-productive. Now that I've had you, I can't fathom how I ever even tried to push you away like that."

"Well, you can't push me away, because you're a part of me. Not possible."

"You're seriously crazy, Chelsea, for wanting a life with me at this point. Thank God for you. I thank God for you every day." He kissed me hard then said, "I want you to come with me to my next doctor's appointment. I really want your input. I think for now I'm gonna hold off on the surgery, though. But I'm keeping an open mind about it."

"I want to know everything there is to know. I don't want you to hide anything from me, especially on those days when you're not feeling well, and I definitely do want to go to those appointments. So, yes, please make sure you include me."

"Okay."

"No more secrets, Damien."

"No more secrets."

"What's the H stand for, then?"

He tickled me under the arm. "Nice try. That one is the exception."

I playfully threw a pillow at him. "Oh, come on."

♦ ♦ ♦

My apartment across town was merely a glorified storage closet now that all of my time was spent at Damien's.

The old apartment next door still sat empty. Damien couldn't exactly show it to potential renters with the gigantic unicorn on the wall. So, we needed to figure out whether I was going to try to break my lease in order to move back into my old place or whether I would move in with Damien permanently. Even though we were basically shacking up, he hadn't exactly asked me to live with him. I wasn't going to be the one to approach the subject, though.

Jade and I were chatting about it on the phone one afternoon while Damien was out with the dogs.

"Are you keeping a toothbrush there?" she asked.

"Yes."

"Then, you're totally living with him."

"I suppose I am...unofficially."

"I was planning on staying with you when I came home after the New Year, but maybe I'll stay with Mom and Dad instead."

"Why?"

"I don't want to impose on you if you're there with him. I wanted to come for Christmas so badly, but the show is busiest around the holidays, since everyone is visiting the city. They don't want the understudies performing during peak times. So, none of the leads are allowed to take time off. There was no way I could get out of it."

"Damien wouldn't mind if you stayed here, but I'm still under lease at the other place. We can just stay there together and have a girls' week."

"Maybe I should just stay with the hot brother instead," she joked.

Jade didn't even know what Tyler looked like. She was just basing her opinion on what I'd told her about his resemblance to Damien. She also knew that he, too, was an actor.

"I have no doubt that Tyler would love that. He's apparently dating someone now, though. I'm supposed to meet her over Christmas."

"Well, nix that plan, then."

"Yeah, she might not appreciate a six-foot tall, gorgeous blonde who looks like a model shacking up with her boyfriend."

"Wouldn't be the first time I shacked up with a guy and girl," Jade said. "Except I was the girlfriend getting screwed over in that scenario."

"What an asshole."

"I don't want to talk about him. Change the subject."

"Okay...well, back to my living with Damien, I don't want to assume it's official, so let's plan on you staying with me at my place when you come visit."

"Okay. Sounds like a plan."

Three weeks later, Damien would finally make it known where things stood as far as my living at his place.

I'd been enjoying spending time there with no expectations for however long it lasted. It wasn't uncommon for me to wake up in the morning with Damien's face in between my legs. I loved rolling out of bed on weekends and having breakfast with him and the dogs. I loved everything about spending time with him, and it didn't matter to me if he put a label on it.

One thing I learned over time about Damien was that when he did something important or made a big decision, he typically did it in a spontaneous way. Case in point, the first time we'd made love when I found him painting the wall.

So, when he finally decided to acknowledge our living situation, it also wasn't in a way that I ever could have predicted.

One afternoon, I returned to his apartment after work to find a massive pile of rubble where his office used to be. Damien was with two other men and wore a mask covering his face. There was dust everywhere, and the wall separating our two apartments was completely gone. It was all just one huge open space.

"Damien? What did you do?"

"We'll go get your stuff next week when the dust settles. I talked to your landlord—mentioned some more violations on his property that I happened to notice. He said he'd be happy to let you out of your lease." He pulled down his mask, flashed a huge smile and gestured to the massive space around us. "I'm giving us a penthouse suite."

And *that* was how Damien asked me to move in with him.

CHAPTER **TWENTY**

Under the Camel Toe

I had to wonder what I was thinking when I'd insisted on hosting a Christmas Eve get together at our place for a few of our closest friends and family members. It seemed like a great idea at the time, but with only three hours left to prepare, I was seriously kicking myself.

There was a lot to be thankful for this year, and that made me want to do something to celebrate. Everything seemed to be going our way. Damien's most recent checkup turned out okay, and he was feeling well most days.

The apartment was looking spectacular—totally fit for a party. Damien had done most of the renovation work himself after the initial wall demolition. It was now basically one gigantic love nest. He'd removed my old kitchen altogether, and my former bedroom was now part of our living room. We kept the other bathroom as a spare, and he'd closed off an area into a small guest room. The dogs had more space to putz around the house, too.

The door swung ajar to reveal Damien shoving a freshly-cut Christmas tree through the opening. The scent of fresh pine filled the air. It definitely smelled like Christmas all of a sudden.

"It's huge!"

"Why thank you. So, is this tree."

"Seriously, that tree is massive!"

"Don't you know by now that I do everything big, baby?"

"Yes, but we didn't need one *that* big."

"Actually, all the small ones were gone. Most people have their Christmas trees set up by now. This is what happens when you procrastinate until Christmas Eve."

"That's true. We've been bad. And I have to send you out to the store again, too, because I forgot a few things."

After setting the tree down in a corner, Damien brushed off his hands. "Where are the Ds?"

"They're playing with some wrapping paper in the other room."

"Okay, good. Maybe they'll let me set up this tree in peace."

"Is Jenna coming to pick them up before the party?"

"She was being kind of a bitch about it because she has a party to go to herself, so I'm not sure if she'll show."

"So, let them stay. I'm in no mood for an Ex-mas anyway."

"I want her to show up just so she can get a load of you in that little white dress. Steam is going to be blowing out of her ears."

"You like it?"

"Yes. I love it. In fact, I'm thinking this tree decorating might have to wait."

"We don't have time."

"Yes, we do."

"No, we don't. Look at the clock."

"Fuck. Alright, but I'm gonna need a quickie later when everyone's too drunk to notice us slipping into the bedroom."

"You're nuts."

"You love my nuts."

"I *do* love your nuts. Oh, speaking of which...I need you to get some mixed ones to put out on the table. I also never bought soda. We can't only have alcohol and water with nothing else to drink. So, get some cans of Sprite and Coke. They have the ones with the Christmas logos at the store."

"I'll give you a Christmas Coke can right now."

"Why oh why did I ever put that idea in your head?"

"You've just said nuts, Coke can and head in the past thirty seconds. How the fuck am I supposed to focus on decorating a tree?"

Damien began opening the packages of bulbs and other ornaments he'd bought along with bags of tinsel. It was going to be a half-assed tree, but at least we'd have one.

I really needed a glass of wine to relax while I finished preparing all of the appetizers. Normally, I drank white, but since Damien had decided to open a bottle of red last night, I just took from that. The bottle somehow slipped out of my hands, shattering to the floor and splattering red wine all over my new white dress.

"Shit!"

Damien dropped his tinsel and immediately began to clean up the mess from under me. One of the things

I loved about Damien was his take-charge attitude. He never wasted time taking care of things. He continued to clear away the glass and mop up the floor as I stood there in shock.

He stood up. "Fuck. Alright. We gotta get you changed. I've been dying to get you out of that dress anyway."

"Are you serious right now?"

A smirk spread over his face. "Let's go pick out something else."

We entered the bedroom, and the dogs fled like bats out of hell. They'd shredded tons of wrapping paper and were probably thinking Damien was going to reprimand them. They didn't realize that my hornball boyfriend had nothing on his mind besides figuring out a way to take advantage of my undressing situation.

"I have nothing to wear now."

"I'll pick something out for you."

Damien actually had pretty good taste. Whenever I got stressed about what to wear, he'd often take over and pick out my outfit.

Perusing through my closet, he chose a pair of fitted black pants that were almost like shimmery leggings along with a flowy red shirt that had a sequin neckline.

"Those pants are really tight on me."

"I know. I love your ass in them."

"We don't have much time. I'll just wear them."

Damien stood with his arms crossed, watching every movement as I undressed.

"Let me shave your pussy," he blurted out.

"What?"

"It's getting a little bushy. Let me do it real quick." Without waiting for my answer, he rushed to the bathroom.

I yelled after him, "This is not the type of bush trimming you're supposed to be doing right now."

"I know." He clicked the razor buzzer on. "This is way more fun."

Damien shaved a neat landing strip onto my vagina. After he finished, he looked down at me. "Fuck. I can't wait to hit that tonight."

Placing my hands on his broad shoulders, I pushed him out of the room. "Okay, you really need to leave. I have to get dressed."

He snickered. "I'll go finish the real tree trimming."

As he was leaving, I called out, "Damien?"

He turned around. "Yeah?"

"Thank you." I smiled.

He blew me a kiss and ventured back out into the living room. Not even a full minute passed before I heard him swearing.

"Fuck!"

I ran to the living room, still buttoning my shirt. "What happened?"

"The dogs apparently took it upon themselves to pee in the bushes like they normally do, but in this case, said bushes would be our fucking Christmas tree. There's a massive puddle, and I just stepped in it!"

"Shit."

Dudley and Drewfus were now hiding in the corner of the room.

His anger turned to laughter. "I can't even get mad at them because I think they were confused. We've been so busy, we forgot to take them out. They thought we were bringing the bushes to them."

"Well, they were spreading the holiday cheer."

"At least it wasn't Christmas logs of shit."

I cracked up. "True."

"Well, I guess I don't have to take them for a walk anymore."

"Have they ever done that before?"

"I've never had a Christmas tree with them."

"Really?"

"Yeah. Jenna is Jewish and to be honest, I probably wouldn't even be celebrating Christmas if it weren't for you."

"Why not?"

"I never really got into it. After Dad died, Mom didn't celebrate it anymore. The holidays always sucked. This will be the best Christmas I've had since childhood." He walked toward me and fixed one of my buttons that I'd apparently put into the wrong loop, then said, "Christmas is about happiness and love. When you're lacking those things, it can be one of the most painful times of the year. But when you suddenly realize that you're happier than you've ever been, Christmas comes alive again. So, fuck the spilled wine and the dog piss. It's all good, because this is the best Christmas ever."

As if on cue, one of the dogs barked. *"Woof!"*

He chuckled. "They agree."

"I'm lucky to have found you guys. Last Christmas was the worst of my life. What a difference a year makes."

"Anything can happen in a year, sometimes horrible stuff, sometimes amazing things. I'm glad this year was the latter for me."

"This year was life-changing."

Returning to the kitchen counter to finish arranging the appetizers, I admired Damien's body as he decorated the top of the tree. His fitted red shirt rode up every time he reached his arm out to position an ornament.

Mixing some onion soup mix into sour cream, I said, "It's not every day I get to watch a hot man in a Santa hat decorate my tree."

Damien turned toward me and raised his forehead. "Stop looking at me like that, Jameson, or the only thing wrapped under the tree will be your legs around my back."

I'd better change the subject.

"So, who's coming tonight for sure from your end?"

"Tyler is picking up my mother and bringing her here along with his new girlfriend."

"What's her name again?"

"Nicole."

"Hmm. Okay. I'll try to remember that. Who else?"

"I invited Murray and his wife. That's it. You know me. I don't need a big crowd."

"My parents are coming a little late. They have another party to stop at first. I also invited my friends Laura and Courtney from the youth center. We're only talking ten or eleven people max."

"It'll be nice to see people, but personally, I'm looking forward to our Christmas morning alone more than anything," he said.

"Me, too."

We planned to spend tomorrow morning together, exchanging our own presents before heading to my parents' in Sausalito later in the day for dinner with Claire and Micah. So, my Christmas morning would surely consist of an awesome homemade breakfast and lots of sex.

Damien had finished the tree just in the nick of time. While he was out buying the few items I'd forgotten earlier, the doorbell rang.

The first to arrive were Tyler and Nicole.

Tyler looked really handsome in a fitted black collared shirt and dark jeans. Nicole was cute. She was petite like me, except she had long brown hair and big brown eyes. She was beautiful, everything I would expect from someone Tyler would bring home, although she seemed even sweeter than I might have imagined. I didn't know why, but I kind of pictured him with someone a little bit more stuck-up.

"It's so nice to meet you," I said.

Tyler looked beyond my shoulders. "Where's D?"

"Out getting some last minute stuff."

"I was telling Nic the story of how you and Damien met."

"There were lots of ways Damien and I technically got to know each other. Which story?"

"The time you almost burned down the building."

"Ah, yes, my most famous claim to fame." Turning to Nicole, I asked, "How did you guys meet again?"

"I'm a makeup artist for Tyler's show."

"Oh, okay. It must be a tough job making that face look presentable." I winked.

"Actually, it's tougher making him look ugly for certain scenes."

"It seems like it would be fun to work in that environment. My younger sister is a stage actress in New York."

Tyler nodded. "Damien was telling me. Is she on Broadway or off-Broadway?"

"She's done both, actually. Right now, she has a starring role off-Broadway."

"When this run is over at the Bay Repertory, I was thinking of moving to L.A. or possibly New York if an opportunity was there. I really don't want to leave California. It's not easy in this business, though. You sort of have to take what you can get."

Nicole looked at him affectionately. "At least I can do makeup anywhere."

"I might take you with me if you're good."

"I just might go." She smiled.

It sounded like this was getting pretty serious.

The door opened, and Damien emerged. "For my lovely lady, I come bearing Christmas Coke cans, nuts and sticky balls."

I took a small box from him. "Donut holes. Great. Those weren't on the list."

"No. But I couldn't resist completing the trifecta just so I could say sticky balls." He turned to Tyler's girlfriend and extended his hand. Glancing down at it, he joked, "I promise it's clean. Nice to meet you, Nicole."

Looking between the two brothers, she said, "Wow. You guys look so much alike."

I chuckled. "Your reaction reminds me of mine the first time I saw them in the same room. I thought I was seeing double at first, but they actually look less alike to me the more I see them together."

Damien turned to Nicole and cracked, "We look alike, but surely you find me the better looking one?"

"It's a toss up," she said.

A twinge of jealousy crept in at the thought of her finding Damien attractive.

Damien smacked Tyler on the shoulder as he addressed her, "I'll help you figure it out. I'm the better looking one, but I'll give my little brother the distinction of having the better personality. He's way more outgoing than I could ever be. And he's a great actor."

"Don't sell yourself short," Tyler said before looking over at Nicole. "Damien here has been playing the role of an elusive artist quite well for a few years now."

"Shut the fuck up." Damien laughed.

Nicole whispered to me, "Do they spar a lot like this?"

"Yes. It's kind of cute. You can smell the testosterone like burning rubber whenever they're together."

Damien looked around. "Where's Mom?"

"I couldn't get her to come. She said to tell you she was sorry, but that she wasn't feeling very festive. I think she's in the middle of a depressed episode."

"Fuck."

Rubbing Damien's back, I said, "Shit. I'm sorry."

"Christmas is really tough for her. She doesn't want people to look at her and be able to tell she's sad," Tyler said. "So, she chooses to stay away."

Damien looked at me. "When we went to stay with her, she was actually having a really good couple of days. This is more typical." Taking a deep breath and wrapping his arm around my waist, he said, "Anyway, you guys are probably hungry. My little lady made a bunch of stuff, none of which she burned, so help yourself."

◆ ◆ ◆

Everyone seemed to be having a great time. The appetizers were getting gobbled up, and the drinks were flowing. Damien had even put on Christmas music in the background.

Jenna never did come for the dogs, so we made the best of it, throwing some reindeer antlers on them. They hadn't pissed in the tree again and were having a field day fetching everyone's scraps; we would likely be paying for it tomorrow.

I was in the midst of listening to a conversation my parents were having with Tyler about the play he was in when Damien came up behind me. The heat of his breath in my ear gave me chills.

"I'm ready for all these people to leave. Those pants are so tight on you that they're making *my* pants tight."

"Behave," I whispered, even though I wanted nothing more than for him to stay pressed against my back.

He groaned, "I need your help with something."

"What?"

"It's in the other room."

"I think it's in your pants."

"For now it is, yes."

"You're bad."

"Come on. No one will miss us for five minutes."

Before I could answer, Damien locked his fingers in with mine. When it seemed like no one was paying attention, he started to lead me into the bedroom. He locked the door behind us before backing me against the wall.

I closed my eyes as he showered my neck with kisses. Tugging on my shirt, he began to undo the buttons before taking it off.

"These pants have had me looking down all night." He knelt to the floor. "They look so fucking good on you, but they're snug as hell. Thank God your shirt was covering this." He pointed to my crotch, which displayed a massive camel toe. Damien spread my legs and began to kiss me there.

"What are you doing?" I muttered.

"It's Christmas. I'm kissing you under the camel toe."

Shaking with laughter, I said, "I thought it was the mistletoe."

"Not anymore."

Pulling down my pants, Damien said, "Everyone's talking and laughing out there, and all I could think about is burying my face in your pussy."

When my pants were off, he did just that as I spread my legs apart. Still leaning my back against the wall, I dug my fingers into the back of his head as he continued to eat me out.

He came up for air. "Falalalala to me. You taste better than any Christmas treat."

I laughed. "We have to get back out there." Panting, I said, "I need to come."

"Don't come yet," he growled.

Standing up, he flipped me around so that I was facing the wall.

"Come now," he said as he entered me. It took me all of ten seconds to spasm around his cock at the exact moment he released inside of me.

"That was the very definition of a quickie," I breathed out.

He was holding my hair back as he spoke against my neck, "That's what happens when you work me up all night."

"Go ahead of me. I need to use the bathroom."

He pulled his pants up and went back out to the party.

After I emerged, Damien was leaning against a table in the corner casually sipping a beer as if our fucking in the next room hadn't ever happened. Meanwhile, I felt like the word SEX was written all over my face in flashing Christmas lights.

When he noticed me from across the room, I think he could tell I was embarrassed. As I stood behind the counter preparing the dessert tray, he just continued to sip his beer with a smirk on his face as he looked at me. I randomly burst out into a laughing fit while Damien started to crack up from across the room.

No one else knew what the heck was going on. They were talking away amongst themselves. The dogs were playing with some of the ornaments that had fallen off of the tree. Damien and I, in the meantime, were in our own little world.

When we stopped laughing, he just continued to gaze at me from afar with a look that was a mixture of lust...and love. This truly *was* the best Christmas of my life.

I knew that Damien and I likely had some tough times ahead, but tonight—this moment in time where the two of us were oblivious to everything but each other—was perfect.

CHAPTER **TWENTY-ONE**

Le Nombril

Damien and I'd stayed up until the middle of the night cleaning up the mess from the party. It was worth it to be able to sleep in on Christmas morning.

I woke up to the amazing feeling of Damien's hard dick sandwiched inside the crack of my ass. It was our own special version of spooning.

Damien spoke against my back. "Merry Christmas."

I turned around. "Merry Christmas, baby."

Massaging my fingers through his hair, I admired his beautiful jawline but noticed the look of worry on his face.

"What's wrong?"

"I was just thinking about stuff while you were sleeping. I was up a lot last night."

"Like what?"

"I was thinking about the future."

"What about it?"

"Promise you won't get mad if I bring this up again?"

My heart sank a little. "I promise."

"I was thinking about children again, and how much I don't want to hold you back from having a child of your own. I know we've had this discussion, but I guess I still can't wrap my head around your decision. Whenever I think about it, it makes me ill."

Closing my eyes, I tried as best as I could to gather my thoughts on the matter so that I could explain myself. "Our need to procreate is a selfish one anyway, right? Why do we need to have children as long as there are children in the world who need good homes?"

"Don't fucking pretend you wouldn't want one of our own someday."

"I *do* want one. I *do* want to experience that with you, but I understand the scenario we face. If you can't live with the risk, I understand that completely. You mean more to me than anything. I want *you* more than anything, and I'm not lying when I say that."

"I just want it to go on record that I'd understand... if you couldn't accept it."

"You'd understand if I left you to become impregnated by some man I didn't love?"

He looked like he was seriously pondering my question. "Fuck that. No, I wouldn't understand. I'd end up killing someone. Or kidnapping your pregnant ass and raising the baby with you." He suddenly pulled me close. "I'm such a lost cause."

"Well, you're lucky I'm not going anywhere, then."

"When I'm old and crusty and no longer hot, you're gonna wish you had some children."

"And I will. *We* will. Even if they're not biologically ours."

He was looking so deeply into my eyes. It was as if he was looking beyond them. "Do you have any idea how much I love you?"

"I think I do."

"No. I don't think you do. There's something I need to say, and I need to make sure you *really* understand it."

"Okay..."

"I know it's always at the back of your mind, because I know you so well. You wonder whether you're gonna wake up one day and find that my feelings have changed—like his did. You won't allow yourself to believe that this could be forever, because you want to protect yourself in the event that history repeats itself. I need you to believe that as long as I'm walking this Earth, I'm going to love you. I'm not gonna hurt you like he did. I can promise you that. You're it for me. Maybe you've heard that before, but this time, the person saying it means it. I need you to understand that."

So overcome with emotion, I could barely mutter, "I do."

"Good." He abruptly got up.

"Where are you going?"

"To make you coffee and breakfast."

Feeling undeserving, I watched every movement of his gloriously naked body as he slipped on some sweatpants and sauntered toward the kitchen.

Stretching my arms, I yawned and lifted myself off the bed in search of one of his t-shirts.

I could hear Damien from the kitchen. "Shit. There's no coffee left in the can. I meant to buy some when I was out last night."

"How the heck could we be out of coffee? You buy that gigantic one."

"Have you seen how much coffee we drink?"

"Crap."

"Alright." He sighed. "I'm gonna get some from the bodega. I saw a sign the other day saying they'd be open today."

Looping my arms under his, I said, "It's Christmas Day. Don't leave. We'll make due."

He turned around and kissed me on the forehead. "You think you're really gonna be able to survive with no coffee?"

"I'll try."

"Well, I'm a beast without it. Not an option for me."

"You're a beast either way, but I agree. You need your coffee more than me."

"I knew I was forgetting something at the market yesterday."

"You remembered the sticky balls but forgot the most important thing. Maybe if you came up with a coffee innuendo, you would've remembered."

"Chock Full o' Nuts?" He winked.

"Damn, you're fast."

"You like that brand, right?"

"Yes. Don't be long!"

"I won't."

After the front door shut, I returned to the bed, slapped my thighs and waved to the dogs, prompting them to hop in with me. "Psst. Guys. Come on. Your daddy is gonna be so mad at me, but I want to snuggle with you on Christmas." It was our little secret that we would hang out in the bed when Damien wasn't home. I was pretty sure Damien was ignoring the evidence since they always left plenty of hair behind.

Dudley and Drewfus wasted no time jumping up on the bed and licking my face. They smelled like the biscuits we'd given them to open as presents last night, and now, I, too, smelled like them.

After forty-five minutes passed, it dawned on me that Damien was taking an awfully long time to get coffee. The bodega was only a few blocks away, and he'd driven his truck on top of that. The more time that passed, the more concerned I became.

Finally, the phone rang.

"Damien?"

"Yeah, baby."

"Where are you?"

"I was just about to call you. I'm at the hospital. Memorial."

"What?"

"It's okay. I took myself."

"What happened? You just went to get coffee. I don't get it."

"I was at the cash register. They were ringing me up. I started feeling this chest pain I'd never experienced before. It scared the shit out of me. I didn't want to risk coming home, so I went straight to the emergency room."

"What's happening now?"

"They're admitting me."

"I'm coming there."

"Please don't get into an accident. Take your time. I'm gonna be fine, okay?"

"Okay."

He could tell I was starting to tear up. "Chelsea... please. Don't cry, alright? Be strong for me. I'll be okay. I'm just gonna get checked out, and then we'll be back home having our coffee by the tree in no time."

"Alright. I love you."

The ride to the hospital seemed to take forever. When I got to his room, Damien was sitting up in bed.

Rushing to him, I started to sob.

Damien took me in his arms. "Calm down, baby. I'm fine." He wiped my eyes.

"You were saying all those things to me. And then...I was afraid that..."

"That I'd be dead when you got here? Because I'd just told you I would love you until the day I died?"

I sniffled. "Yes."

"That would be horrible timing. You've been reading too many shitty romance novels." He forced a smile.

I returned it. "I'm just glad you're okay. What can I do while we wait?"

He took my hand and kissed my knuckles. "Just stay with me. That's all I need."

"Like I could be anywhere else right now."

♦ ♦ ♦

We ended up spending most of Christmas day into the evening at the hospital. They'd run a series of tests then let Damien go with the understanding that he would see his doctor as soon as possible after the holiday.

The following Tuesday, we were able to get in to see Damien's cardiologist at Stanford.

Dr. Tuscano was mild-mannered and did his best to put me at ease. After the examination winded down, he smiled over at me. "I've been seeing Damien for some time now. I have to say, he's never seemed this happy."

"Thank you."

"Doc, I brought Chelsea with me so that you could personally answer any questions she has. I still haven't made any decision about surgery, but I want her to be informed."

"It's my pleasure to do that." The doctor took a seat on a small stool. "What can I answer for you specifically?"

Clearing my throat, I said, "I guess, I just want to learn more about the risks versus the benefits."

"Okay, well, as you probably already know, the procedure we would be performing is called a septal myectomy. We would be removing a small amount of the thickened septal wall surrounding his heart to eliminate the obstruction. This will make it easier for the heart to pump blood. We've always felt that he's a good candidate for this procedure, because Damien is fairly young and because of his significant septal thickness."

When I drew a blank, Damien decided to embarrass me. "Sorry, Doc...you said thickness, and her mind must have gone to another part of my anatomy."

The doctor chuckled but otherwise decided to ignore the comment. "Anyway, the surgery will likely provide him with relief from his symptoms, but more than that, it can lengthen his life expectancy."

"Is it safe?"

"It is generally very safe, yes. As with any surgical procedure, there are risks, albeit very low."

"What are those risks?"

"Infection, heart attack, stroke or death. But we do everything in our power to reduce the chances of anything like that ever happening."

"I've read a lot of conflicting things about whether this operation actually impacts life expectancy."

"You're right. There have been differing schools of thought on that. But the newest research has shown that for individuals like Damien who are symptomatic, myectomy may actually normalize their life expectancy. Ten-year survival would be ninety-five percent, which is on par with the general population."

"What's the ten-year survival for those who don't have the operation?"

"About seventy-three percent."

"Wow."

"There are no guarantees, Chelsea. Even with the surgery, we wouldn't be able to say with absolute certainty that sudden cardiac arrest won't happen. But given his family history, with his father dying so young, we recommend being as proactive as possible. He'll, of course, continue taking his medications either way."

Dr. Tuscano continued answering my questions. My feelings went up and down on the matter. Just when I would conclude that the operation was the way to go, I'd look over at Damien and shudder at the thought of him having open-heart surgery. Even though the doctor had said dying during the procedure was rare, it *has* happened. I'd read a couple of stories online that terrified me. I would never be able to forgive myself if I encouraged him to do it and God forbid, he died on the operating table.

At the same time, what if we put it off out of fear and something happened to him that could have been prevented? It was impossible to feel comfortable with either scenario. The only thing I was sure of was that it needed to be *his* decision and that I would support him no matter what.

♦ ♦ ♦

The Wednesday after Christmas, Damien left me a huge surprise on the kitchen counter.

Printed out were two e-tickets for direct flights from San Francisco to JFK.

"Damien? What are these?"

"It's my apology for fucking up our first Christmas."

"We're going to New York?"

"Yes...for New Year's Eve. You can see your sister. I know you said how much you missed her, since she couldn't be here over Christmas."

My eyeballs moved back and forth as I examined the details. "Okay...these are first class! During the holidays? These tickets cost a fortune."

"We can afford it."

"Are you serious?"

"We never go away, and we fucking deserve it. We need a change of scenery to try to forget about all of this depressing shit for a few days."

Reaching on my tippy toes to embrace him, I cried, "I could hug you!"

"I hope I get a little more than that."

"Oh, you'll get *a lot* more than that."

He lifted me into a kiss as I wrapped my legs around him. When he put me down, his expression turned serious. "I can tell you've been worried since the appointment yesterday. I just need a little more time living in denial with you, okay?"

"I can handle that."

He put me down. "Let's have some fun."

♦ ♦ ♦

New York City was a welcome change of pace.

We'd just gone to see Jade's evening performance and were out to eat at a restaurant not far from the theater district. I'd gone to the bathroom when I heard two of Jade's friends enter. One of them had apparently just arrived.

"Oh, my God, who is that guy out there sitting next to Jade?"

"That's her sister's boyfriend. His name is Damien."

"Holy hell."

"I know. He's fucking hot. He's visiting from California."

"They grow them well in California, then."

"Seriously. Makes me want to visit the West Coast. I'm sick of the guys here."

When I emerged from the stall, the one I'd met previously bit her tongue.

"Oh, hey, Chelsea." She turned to her friend to introduce me. "This is Jade's sister."

The other girl looked horrified. "You heard us."

"Yeah."

"Sorry. Your boyfriend is gorgeous. We were just admiring him and didn't mean any harm."

"Thank you. I know. None taken."

Even though I couldn't blame them, I still felt like strangling someone. As I washed my hands, I thought about the fact that I'd never felt this possessive over my former boyfriends. My feelings for Damien were at an entirely different level. The idea of someone trying to steal him—even just someone coveting him—made me crazy. Thankfully, he only ever seemed to have eyes for me.

When I returned to my table, I noticed he had moved seats and was talking to Jade. She smiled at me when I approached, and I suspected they were talking about me.

"You okay?" he asked.

"Yeah," I said, still flustered by the bathroom incident.

Sensing my mood, Damien placed his arm around me and gently scratched his fingertips along my back. When the two women from the bathroom returned to the table, I possessively took his hand and wrapped my fingers in his.

A few minutes later, Jade's co-star, Craig, showed up. He was the ginger guy I'd hung out with during my last visit here—the one Damien had seen me photographed with on Facebook. Damien immediately gave me a look that signified he recognized him.

When Jade introduced them, Damien offered him a firm but reluctant handshake.

Craig looked over at me. "It's so good to see you again, Chelsea. I didn't think you'd be back so soon."

"I know. This was a surprise trip." I smiled, squeezing Damien's hand tighter.

Together, we were a lost cause.

After dinner, Damien whispered in my ear, "That guy keeps staring at you, even with me sitting right here."

"No, he's not."

"Yes, he is. I've been watching him."

He suddenly let go of my hand, got up, and headed toward the bathroom.

My phone buzzed.

There's no one in the men's room right now. Get in here.

I slowly opened the door. Damien was standing right there and immediately pulled me into the handicapped stall.

"What are you doing?"

"Marking my territory."

"Are you gonna pee on me?" I joked.

"Only if you want me to."

"I don't."

"I'll do better than that," he said, flipping me around and lifting my skirt. He let out a deep breath onto my neck as he pushed deeply into me. With each thrust, I became wetter for him.

Spontaneous sex with him always felt good, but this time felt better than I could ever remember. As he fucked me from behind against the bathroom stall, he had no clue that I was just as revved up by jealousy as he was.

We could hear the main bathroom door open. That didn't stop our pace. In fact, whenever Damien and I were close to getting caught, it often made things more frantic. I opened my mouth into a silent scream as I came hard and fast. I could feel his hot cum shooting into me.

His hands were on each side of me locking me from behind against the stall. "I love when you clamp down on me like that with your pussy."

"We'd better go before Jade and her friends figure out what we're doing."

"Fuck that. I hope they do."

◆ ◆ ◆

The following day, Damien had taken a walk down the street from Jade's to pick up takeout for lunch. The three of us were going to hang out at the apartment until she had to leave for her evening show.

It was the first time Jade and I were left alone, and I had to ask, "So, last night at dinner, when I was coming out of the bathroom, what were you and Damien talking about?"

"He apologized for cornering me at the restaurant but said he needed to know my opinion. He said he knows you open up to me and that he figured I knew everything that was going on with you guys. I told him I did. Then he wanted my opinion on whether I felt that you were truly okay with the no-kids thing."

I blew out a breath of frustration. "I've been through this with him."

"I know, but he realizes that I know you better than anyone. He just wanted a second opinion to make sure that I didn't think you were kidding yourself."

"What did you tell him?"

"I told him that you are the most selfless person I know, but that I also know you wouldn't do or say anything you don't truly mean."

"He said that after we figure out whether or not he's gonna have heart surgery, he's gonna get a vasectomy so that I don't have to be on the pill forever."

"God, that seems so final."

"I know."

"Do you have any doubts? You'd tell me, right?"

"Yes. I swear. I'm not gonna lie and say that it doesn't make me sad, because it does, but I know how adamant he is. I can't live without him, so I have to live with his decision."

"Okay."

When Jade hugged me, my eyes watered. It was the first time I'd actually cried thinking about not ever having babies with Damien; I vowed that it would be the last time I would cry over it.

The door opened, and he walked in carrying paper bags of Chinese food. I quickly rubbed my eyes, but it was too late. He'd noticed my tears.

Examining my face, he said, "Everything okay?"

"Yes. I promise. We were just talking, and I got a little emotional."

Seeming doubtful, he looked over at Jade then at me. "Alright."

◆ ◆ ◆

Early that evening, Damien and I were walking hand in hand through SoHo when he said, "So, I've been keeping something from you."

"Not again?" I teased.

"This is a good thing, my little wiseass."

"What?"

"A friend of mine, who I met through an art forum, opened up a gallery here that's dedicated to spray paint art. That's why I wanted to come to this neighborhood before we left."

"That's so cool. Is that where we're going now?"

"Yes, but that's not all. I actually gave him one of my paintings."

"It's there?"

"Yup."

"Which one?"

"You'll have to wait and see."

The gallery was small. Large canvases of spray paint art were mounted onto the brick interior walls. Faint jazz music played in the background.

"Let's see if you can guess which one's mine."

We walked slowly through the gallery, stopping at each work of art. The images ranged from people to abstract shapes and colors.

"What is that?" I looked closer at the title of one piece in particular.

Le Nombril by Damien Hennessey.

"I guess I don't have to guess anymore. This is it!" I tilted my head. "What is it?"

"Look closely." He stood behind me, wrapping his arms around my waist and resting his chin on my head. "It's you."

"Me? It just looks like a big swirly hole." I suddenly felt hot. "That's not my vagina, is it?"

His laughter vibrated against me. "Not *that* hole, baby, although, I could spray that all day long if you want. In fact, it would be my pleasure." He guided me away from the canvas. "Step back."

I finally saw it. "It's my belly button. That's right! You mentioned once that you'd painted it."

"You are correct. That's your belly button. My beautiful navel, otherwise known as *Le Nombril*. That's the French term."

"How did you manage to paint it?"

"Well, a long time ago, I did one from memory. You'd worn this half-shirt over to my apartment, and I took a mental picture. This version is the replication of an actual photo I took of you more recently while you were sleeping. I know you probably wouldn't know the difference, but see all those grooves? They're actually a pretty accurate depiction of yours. You'd be surprised how challenging it is to capture the details of a navel. One of the hardest paintings I've ever done, but it's pretty much my favorite."

"Is it for sale?"

"No. No way I'm giving that away to anyone. This is just for display."

"Well, I think you're the only person in the world who'd appreciate it."

"I truly love every inch of you."

I looked into his eyes and knew he'd meant that with all of his heart and soul.

◆ ◆ ◆

New Year's Eve in Times Square was just as spectacular as I'd always imagined. Swimming in a crowd of people, I cuddled with Damien who wrapped me in his shearling-lined coat as he hugged me from behind.

When the ball dropped, we kissed so hard it felt like my lips were going to fall off.

Damien flipped me around toward him and repositioned the coat over me as a blanket. "It freaks me out to think that this time last year, I was watching all of this, staring at Ryan Seacrest on the television and thinking it was just going to be another year of the same. I'd automatically assumed I'd be stuck in the same rut, screwing around with women I didn't care about, painting all day. I didn't think that was a bad life, but I really didn't know better. I thought I was pretty happy. Turns out, I didn't know happy from a hole in the wall."

I smiled, appreciating the wall reference as he continued.

"I didn't have a fucking clue. I didn't know that true happiness would only come from a girl I hadn't met yet. It's hard to believe that this time last year, I didn't even know who Chelsea Jameson was. Now, I don't even know who I am without you."

My heart felt like it was bursting with a mixture of love and fear. There was so much I wanted to say, but I couldn't seem to form the words. It was very hard for me to articulate what I was feeling, so I simply buried my head against his heart and said, "This is gonna be a good year, Damien. I just know it."

Damien was right. The New York trip had been a much-needed change of scenery. It went by all too fast.

The next day, on our flight home, Damien held my hand as our plane slowly descended in preparation for its landing in San Francisco. The sun was shining into the aircraft, illuminating his beautiful eyes as he looked at me and said, "I think I'm gonna do it."

My chest tightened. I knew full well what he was referring to but asked anyway.

I braced myself. "Do what?"

"The surgery. I'm gonna do it. I'm gonna schedule it when we get back."

Squeezing his hand tighter, I put on a brave face and smiled despite filling with fear. "Okay."

I suddenly wished that we could have just stayed airborne.

CHAPTER **TWENTY-TWO**

Unintentional Vows

Damien's surgery was scheduled for the twenty-eighth of February, which was a little over a week away.

I'd been doing everything in my power over the last month and a half to remain strong for him. He didn't need to see that I was scared shitless; that wouldn't help anything. So, I quietly dealt with my anxiety on my own. I went and saw a therapist a couple of times during my lunch breaks and began taking something mild to take the edge off.

The past few weeks had consisted of lots of special appointments in preparation for the surgery. Damien had to have an echocardiogram; he met with his surgeon and anesthesiologist and also underwent a number of blood tests.

We'd decided that the upcoming weekend before his surgery was going to be low-key. We would do something relaxing and try to get our minds off of things.

Damien and I were sitting on the couch watching TV Monday night. I was pretending to be immersed in the movie. Instead, I was ruminating about the surgery.

He looked over at me at one point, and I just knew he could tell I wasn't really paying attention to the television. When he kissed me softly on the forehead, I took it as an unspoken acknowledgement that he knew what I'd really been thinking about. It was so tiring trying to pretend that I was fine all of the time. I wanted these days to pass so that we could have the surgery behind us. At the same time, I wanted them to drag, because I was scared.

He kissed my head again then asked, "Have you thought about what you want to do this weekend?"

"I thought we were just gonna hang out here, have some private time at home."

"We could do that, or maybe we could do something else."

"What did you have in mind?"

"Maybe we could get married."

My heart started to race. *Did he just say what I think he said?*

He'd rendered me speechless. "What?"

"We could get married...you know...if you wanted."

At first, I thought maybe he was joking, but the seriousness in his expression negated that. He was nervous. There was no way he was kidding.

"I don't understand."

"I know it's out of the blue."

"Yes. It is."

He took both of my hands in his. "Hear me out."

I blew out a deep breath. "Okay."

"It's all I've been able to think about ever since I made the decision to have the surgery. I truly believe I'm gonna be okay, Chelsea. Alright? But if there's even a miniscule percent chance that I'm not...the one thing I would regret the most in this life is not having seen you walk down the aisle toward me. I'm not trying to sound morbid, because again, I really trust my doctors, but it's still all I can think about. I want you to be my wife."

The tears I'd been holding back could not be contained any longer. "I want that, too."

"Are you not ready? Do you think it's too soon?"

"Maybe I *should* think that, but I don't."

"Me neither, baby. When they put me under and tell me to count to ten or whatever it is they do, I want to think about the memory of you in that white dress. I also want to know that when I wake up, we'll be married. But full disclosure...I also want you to have the legal right to have access to me at all times and to make decisions if needed."

When I just nodded in silence, he continued.

"I don't want you to think that I'm only asking you because I'm scared. I've known for a long time that you're it for me. I was gonna ask you on Christmas morning. You know that was before I even decided to have the surgery. Obviously, my going to the emergency room ruined those plans. Then, I was going to ask you in New York, but by that time, I'd decided on the surgery and changed my mind, thinking it would be better to wait until after. But as we've gotten closer to the date, I've changed my mind again because I'm realizing I just *can't* wait any longer. I want it now. Fuck that, I want it yesterday."

"You were really gonna propose to me on Christmas?"

"Yeah. I have the ring and everything." He dropped his head. "Fuck, I royally screwed up this proposal, didn't I? I just basically asked you to marry me with no ring."

"No. This is so you, Damien. It's as spontaneous as anything you've ever done. I'll see the ring on our wedding day. I want to be surprised."

"Are you sure? Because I could just casually walk to the bedroom where I'm hiding it and hand it to you right now. That would make this proposal even lamer."

"There's nothing lame about you saying you can't wait another day to marry me. You are the most unintentionally romantic person I have ever met."

"That's a good way of putting it."

"Will we tell people?"

"I think we should keep it to ourselves. You can tell Jade. I'll probably tell Ty. But we'll keep it on the down low. We'll still have the big wedding in the near future. You deserve that."

"Who's gonna marry us?"

"I'll take care of those details. I was thinking Santa Cruz Beach at sunset. The forecast looks nice. It's gonna be warmer than usual for this time of year. What do you think?"

"I think that's perfect."

"You just need to worry about two things. One...buy a white dress that will make me want to rip it off of you later that night. Between you and me, that just means any white dress. And two...take some time off tomorrow so we can get our marriage license in time for Saturday."

"I feel so sneaky doing it like this, but there's also something really exciting about the whole thing."

"We're good at sneaking around. It's what we do."

"You're right about that, except usually it has to do with you corrupting me, not making me an honest woman."

He flashed a devilish smile. "So, we have a date, Mrs. Hennessey?"

"We have a date."

♦ ♦ ♦

"We're here to apply for a marriage license," Damien said.

We'd just arrived at the county clerk's office. The woman at the desk looked less than amused when Damien began kissing my neck as we waited for her to gather the paperwork. We looked like two horny kids. She had no idea how serious our lives had been as of late.

He took one look at the form and said, "Oh, shit."

"What?"

"I just realized you're about to see my middle name. They make me enter it here."

"Were you seriously never gonna tell me?"

"Probably would've told you eventually, but it's been too damn fun keeping you wondering, Chelsea Deanna."

"You go first. Put your name down," I said.

With bated breath, I watched every stroke of the pen as he wrote it: *Damien Homer Hennessey*.

"Homer?"

He nodded without taking his eyes off the paper. "Homer."

I chuckled. "Homer...as in—"

"Simpson. Yup. Homer Simpson. *The Simpsons* show had just started airing around the time I was born. My father was a huge fan. So, he decided that out of all the names in the world he could've given me for my middle name, Homer was it."

"Your mother went along with it?"

"You see how crazy about him she is. He could have sold her on anything." He clicked the pen and gave it to me. "You know what, though?"

"What?"

"It could always be worse."

"How so?"

"Tyler got Bart."

City Hall echoed with the sounds of our laughter. An elderly couple walked by, giving us a dirty look for disturbing the peace.

Damien smiled impishly over at them and proudly proclaimed, "We're getting hitched."

When they continued to stare at us funny, Damien looked at me and said, "I can't believe Daddy gave us his blessing." He turned to them, pulling me into his side and joked, "She's my stepsister."

The couple walked away, looking mortified.

♦ ♦ ♦

Damien was intentionally keeping me in the dark about his plans for the beach ceremony.

My one mission was to find that perfect dress on Friday afternoon. I ended up hitting one local wedding boutique that had a lot to choose from. Since there wasn't a great deal of time to go from place to place, I vowed to make a decision there. The dress I finally chose was a very unconventional style, but it fit me better than any of them.

It was technically a gown but had four thigh-high slits, two in the front and two in the back. The frock was revealing yet whimsical with a few large strategically placed flowers sewn atop the strapless bodice. The bottom material was sheer, so you could see my legs right through it. It reminded of something a sexy fairy would wear. The fact that it showed off a lot of leg seemed appropriate for a beach setting.

When I texted a picture to Jade from the store, she immediately called me.

"Damien is going to lose it! That dress is hot."

"You think so?"

"I really do. It's so gorgeous on you. You need to wear your hair down with beachy waves." She was silent for a bit then it sounded like she was starting to get choked up.

"Are you crying, Jade?"

"Maybe a little."

"You know we're gonna have another wedding, right? You'll be my maid of honor, standing right behind me."

"I know. That's not why I'm crying." She paused. "I'm just so happy for you. And I think this is just about the most wildly romantic thing I've ever heard of—two people just getting married for the simple reason that they can't wait any longer and keeping it an intimate experience."

"I never thought I would have the balls to do something this sporadic, but it feels right for some reason."

"If it feels right, then it is. Tomorrow don't you dare think about next week or anything negative, for that matter. You hear me? I want you to enjoy every single moment of it. I know it's private, but please send me one picture of the two of you. Promise?"

"I promise."

"I'll be with you in spirit every step of the way."

That evening, when I walked in the door holding my dress inside of a wardrobe bag, Damien got up from the couch to greet me.

"Did you find one?"

"I did."

The excitement that filled his eyes made me even happier that I'd said yes. "I can't wait for tomorrow." He beamed.

"So, how is this going to play out? You can't see me before the ceremony."

"I remembered how adamant you are about that, so I have a car coming to pick you up here. I'll get dressed over at Ty's and will head to the beach early to set up. We'll meet there at exactly eight. I'll give the driver the precise location. All you have to worry about is looking pretty, which is really not a concern because you could show up wearing a paper bag, and you'd still be the most beautiful girl in the world to me. So, scratch that. All you have to do is show up."

"I can swing that."

♦ ♦ ♦

Saturday just felt different from the moment we woke up. It was unseasonably warm by about ten degrees for northern California, so it was in the seventies. Damien and I had our coffee together outside in the courtyard as we admired his mural, which was still a work in progress. In one spot, he'd replicated the famous unicorn he'd previously painted for me. The one he created on my old bedroom wall had to be torn down during the apartment renovations.

It surprised me that I wasn't nervous at all, not about the ceremony or the surgery this coming week. I was instead experiencing a day of respite, a day of peace where I could just experience living in the moment with him.

He left sooner than expected to get things ready for the beach. I wouldn't see him until the wedding. Getting ready all alone felt strange yet serene. The dogs were with Jenna this weekend, so I was all alone as I stepped out of the shower and prepared to get dressed.

My hair took the longest. I decided to wear it half up half down and used an iron to make loose curls.

I was doing really great in not getting too emotional until *The Fighter* by Keith Urban and Carrie Underwood came on the radio just as I was applying my mascara. I lost it. *Totally* lost it.

Sometimes, a song eerily comes on at just the right time. The lyrics could have been Damien speaking to me. It was the story of my life: a girl hurt so badly by a relationship, so afraid to trust in love. Then along came a man who would truly protect her and fight for her. He was my fighter. Of course, later this week that would also take on a whole new meaning.

Keep the surgery out of your mind, Chelsea. Not today.

I stood in the bathroom leaning against the sink and sobbed. They were tears of joy—not fear or sadness. Allowing myself to have one good cry before having to face Damien, I let the mascara run and vowed to reapply it.

It took me two hours to get ready after that. Every time I would start putting on my eye makeup, I would think about the song and tear up again. Eventually, I was finally able to pull myself together as I slipped on my dress. Looking in the mirror, I added the final touch, clipping a simple short veil to lay low in the middle of the back of my head.

A car horn beeped outside. I grabbed my silk bouquet of white hydrangeas and a small rolling suitcase before heading out the door.

Damien had sent a town car to come get me. A nice older man opened the door for me and placed my suitcase in the trunk.

The leather seats were cold from the air conditioning as I situated myself in the backseat. I gazed out the window at the sunset during the ride to Santa Cruz.

After the amount of crying I'd done, my body felt relaxed. So much so, that when *The Fighter* ironically played faintly on the town car radio, I was able to listen to the words without tearing up this time.

My heart began to pound as the signs for Santa Cruz Beach started to appear along the highway.

When the car pulled into a parking spot near a private section of the beach, I took an Altoid mint out of my small white clutch and nervously chomped on it.

"Here we are, Miss. Follow the lights."

"Thank you for the ride," I said, handing him a ten-dollar bill.

Follow the lights.

I looked to my left and saw nothing. Then, I looked to my right and understood exactly what the driver meant. In the distance, was a long line of tall tiki torches. There had to be at least twenty of them on each side.

The waves were crashing as I made my way toward the flames. When I finally arrived at the beginning of the line of flickering bamboo sticks mounted into the sand, I paused and took a deep breath before looking over at him in the distance.

Damien looked breathtaking as he stood tall with his hands crossed one over the other. He was wearing a light-colored vest with a thin tie over a fitted white shirt that complemented his muscular arms. His sleeves were rolled up, and his beautiful dark hair was disheveled from the wind. He was the sexiest groom I'd ever laid eyes on.

My eyes started to water when it hit me that he wasn't alone. Flanking Damien were the Double Ds—Dudley on one side, Drewfus on the other. They were standing at attention, more well-behaved than I'd ever seen them. I hadn't expected him to bring them, but it was an amazing surprise.

My heart beat faster with each step closer to the end of the line. I could finally make out Damien's face. He seemed overcome with emotion, and it shocked me to see him wipe his eyes. I'd never seen Damien cry and honestly didn't expect it today. That, of course, made me break out into my own tears before I even got to him.

The dogs left their spots to greet me, and I bent down to pet them. Damien had put little bow ties on them; it was the most adorable thing I'd ever seen. I then noticed that the town car driver suddenly appeared again and took Dudley and Drewfus to the side.

Damien whispered, "He's gonna take them back to Jenna's in a little bit." Placing his head on my forehead, he simply said, "Hi."

"Hi."

He pulled back. "You look..." he seemed to lose his words then looked me up and down. "That dress. Baby, you look like an angel."

"I'm glad you like it."

"I really do."

Holding both of his hands, I looked around at the torches surrounding us. "This is amazing what you've done."

"I figured you'd appreciate the fire, even though this one is controlled." He winked.

"I do."

There was a vague awareness of a man standing to our left, holding a book. Whoever he was, he was being patient, letting us have our private moment.

Damien and I continued to be in our own world, holding hands in silence. I momentarily closed my eyes and cherished this moment: the sound of the water, the breeze in my hair, the smell of his cologne mixed with the salty ocean air.

"May I start?" the man asked.

Damien squeezed my hands then looked over at him. "Yes."

The Justice of the Peace started his script, saying some generic things about love and marriage. Then, he asked Damien and me if we had written any special vows. With the short notice of our wedding, I hadn't had the time nor the clarity of mind to put my feelings into words.

Damien placed his forehead against mine.

I whispered, "I didn't write vows. I didn't know we were supposed to." I started to tear up, afraid that I'd somehow failed him by not coming prepared with something poignant to say. The thought of putting into words everything I was feeling seemed impossible.

When I looked into his eyes, he was crying.

Damien wiped my tears with his thumbs and wrapped his hands around my face. "I had a thousand things memorized to say to you in this moment, but I can't think of a single one. What you mean to me, Chelsea, defies language. It can't be summed up in words or reduced to a minute recitation. Just know that I love you with all of my heart and soul and that it's limitless. As long as my heart is beating, it will only beat for you."

His bottom lip was trembling.

I placed my hand on his heart and said, "This heart beating for me...these tears...they tell me more than any amount of words ever could. I never thought I'd be fortunate enough in my lifetime to have someone love me enough that it would bring them to tears. I love you more than life, Damien. You're everything I'll ever need. Please don't forget that. I'm so lucky to have found you, so lucky that out of all of the places in the world I could have ended up, I moved next door to you—the one person I was meant to be with."

"It was no accident. It couldn't possibly have been. I'm just so grateful to God that He brought you to me when he did."

The man cleared his throat. "For two people who didn't memorize anything, I would say you did pretty well. Best unintentional vows I've ever heard."

We got a good laugh out of that.

"Do we have rings?"

"Yes." Damien reached into his pocket, taking out a white gold hammered band and a large round diamond that had to have been at least two carats. The stone sat atop an eternity band of smaller diamonds. My eyes practically popped out of their sockets. That ring must have cost tens of thousands of dollars.

"Oh, my God, Damien..." I mouthed.

Damien repeated after the officiant, "I give this ring in pledge of my love and devotion. With this ring, I thee wed." He placed the ring on my finger, and it fit perfectly.

I repeated the same words and slid the thick band onto his hand.

"By the power vested in me by the state of California, I now pronounce you husband and wife."

Damien lifted me into a kiss and whispered over my mouth, "You're my wife, Chelsea Hennessey."

"I love that name. It actually rhymes."

"Chelsea Hennessey. It does have a nice ring to it. Chelsea Hennessey...got married by the sea. And the lucky bastard is me."

"You're a poet now? You have too much talent for one man."

"I plan to show you many talents tonight, wife. By the way..." His eyes traveled down the length of my body. "That has got to be the sexiest wedding dress on the freaking planet. I'm gonna take scissors to all of your dresses and cut four slits into them just like that."

"Wouldn't be the first time you cut my clothing into pieces."

"Clothing on a body like yours is a sin."

"Speaking of which...I'm not wearing underwear."

"Fuck. Really?"

"Yes, you're rubbing off on me."

"Rubbing one off on you...later...for sure."

"I married a dirty, dirty man."

"I married a little perv." He kissed me hard.

I stretched my fingers out. "Can we discuss this ring?"

"Do you like it?"

"It's perfection, but did you sell the building or something to pay for it? It's huge."

"Well, see, I read something in this wedding eti-quette article that the size of the ring should be directly proportional to the groom's cock size, so..."

"Ah...that explains it." Wrapping my arms around his neck, I could see the reflection of the flames in his eyes. "Seriously, it's the most beautiful ring I've ever seen. It had to have cost a fortune."

"Like you always say, I do everything big. I love you big. The ring should reflect that, if the person can afford it. I can't think of a better thing to spend some money on."

"Thank you."

"Don't thank me. No ring in the world could repay you for what you've given me and for agreeing to marry me." His mouth curved into a smile. "Are you ready for our reception?"

"Is there a reception?"

"Yes. The dogs don't know the chicken dance, so there will be none of that, but I brought dinner catered by Mama Rocco's. I figured we could eat here on the beach under the torches. I also booked us a room at a resort on the mountaintop a few miles away. The driver, Gary, is gonna come back after he drops off the dogs and clean up after us, so we won't have to worry about any of that. I basically hired him for the night."

"You really have everything figured out."

"I haven't figured out how to get you out of that dress and fuck you on this sand without getting arrested. Seriously, I can't wait to get back to the hotel."

Remembering my promise to my sister, I said, "Oh, I promised Jade we'd take a picture."

"Gary will do it. He snapped a bunch during the ceremony, too." He waved Gary over. "You mind taking some pictures of us?"

Activating the flash, Gary took several snapshots of us with the torches as a backdrop.

"Thanks, man."

When our pseudo photographer was out of earshot, I asked, "Who is that guy anyway?"

"Gary? He's the new tenant downstairs. Nice guy. He couldn't pay his rent, so I told him if he worked for me all day today, I'd let it slide just for this month only. He's at our beck and call."

"Well, that's win-win, I guess."

The dogs sat by us throughout our picnic-style dinner atop a blanket before Gary left to take them back to Jenna's, leaving Damien and me alone under the stars.

We couldn't have asked for a better night.

♦ ♦ ♦

Damien carried me over the threshold as we entered our suite at the mountaintop retreat, which overlooked Monterey Bay and the Santa Cruz mountains. He'd arranged for a massive bottle of champagne to be sent to the room, and there were rose petals scattered throughout.

"How on Earth did you find the time to do this?"

"Gary really earned his rent today." He grinned.

"I should have known."

"I wanted this day to feel as much like a real wedding night as possible."

"It's way better than an average wedding. We basically cut out all of the bullshit and made it about us, which is the way it should be."

"Lie back on the bed. I want to look at you in that dress one last time before I take it off."

Lying back against the plush down pillows on a bed of roses, I watched as my gorgeous husband kneeled at the foot of the bed while he gazed at me for several minutes.

"Alright. I'm done looking. It's burned into memory. Now I need to put those slits to good use."

Damien slowly undid his tie; there was something so sexy about that simple act. He then crawled over to me. "Let's give new meaning to tying the knot," he said as he took my hands and wrapped the tie around my wrists, pinning them over my head.

He took off his vest and shirt, throwing them aside before lowering his warm chest onto me. I wanted to touch him, but my hands were tied. He knew I loved this kind of torture, though.

Damien feasted on my body, starting with my neck and eventually making his way downward.

Burying his face under the material of my dress, he used his tongue to fuck my bare pussy as he bore down on my clit with his thumb. I wriggled beneath him, desperate to hold the back of his head as he did it.

When he sensed I was going to come, he suddenly got up to quickly untie my wrists before he undid his pants. He pushed my dress up, and within seconds, he was inside of me. Rocking his hips in a rhythmic motion, he penetrated me slowly and deeply. It was unlike his usual pace. With his eyes closed, he was cherishing every single movement. What it lacked in speed, it made up for in intensity. We'd fucked in just about every which way since we'd gotten together. Every time was somewhat different from the last. But *this* time felt different from all of the other times.

This definitely felt like a husband making love to his wife.

CHAPTER **TWENTY-THREE**

The Fighter

As magical as our wedding night in Santa Cruz was, it wasn't powerful enough to slow down time.

The day of Damien's surgery came faster than I'd hoped. Well, if I'd had my way, it wouldn't have come at all.

He didn't let go of my hand once as we drove to Stanford in the wee hours of the morning. We were both eerily quiet.

After parking his truck in the hospital garage, we lingered after Damien turned off the ignition. Understandably, neither of us was ready for what faced us inside. He looked over at me. I could no longer mask my fear.

"It's okay to be scared, Chelsea. You've forgotten I can see right through you."

"I want to be strong for you."

Squeezing my hand tighter, he said, "Everything's gonna be alright, baby. It's okay to show your fear, though."

Once inside, I likely wouldn't be able to tell him everything I wanted to say. The words I couldn't form felt like they were choking me.

I was breaking down and could hardly talk. I managed to say, "You'd better be okay, because I can't live without you."

Blinding tears filled my eyes. I had one job—to be strong for him—and I had totally failed.

"When I'm in there, I want you to think about all the things we have to look forward to this year, like planning our other wedding. Just focus on the good and then every hour that passes, we'll be closer to having this behind us."

I nodded as if it were really possible to look forward to anything in this moment.

He went on, "Nothing is gonna happen, okay? But God forbid, if something did, I need you to know that what I said that one time about not wanting you to ever move on, that was irresponsible. I would want you to move on and be happy."

I shook my head profusely. "I can't have this conversation, Damien."

"Yes, you can, because nothing's gonna happen, but I just need to say this. Please."

"Alright."

"I don't want you to stay alone or feel guilty for moving on someday if something ever does happen to me."

I nodded just to make him feel better, but I knew deep in my heart, that there would be no moving on if something ever happened to Damien. It was *that* kind of love. The once-in-a-lifetime kind. The kind that his mother and father had. The kind that I couldn't have with Elec or anyone else, because it would have only been possible with Damien.

"You're my soulmate, Damien. My fighter. Have you ever heard that song, *The Fighter?* The Keith Urban one?"

"I've heard it come on the radio. It reminds me of us," he said.

It shouldn't have surprised me that he'd picked up on that, too. We were connected that way.

He nudged his head. "Let's go. Let's get this shit over with. I have a wife and dogs to get back to."

"Okay. Let's do it."

Inside, Dr. Tuscano addressed any last minute concerns we had.

"So, we're clear on everything that's gonna happen? The incision will be made down the center of Damien's chest. The cut muscle will eventually heal on its own. We use a heart-lung machine during the procedure, which helps protect the other organs while the heart is stopped. Once the operation is over, Damien's heart will start beating on its own again with no problems."

The doctor noticed Tyler and Damien's mother waiting outside the door and waved them in. They looked just as nervous as I did. Damien was being stronger than all of us.

Dr. Tuscano finished answering some questions that Monica had before he said, "Surgery should take about five to six hours. Don't be alarmed if no one comes and updates you. We typically need full surgical staff to remain in the operating room for this procedure."

Damien hugged Tyler and kissed his mother. They were just about to leave to allow us a moment alone when Damien called after his brother.

"Dude, keep Mom and my wife sane out there. I'm counting on you."

"You got it, man."

After the door closed, Damien whispered, "By the way, when I said you should move on with another man, that doesn't include Tyler. I'd find a way to come back from the dead to castrate him if he ever made a move on you."

He'd managed to make me laugh a little. "Understood."

After a long silence, there wasn't anything left for him to say except, "I love you."

"I love you so much."

"Be strong for me, okay?"

"Okay."

Dr. Tuscano was all suited up when he came in with a staff to wheel Damien out. "Ready?"

Damien squeezed my hand one last time before letting it go. "Yep."

As they took him out of the room and down the hall to the operating room, I started to feel weak, like my legs were going to give way. Just when it seemed like I was going to collapse, I felt Tyler's hands on my arms, gripping them and essentially holding me up.

"He's gonna be okay."

I just kept shaking my head, desperately trying to convince myself of that. "I know."

He had to be.

♦ ♦ ♦

The first hour was the hardest. It went by painfully slow. As much as Damien had asked Tyler to look after us, it seemed Ty was just as nervous as we were and needed us just as much as we needed him.

Damien clearly underestimated how hard this would be for his brother, who'd been his closest confidante long before I ever came into the picture.

Tyler held my left hand and Monica held my right. Damien was our common denominator, the person each of us loved most in this life.

At one point, Tyler looked down at my ring. "Holy shit. He wasn't kidding when he said he spent a fortune on that thing."

Staring down at my rock, I agreed. "He's crazy."

Monica chimed in, "No, he's not. He just loves you so much." She sighed. "Congratulations. I know it was supposed to be a secret, but he told me everything. I'm looking forward to being there for the big one."

"We didn't mean to exclude anyone."

"I know that. I'm not trying to make you feel guilty. I'm so happy you did it the way you did."

"Thank you."

Tyler grinned. "I'll never forget the first day he told me about you. He said, 'Ty, there's this girl who moved in next door. She's quirky, a little fucked-up in the head, can't get out of her own way, but she's beautiful, like the most natural beauty you've ever seen and the realest person you'll ever meet. She came to complain about the dogs, and all I wanted to do was kiss her senseless."

"He said that?"

"He did."

Once the somber first hour of waiting passed, the mood changed drastically. It all started with a pizza.

A deliveryman showed up to the waiting area.

"I have a pizza order from Damien?"

"Damien couldn't be ordering pizza. He's in surgery," I told him.

"Nope. He scheduled a delivery."

"When did he call?"

"I don't know. Anyway, I'm supposed to bring the pizza here and give it to Chelsea with this note." He handed it to me.

"Thank you."

The pizza box felt hot on my lap. The smell of the cheese and sauce reminded me that I hadn't eaten anything. I ripped off the paper that was taped to the top and read it.

It's not as good as mine, but I'm a little busy
at the moment and couldn't bake you one.
So, this will have to do. I knew you
wouldn't eat unless I brought it to you.
—D

If we thought that was the only waiting room surprise, we were wrong. The next hour came a ginormous fruit bouquet from Edible Arrangements along with a note.

I know my mother probably didn't touch the pizza. She'll claim to be too upset to eat, but she's never seen a chocolate-covered strawberry she could refuse.

He was right. Monica had refused the pizza but ended up devouring the strawberries.

The third hour brought the biggest surprise of all. In walked our tenant, Gary, who was apparently still slaving away as a personal assistant to Damien in lieu of paying rent. He was leading the Double Ds on two leashes into the waiting room.

"They let the dogs in here?" I smiled.

Gary shrugged. "I guess? No one said anything."

Letting them lick my face, I said, "I can't believe they're here."

"Damien thought it would cheer you up to see them."

"He was totally right."

Gary handed me a wrapped gift. "He also wanted me to give you this."

"Where is it from?"

"I have no idea. He gave it to me already wrapped like this."

I opened it but had to quickly shield the contents from Tyler and Monica. It was a ménage book titled, *Three Times A Lady*. Of course, there was a note.

I figured if anything could take your mind off me going under the knife, this would be it. Still a few hours to go. Happy reading.

Gary handed me one more item. "He also gave me this envelope but said you can't open it until the fifth hour."

I took it. "Okay, thank you."

When the final hour rolled around, I opened the envelope. It was a simple note.

It's almost done. I know you must be exhausted and scared, waiting for me to get out. Believe me, no one wants to get out of there more than me. I just wanted to remind you that even though a machine might be taking over my heart right now, it's still only beating for you. I love you. Kiss my mother for me. Do NOT kiss Tyler. See you soon.

The expected six hours had come and gone, and there was still no word from the doctor. Even though Damien's tactics had worked to seriously calm us down up until now, I was starting to get really nervous again.

Really nervous.

Panicked.

What could be taking so long?

I just wanted so desperately to see him.

I turned to Tyler. "Do you think everything is okay?"

"I'm sure it is. The doctor said it could go over the six hours."

"I just wish someone would come out to give us an update, let us know that everything is going as expected."

Monica was quiet and just took my hand again. The mood was quickly dampening with each excruciating minute that passed. It seemed like forever since I'd touched him or heard his voice.

Finally, thirty minutes later, Dr. Tuscano appeared, walking down the hall toward us. My heart beat faster with each step he took closer. The three of us stood up.

He pulled down his mask and said, "Surgery went well."

It felt like someone had released a thousand-ton rock off of my chest.

"The procedure turned out to be a bit more complex than we anticipated, which is why it took a little longer, but we were successful in doing what we needed to. He's in recovery right now. I've asked a nurse to come out in just a little bit to escort one of you at a time to see him. He'll be in recovery for a while before they move him into the intensive care unit."

"Thank you so much, Dr. Tuscano, for everything."

"It's my pleasure. Damien is one of my favorite patients. I'm glad we finally decided to do this. I'm sure I'll be seeing you a lot in the coming weeks during the post-operative period. You have my cell phone number and email if you have any questions at all."

"Yes. Thank you."

After he walked away, the three of us embraced in collective relief. A nurse approached soon after, and Monica and Tyler agreed that I should get to see him first.

My heart nearly skipped a beat at the sight of Damien sleeping in the recovery room. There was a tube coming out of his chest that seemed to be draining fluid. A nurse was monitoring his heart rate.

"Is he awake?"

"The anesthesia is still wearing off, but he woke up fine. He seems to be dozing off again, though," she said.

I waited patiently for him to open his eyes. When his eyelids began to flutter, I said, "Baby, it's me...Chelsea. I'm here with you now. You're fine. You made it through. We have it behind us."

Damien blinked repeatedly and seemed disoriented. It was hard to see my strong man in such a vulnerable state.

I just kept talking. "Welcome back to the living. You're gonna be okay."

"Chelsea," he whispered.

Thank God.

"Yes, baby, it's me. And your mom and Tyler are here, too. We're so happy you're out."

He repeated, "Chelsea..."

"Yes. I'm here. I love you."

"Where is she?"

"Your mom? She's just down the hall. She'll be coming in soon."

"No."

"What?"

"Where is..." He hesitated.

"Where is who?"

"Where's our baby?"

"Our baby?"

"Where's our baby?" He repeated. "I saw her. Where is she?"

"We...we don't have one. There is no baby."

He just stared at me, looking confused until his eyes closed again. I didn't know what to make of it and concluded that he was just delusional from all of the medication.

♦ ♦ ♦

A few hours later, Damien was moved into the intensive care unit. His clarity had returned, and he no longer mentioned anything about a baby. He probably had no recollection of it. Still, hearing him ask to see our baby—a baby we would never have—was definitely painful. It made me wonder whether on some subconscious level, Damien was longing for a child more than I thought.

"Did you receive any special deliveries while I was under?"

"Oh, we sure did. You're very clever."

"The next couple of months are gonna suck," he groaned.

"Why?"

"That's how long it's supposed to take for a full recovery."

"I'll be your private nurse. Don't worry."

"Mom, block your ears." Damien spoke in a low voice, "That's not gonna work. I can't have you looking all cute and tending to me when we can't have sex for at least three weeks. I'm gonna end up breaking the rules, and if I end up dead…"

"It'll be all my fault?"

"No. I was gonna say, it will all be worth it."

"We'll figure something out, so that doesn't have to happen."

"I just want to go home."

"I know. I just want you home, too."

◆ ◆ ◆

Damien was approved to be released after five days. There were no surprises or complications as far as his prognosis was concerned. We were so grateful to God that we would finally be able to slowly but surely move on with our lives.

It felt like I could finally breathe after months of worry.

That feeling wouldn't last.

A few weeks into Damien's recovery at home, one of my biggest fears would come true.

CHAPTER **TWENTY-FOUR**

God's Plan

"**N**otice how they never show these pretty boy hosts doing any work for more than a few seconds. How much money you want to bet they're not really doing shit when the camera stops rolling?"

As Damien lay on the couch watching a home improvement channel with his big feet on my lap, I stared at the red line that ran down the middle of his otherwise flawless, rock-hard chest. The scar was a permanent reminder of the risk he took for us.

I knew he'd made the decision to have the operation, not only to better his quality of life, but also so that he and I could have a better chance at a longer life together. The scar was also a constant reminder of the fragility of life.

I had to leave the room. Whenever I got overly emotional, I was afraid he would be able to see right through me. I couldn't let him see that something was seriously wrong. I wasn't ready to face it myself, and I sure as hell wasn't going to put him through any kind of stress over nothing—over speculation.

Another day...another denial.

My period was now officially three weeks late. Even though I'd never missed a cycle in my life before, I refused to believe that could mean I was pregnant. I wouldn't take a test, because I was too scared of the consequences, unable to even fathom that possibility, unable to fathom what Damien's reaction would be. So, I just kept letting the days pass.

Not to mention he was still in a fragile state. He was only just beginning to get back to normal, certainly nowhere near one hundred percent. I couldn't risk putting him under any kind of unnecessary stress. There was still a chance it was nothing. I'd read that stress could potentially delay a menstrual cycle. I'd been under so much stress in the weeks before his surgery that it was easy to see how that could have technically happened. I was on the pill, which was ninety-nine percent effective.

Still, as much as I tried to talk to myself, the not knowing was starting to eat away at me.

"Hey. What's wrong?"

"Nothing."

"Bullshit. Come here." He moved closer to me. "Sit down right here." Pointing to the floor in front of him, he positioned my body between his legs and began to massage my shoulders. "Has this been too much for you?"

"What?"

"Having to take care of me while I recover?"

I looked behind to face him. "Of course not. It's been my pleasure to take care of you. Don't ever think that."

He dug the base of his palms deeper into my muscles pressing in a circular motion. "What's going on with you, then?"

"I think the stress of the past month is just catching up with me. Everything is okay," I lied.

After a half-hour of sitting in the same position, I lifted myself off the ground. "You know what I just remembered? We are all out of shredded cheese. I was going to make tacos tonight. I'm gonna head to the store and get some."

"Alright."

I left the apartment in a hurry.

Once around the corner, I leaned against the side of the building and took a deep breath, taking out my cell phone and praying that Jade picked up. I'd told her about my late period earlier in the week.

When she answered, I said, "Oh, thank God."

"Is everything okay?"

"I think I'm having a panic attack."

"Okay, calm down. I'm here. Where are you?"

"I was sitting down watching TV with Damien, and I had to get out of the house. He's starting to catch on that something is off with me."

"Listen. You need to do a test. I know that you don't want to know, but you need to grow some balls and do it. Not knowing is the problem right now."

"Okay. I'm out now. I'll buy a test and do it. I told Damien I was going to the grocery store."

"I'll stay on the phone with you. Can you use a public bathroom?"

"I'll find something."

After purchasing a pregnancy test at the drug store, I asked if I could use their employee bathroom in the back. I put Jade on speakerphone while I followed the directions and peed on the stick.

Placing my head between my legs on the toilet, I sighed. "Now we wait."

After a few minutes of waiting in silence, Jade said, "Breathe, Sis. Breathe. If you are, then it's a freak accident. He's going to understand."

"Damien spent enough years worrying about his health. I didn't want him to have to worry anymore. This is going to be a nightmare for him, especially given that he's not even fully recovered. I—"

"The time is up," Jade interrupted. "I've been watching the clock. Time to check."

When I reluctantly looked over at the stick sitting on the sink, the red symbol that met my eyes wasn't really a surprise in the least. "It's a plus sign."

Jade blew a deep breath into the phone. "Okay. Okay. We're gonna handle this. It's going to be okay."

I covered my mouth. "Oh, my God."

"You need to tell him soon."

"I need more time. He needs more strength before he can deal with this. I don't think I'm gonna tell him for another couple of weeks at least. I can't do this to him. I also need to confirm it with a doctor first."

"Okay. Make an appointment this week, but promise me you won't put off telling him for too long."

"If I could, I would never tell him."

♦ ♦ ♦

"Congratulations, Mrs. Hennessey. We have the results of your blood test, and you're definitely pregnant."

I probably looked like she'd told me that someone died.

"Is this not good news for you?"

Holding onto the arms of my chair for balance, I shook my head. "It's not, no."

"This was unexpected?"

"My husband has an inherited heart condition. We'd made a firm decision not to have biological children to avoid passing it on. There's a fifty percent chance of that, and he didn't want to take the risk. I'm on the pill, and he was also planning to have a vasectomy soon. This is like my nightmare, and I don't really understand how it happened."

"I'm sorry to hear that this is not positive news for you."

"The pill is supposed to be nearly one-hundred percent effective, and I never missed a single one. I've always been so diligent. How could this have happened?"

"Well, there are certain things that can counteract it. Were you taking other medications, for example?"

Suddenly, a light bulb went on.

Oh, no.

"I'd been experiencing a lot of depression and anxiety over my husband's surgery. He's been in recovery for about a month. I didn't want to go on antidepressants, but my therapist recommended St. John's Wort, so I started to take that."

Dr. Anderson momentarily closed her eyes in understanding and nodded. "Yes. Unfortunately, that is well-known to interfere with the pill."

"Well-known to everyone but me apparently. Fuck. I'm sorry for swearing, but...fuck." I lowered my head into my hands.

"Your therapist should have known that before recommending it to you."

"No. I should've checked myself. It's my fault. How could I have been so stupid?"

"You'd be surprised how many people take things without reading the fine print or looking into the side effects."

"I was trying to make things better by quietly handling my issues, and I ended up ruining everything."

"You do still have the option to terminate."

Even just hearing her allude to that felt painful. "No. I could never do that." This was still Damien's and my child, and as scared as I was, I knew without a shadow of a doubt that I was already hopelessly in love with it.

"Okay. Understood."

"What's next?"

"We'll make an ultrasound appointment for you soon."

"Okay." I swallowed. This was getting far too real given the fact that Damien still had no clue. The clock was ticking.

I left the office in a daze. If I thought it was difficult accepting the pregnancy before, knowing that it was totally my fault made it completely unbearable.

◆ ◆ ◆

I didn't know how to be around Damien. Carrying the burden of this secret was too much to handle. Whether I realized it or not, I had been shutting him out, and he was starting to sense that something was really wrong with me. I doubted he realized what it was, though. God only knew what conclusions he might have been drawing.

Two weeks passed since the doctor's appointment. Each day, the plan was to come clean to him about the pregnancy, and each day, I would completely chicken out. I would tell myself that he needed more time to heal before dealing with the news, but the truth was, he would never be ready to hear it.

He seemed to suspect something was off and kept asking me if I was okay. I just didn't know how to tell him the truth.

Lately, I'd been taking several trips to the "store" just to be able to talk to Jade privately. With Damien's sensitive hearing, any conversations I had with her in our apartment were within his earshot even when I was whispering behind closed doors. Jade was seriously pissed at me for not having yet told him, but she still agreed to support me until I finally garnered the courage to come clean.

One afternoon, I'd returned home from having snuck out to call her. Damien was standing in the middle of the living room with his arms crossed. Adrenaline rushed through me when I caught a look at his expression.

"What the fuck is going on?" He had never spoken to me with such an angry tone.

"What do you mean?"

"You said you were going to the store. Instead, you were talking on the phone in the alleyway around the corner."

My mouth dried up. "How did you know that?"

"Answer me first. What are you hiding?"

"You had me followed?"

"I was worried about you. When you bolted out of here this time, I called Gary and asked him to keep an eye on you, because I knew something wasn't right. But I never expected him to tell me that."

"So, you had Gary follow me. What exactly do you think is going on?"

"Fuck if I know, but it's not leaving a warm and fuzzy feeling, Chelsea. What's happening? Who were you talking to on the phone?"

I had to tell the truth.

My answer was barely audible. "Jade."

Squinting his eyes, he asked, "What are you talking to Jade about that you can't say in front of me?" He began to walk slowly toward me, and the false conclusion he was starting to draw nearly broke my heart. "Are you regretting all of this? Marrying me?"

I had to tell him.

Now.

"No! No. Never. Damien, I'm..."

"What?"

"I'm...pregnant."

He practically fell back as if the proclamation had knocked the wind out of him.

"What?"

My eyes were getting moist. "Yes."

Placing his hands on his head, he just looked at me in shock. "How could you be pregnant? You're on the pill."

"I made a terrible mistake. In the weeks before your operation, I was trying not to show you how scared I was. I started taking something homeopathic to take the edge off—St. John's Wort. I thought it was harmless, but it turns out, it interferes with the pill's effectiveness." I began to pace. "This is all my fault. You asked one thing of me in this life, one sacrifice, and I couldn't get it right." I looked at him with pleading eyes. "But I can't terminate it, Damien. I just can't."

He suddenly snapped, "I would never ask you to do that. *Never*. Do you understand?"

"Yes."

He just stood there in shock for an indeterminate amount of time.

Grabbing his jacket, he suddenly headed toward the front door.

"Where are you going?"

"I just...I need some air, okay? I'll be back. Don't worry. I'll be fine."

After he shut the door, I collapsed onto the couch in tears. As much as telling him the truth had hurt, it was an enormous release to have finally let it out. The weight of keeping it a secret had been killing me.

Sleep had evaded me for days. This was the first moment I felt like I could relax enough to even close my eyes. Exhausted, my body shut down, and I ended up falling asleep on the couch while waiting for Damien to return.

After an unknown amount of time passed, I woke up to find his head on my stomach.

Running my fingers through his wavy hair, I spoke softly, "You came back."

"Of course I did. I'm sorry I ever left. I shouldn't have left you like that. I just felt like I couldn't breathe and needed to process it alone."

"I'm so sorry."

"This is not your fault. You didn't do it intentionally." He bent down and kissed my stomach tenderly then spoke over my skin, "I thought I was losing you. For weeks, I thought I was losing you, Chelsea. I had no clue what was going on."

It hurt to think that he actually believed I was having doubts.

"Never, Damien. I would never leave you."

He sat up suddenly. "I have to tell you something."

"Okay." I sniffled.

"I never mentioned something that I experienced when I was coming out of the surgery. I thought it was just a dream, but now I have to wonder."

"What?"

"I saw something...or someone. I just somehow *knew* it was our child. It didn't present clearly as a girl or a boy necessarily. It was just like the spirit of a child. I couldn't make out a face, but I do remember seeing blonde curls. So, I guess I assumed it was a girl." He ran his fingers through my hair. "Anyway, I just knew it was ours. This thing...spirit...whatever you want to call it... was trying to leave me. I kept asking it to stay—begging it to stay. In this dreamlike state, I knew about all of the risks, that I wasn't supposed to keep it with me or ask it to stay, but it didn't matter in that moment. My love for it was too powerful. I still don't understand what that experience was—a hallucination or otherwise. It seemed real at the time. I was never going to tell you about it."

"You don't remember what you were asking me when you were coming out of the anesthesia?"

"No."

"You asked me where she was."

"I did?"

"When I asked you who you were referring to, you said it was our baby."

"Oh, man. See, I don't remember that at all. But that must have been the very end of it."

Hearing his story freaked me out a little, because I was definitely pregnant that day, even though I didn't know it yet.

He continued, "The point to all of this is...when faced with the scenario in that subconscious state, I chose for it to stay. Despite everything, I wanted it, because my love for it surpassed everything else...all of the risks, all of the fears."

"Do you think it was a premonition?"

"I don't know. And you know what? It doesn't matter. I want this baby. I always did want one with you. I tried to do what I thought was right, but God had other plans."

An immense relief washed over me. "I thought you'd be devastated. I've been so terrified to tell you."

"I'm freaked out, baby. Of course. But there's no question as to whether I want this. I want it more than anything. I'm just scared, but that's irrelevant at this point. Now that she's really here...I want it even more than I could have ever imagined before. I'm petrified, but I'm so in love—in love with her and with you."

"Her?"

"I think so, yeah. It's a girl." He smiled.

"How will you handle this, Damien? The fear and the guilt you've always worried about."

He thought long and hard before answering, "If there's one thing I've learned, it's how to live with fear. I live every day not knowing if I'm gonna drop dead at the drop of a hat. But I refuse to let it dictate my life anymore. So, I'll handle it just like everything else. I'll wake up each day and pray to the same God who brought me you and who helped me through surgery. I'll pray that He protects our child, too. No matter how scary this is, I have to put everything in His hands at this point and thank him for blessing me with all the things I didn't think I could ever have."

He lowered his head down to my stomach again. "Holy shit. We're gonna have a baby."

I let those words really sink in. For the first time, I actually allowed myself to celebrate it, as if it had only now just become real.

I beamed. "We're having a baby!"

♦ ♦ ♦

The following week when we heard our child's heart beating for the first time, it was as magical as it was frightening.

We wouldn't know for several years whether genetics would be on our side. Hypertrophic cardiomyopathy is a condition that, if inherited, shows itself over time, manifesting in young adulthood. We would leave it up to our child to determine if he or she wanted to get tested.

All we knew was that we would do everything that was humanly possible to monitor and protect our baby in the meantime.

CHAPTER **TWENTY-FIVE**

Mountain Out of a Mole Hill

Our big wedding plans would have to be put on hold until after the baby was born. From getting a nursery ready, to preparing the dogs for the new addition, there was just too much going on to have to worry about organizing a giant party.

We'd opted not to find out the sex, although Damien was still convinced it was a girl. He truly believed that the spirit he'd encountered in his dream—or whatever that experience may have been—was female. He chalked it up to father's intuition.

All of the items we'd purchased for the nursery were gray, white and green, although Damien would pick up small pink items when he was out and place them strategically around the space; it was essentially a baby girl's room.

I was carrying small and low, prompting Damien to dub my belly his "little beach ball."

Overall, the pregnancy was a smooth one all the way up until the final month.

We were both under a lot of stress because Jenna had blindsided us with the news that she was planning to move to Colorado with her new boyfriend. She also decided that the dogs were technically hers and that she had the right to take them with her.

Damien tried to convince her that staying in California was in the Double Ds' best interest because it was the only home they'd ever known. She wasn't having it and threatened to take us to court for full custody. It wasn't looking good at all.

I'd gotten so worked up and ended up on bed rest due to high blood pressure. So not only was Damien worried about the dogs getting taken away, but now he had to worry about the health of his wife and unborn child. I was, in turn, worried about the stress that all of the above was putting on his heart.

The dogs were my only saving grace during the bed rest period, since they'd climb next to me and keep me company during the afternoons when Damien had to get things done around the building. He didn't even fight them being in our bed anymore because he knew what a comfort they were to me. They were still banned at night, however. I knew he was terrified that Jenna was going to win and that they'd be gone soon. As a result, the dogs were getting spoiled rotten.

One day, Damien had gone out for a couple of items I'd been craving. He'd taken two hours longer than he should have.

When he finally returned, the front door slammed shut, and I heard him say, "It's done."

"What?"

"It's done. She's letting us keep the dogs."

"What? How?"

"I drew up a contract and paid her off."

"You what?"

"I threw a shitload of money at her, enough that she couldn't refuse it. I wasn't going to let this stress us out anymore. I wasn't going to let her take them away from us."

"How much did you give her?"

"Don't worry about it. We have the funds for it. And they're worth any amount."

Once again, Damien had taken charge of a situation and come to my rescue. Tears of relief began to roll down my face. It was only in that moment that I truly realized how much the fear of losing the animals had been taking its toll on my health and well-being.

Damien normally didn't climb into bed with us, but that afternoon, he squeezed himself into a spot. Lying in the bed with the *Triple* Ds, an enormous peace came over me. The baby was kicking to boot. Our family was complete, and no one could take that away.

You couldn't put a price on that.

♦ ♦ ♦

It was a clear evening, and the dark sky filled with bright stars. Damien and I were sitting in the courtyard the night before my scheduled C-section, fantasizing about all of the things we were going to do once the baby was born.

"I can't wait to have sushi again and to be able to shave my own legs."

Firmly gripping my thigh, he said, "I can't wait to be able to wrap these legs around my back and pound into you without worrying about impaling my kid." He turned to me. "You can go back to shaving your legs, but leave the pussy shaving to me even when you're able to see it again."

"Sure. In fact, I'm counting on that."

"Good." He winked.

"Oh! I can't wait to have my afternoon latte again. That's another thing I miss, being on a caffeine high."

Damien grunted. "You know what I can't wait for? I can't wait to throw that damn stuffed cockblocker out the window. That's gonna be the first thing to go."

That made me crack up. He was referring to the body-length pregnancy pillow that I'd been sleeping up against these last few weeks. It formed a big barrier between us.

"Actually, why don't you just let the Ds have it? I caught them humping it the other day. They were double teaming it."

He wriggled his brows. "Did that remind you of your books?"

I nudged him with my elbow. "No."

He snickered and kissed my cheek.

Tomorrow's C-section couldn't come quickly enough. Because of my preeclampsia, my doctor thought it best to get the baby out a week before its due date, especially since my cervix had not dilated at all.

We were nervous but so incredibly excited to finally meet our baby.

◆ ◆ ◆

Damien looked so funny wearing the hospital-provided shower cap. Being here reminded me of how terrified I was the day of his surgery. As scary as it seemed to imagine the doctor cutting into my abdomen today, nothing compared to the fear I'd felt the day my husband went under the knife.

He surprised me when he said, "You know, as scary as my operation was, I'm way more freaked out by this. I just can't wait until this is over."

The irony of his statement made me smile. I guess that's what it's like when you love someone. The thought of something happening to the other person is far worse than the thought of something happening to yourself.

I looked up at him from my horizontal position on the operating table. "I love you."

He briefly took down his surgical mask to say, "You guys are my whole life."

I felt so grateful that he was feeling well, that he was right by my side.

Damien held my hand tightly as the doctors explained everything they were doing. Because they'd given me a spinal, my entire lower body was completely numb.

They'd warned me that I was going to feel some tugging. Just when I did, Damien squeezed my hand harder.

"Oh, my God, she's coming. They're taking her out."

Then I heard them.

Cries.

Cries.

More cries.

My baby.

Damien's eyes were glistening. "Oh, my God! She's beautiful, baby. She looks like you. Just like you!"

"She does?"

"Yeah. She's fair-skinned. She's an angel. She... she...has...a penis. A penis?"

"It's a boy," the doctor proclaimed.

Damien started to cry tears of joy and laughter all at once. "She has a little cock. It's a boy? It's a boy! Baby, we have a son."

"It's a boy!" I repeated.

"Yes!"

After a few minutes passed, a nurse handed our son to Damien who placed him by my face.

I kissed his cheek, longing to hold him. "Hi," I said ever so softly.

As much as Damien thought he looked like me, I could definitely see Damien's nose.

"You were supposed to be a girl," I cooed. "You had your daddy fooled."

Damien bent down and kissed our baby boy's forehead. "He changed the story."

♦ ♦ ♦

One of the drawbacks of being thrown off guard by the gender of our baby was the fact that we had no name picked out. We'd been so focused on girl names that the boy options fell by the wayside.

Our son was a few weeks old before we finally decided on a name. We opted to announce it to our closest family and friends on Christmas Eve.

It seemed like just yesterday that we'd had everyone over for a holiday party at our place last year. So much had changed since. Back then, Damien hadn't even decided on the surgery, we'd also thought we would never have kids, and we were only just dating. Fast forward a year later, Damien was ten months post-operation, we were married, and we had a son. Not to mention, the dogs were now ours full-time.

Damien had the baby in a carrier on his chest while he put up the last of the decorations. Still recovering from my C-section, I took it slow as I prepared the food in the kitchen. We weren't originally going to have a party, but it was a lot easier than trucking our son from house to house during the holidays. We had everything we needed for him here at our place.

The doorbell rang.

Tyler, his girlfriend, Nicole, and Damien's mother were standing in the doorway with wrapped gifts.

"Hey, guys! Come on in."

Monica hugged me tightly. "How are you feeling?"

"I'm good, still a tad bit sore, but great considering."

Nicole looked me up and down. "You are so tiny. No one would ever know you gave birth a month ago."

Damien yelled over to us, "She didn't even look pregnant from behind in her ninth month. I know this because I spent a hell of a lot of time in that position toward the end." He glanced at Monica. "Whoops, sorry, Mom."

Tyler pushed his way past us over to the baby. "There's my no-name godson!"

Nicole smiled. "Aw, he's wearing a beanie like his daddy."

We'd put a little gray hat on him to match Damien.

Tyler's gaze travelled from the baby back up to Damien when he said, "I never thought I'd see the day, man."

"You and me both, brother."

Tyler spoke close to the baby. "Don't worry, little No-Name. Your uncle Tyler is gonna teach you everything you need to know in this life."

"And then Daddy is gonna tell you to just do the opposite of what Uncle Tyler says," Damien joked.

"When are we gonna get to hear the name?" Monica asked.

"When everyone gets here, maybe after dinner, we'll announce it," Damien said. "We're still waiting on Chelsea's family to arrive."

Nicole meandered over to me as she played with her necklace. "Look what Tyler bought me for Christmas. It's from Tiffany's."

I examined the heart-shaped pendant that hung from a silver chain. "Not too shabby, Ty."

"He did good." She grinned.

"It's really pretty. You two must have just celebrated a one-year anniversary, too, yeah? I remember meeting you for the first time last year around this time, and you guys had just started dating."

"Yup. Still going strong."

Tyler overheard and lifted his index finger. "Which means...I haven't fucked up yet."

Damien smacked his brother on the shoulder. "Seriously, Nicole, it takes a special woman to deal with my narcissistic brother. Bravo to you."

"Touché." Tyler laughed. He then turned to me. "So, who's coming from your side tonight?"

"My sister, Claire, her husband, Micah, and their baby daughter, Clementine. Also, my parents."

"Don't you have another sister?" Monica asked.

"Yeah." I pouted. "Jade couldn't make it home from New York. Her show is always busiest this time of year."

"That sucks."

"Yes, it does. I miss her. She hasn't even met the baby yet. It's killing her, but they literally threatened her job when she asked for time off to come home when he was born." Feeling down, I said, "Soon though. She'll fly out here as soon as she has the chance."

Tyler wrapped his arm around Nicole. "Why don't I get some drinks started?"

"Actually, little brother, I was gonna send you to the liquor store to pick up some beer. I went out earlier and forgot it—the most important thing."

"I can do that." He kissed his girlfriend on the nose. "Nic, you want to stay or come with me?"

"I'll stay."

A few minutes after Tyler left, the doorbell rang. I assumed it was my family, since they were all driving here in one minivan.

My heart pummeled against my chest upon the sight of my sister. She was standing there holding a bunch of bags.

"Jade! Oh, my God!"

We leapt into each other's arms. When she pulled away, she got teary-eyed at the sight of the baby. Without prompting, Damien took him out of the carrier and handed him to his auntie.

Jade admired our son in her arms. "I've been dying to hold him."

I gave her a minute to enjoy him before I asked, "How did you manage to get away?"

"I literally cried, begged and pleaded for just one night off. I have to fly right back tomorrow night. I just couldn't go any longer without seeing him." She looked back down at the baby and said, "He looks like us. But he has Damien's nose."

"That's exactly what I said!"

Damien looked happy to see *me* so happy. "Jade, this is an amazing surprise. You have no idea how stoked you've just made your sister."

She grinned over at me. "I'm so glad I could make it happen."

Everyone else arrived soon after, and they were just as shocked as I was to see Jade standing there holding the baby. She didn't let go until he pooped, at which point Damien came to the rescue so that I could have a little one-on-one time with my sister.

Jade and I were getting food ready in the kitchen when Tyler returned from the store with the beer.

"Tyler, come meet my sister! This is Jade."

Jade, who'd been facing me, turned around to greet him.

He opened his mouth and stopped as if he'd seen a ghost. I couldn't blame him for being speechless at the first sight of her. Many people had that reaction. Jade was tall and gorgeous, a commanding presence who lit up any room she was in. With her blonde pixie cut, big eyes and tiny nose, she looked almost like a real-life version of Tinkerbell.

He stumbled over his words. "Hi. I...uh, I'm..."

Jade answered for him. "Tyler." She smiled. "You're Tyler."

"That's my name. Yup. And you're..." Tyler lost his words again.

"Jade."

He laughed nervously. "Right. She said that. Jade. Nice to meet you." He held out his hand, and she took it.

"I know. Finally, right? Really nice to meet you, Tyler."

Nicole walked into the kitchen at that moment, and Tyler, whose hand had been lingering on Jade's, instinctively let go.

"There you are, Ty. I didn't see you come in. I was beginning to think you got lost out there."

Flashing a disingenuous smile, he said, "Hey. Yeah, too many beer choices these days." He looked over at my sister again. "Jade, this is..."

When he again blanked out, his girlfriend answered on his behalf. "Nicole."

Jade smiled at him. "Yes. She and I met when you were out."

"Great. Okay, then." He gestured back with his thumb. "I'm just gonna...put this beer in the fridge."

Tyler bent down at the base of the refrigerator and was fumbling with the bottles when one slipped out of his hand and shattered onto the ground. "Fuck," he said through gritted teeth. "I'm sorry, Chelsea. I'll get it cleared out.

I'd never seen Tyler act like that. He was normally cool as a cucumber. Was it a reaction to my sister, or something else?

After Tyler and Nicole left the kitchen, Jade just looked at me in silence. I'd seen that look on her face before. We had a way of reading each other's minds without saying anything.

"So, *that's* Tyler." She glanced over to where he was standing in the opposite side of the apartment.

"Yep."

"He's gorgeous," she whispered.

"I know. Damien and he look similar but different, right?"

"Totally." Jade let out a deep breath. She, too, looked a bit flustered.

If there was one thing I knew about my sister, it was that she would never consider moving in on someone with a girlfriend. Jade's last relationship ended with her ex leaving her for someone else—just as mine had done to me. She understood what betrayal felt like. And even if in some alternate universe, he weren't with Nicole, I wasn't sure I could trust Tyler with Jade's heart. As much as I loved my brother-in-law, he wasn't Damien. An actor dating an actor didn't seem like a wise combination, either.

Still, for a fleeting moment, I couldn't help fantasizing about what it would be like to see Damien's brother with my sister. That was all it was—a fantasy, especially since Jade lived in New York, and Tyler lived here.

Lived with his *girlfriend* here.

Okay. Move on, Chelsea.

Later that night, everyone had eaten and exchanged gifts, so it was the opportune time to announce the name we'd chosen.

Damien did the honors.

"So, I want you all to know that we thought long and hard about this, going back and forth between obscure names and common ones. Nothing felt right for the longest time. Then, my little lady put her foot down. She told me there was only one name that felt right. Who am I to refute that? So, I introduce to you...Damien Raymond Hennessey, or as we like to call him, Little D."

After all of the "oohs" and "aahs," Tyler shouted across the room jokingly, "We waited all this time just to find out you named him Damien?"

"Damn straight. And his middle name is after Dad, of course."

Monica was in tears, probably thinking about her late husband.

"I think our choice is pretty representative of our relationship as a whole," I added. "Sometimes, the best things are right under your nose all along."

♦ ♦ ♦

Damien and I were getting ready for bed Christmas Eve, and I had to ask, "Did Tyler say anything to you about Jade?"

"You mean other than, 'Holy shit, how did you not tell me her sister was hot as fuck?' No."

"What did you say to him?"

"I told him that Jade was family now and that I'd kick his ass if he ever fucked with her."

"You did?"

"Hell, yes, I did. That being said, I think he's really into Nicole. The teenage boy in him just came out for a little bit when he laid eyes on your sister."

"Okay." I decided to drop the subject and move on from my apparent obsession with the idea of Tyler and Jade.

Damien prowled toward me on the bed. "So...are you ready for your gift?"

"You said to expect something nuts, so I'm not so sure."

"It's not that crazy." He looked up at the ceiling in doubt then chuckled. "Well, maybe it is."

"What did you do?"

"So, let me preface this by saying...I never loved that mole on my ass. I used to hate it actually...until you told me you dug it."

"Whoa. Now I'm really confused. What are we talking about here?"

"I decided to make a mountain out of a mole hill, baby."

"A what?"

"Rather than getting it removed, I worked with it."

Damien stood up from the bed and slowly pulled down his pants to reveal his muscular, tanned ass. A name was tattooed in the spot where the mole used to be.

Wait.

The mole was still there! It was now used to dot the 'I' in the word he'd etched onto his beautiful derriere.

FIRESTARTER.

EPILOGUE

Damien

New Year's Eve.

This time last year, Chelsea and I were kissing in Times Square.

Now, she was fast asleep next to me with our son on her chest. He'd also fallen asleep while sucking on her nipple. The dogs were out cold on the floor next to them.

They'd all slept right through the crystal ball dropping. Cartons of half-eaten Chinese food sat on the coffee table. We were a sight for sore eyes.

I was the only one awake. The TV volume was on low as I sipped my beer and counted my blessings.

I was here.

I was alive with a wife, two dogs and most of all, a precious son I never dreamt I'd have.

Tracing my finger along little Damien's tiny foot, I marveled at how much a life could totally change in a year. Mine did for the better.

With too much nervous energy to sleep, I grabbed my laptop and started to surf the net. I hadn't checked my email in what felt like ages. When I clicked on the icon, Chelsea's email was open, since she was the last to log in. There was an email from over a year ago that she hadn't deleted. Normally, I wouldn't notice this, but the name struck me immediately.

Elec O'Rourke.

Her ex.

The date on the email was from before Chelsea and I were officially a couple.

I couldn't help but read it.

It was just a brief acknowledgement of the day we'd run into him at Bad Boy Burger way back when. From what I could see, she never responded to his message.

I was feeling incredibly happy tonight—high on life. Revved up. Impulsively, I reopened the email, clicked reply and typed:

You don't know me, but my name is Damien Hennessey. I'm Chelsea's husband—the same guy with the forearm tattoo from the burger joint.

Her email inbox happened to be open, and I stumbled across your message. I felt it warranted a response.

I have very mixed feelings about you. A part of me wants to hunt you down and fuck you up for ever hurting her the way you did. Another part of me wants to hunt you down and give you a big gay kiss on the lips as a thank you for the day you decided that fucking around with your stepsister was a good idea.

That didn't exactly come out right, but you get the point.

I'd always hated you. Mainly, I hated the fact that she'd ever loved anyone before me. But as of today, I'm done hating you or anyone, for that matter.

I have a son.

He was just born a little over a month ago. I need to set an example for him.

So, this isn't hate mail; it's a thank you letter of sorts.

Thank you for screwing your stepsister, and in turn, breaking up with my girl.

If you hadn't, Chelsea would be with you right now, and I would've never realized the greatest love of my life.

--D.H. Hennessey

I put down the laptop and took Baby D off of Chelsea, walking him over to the bedroom. Whenever his little heart beat against my chest, I tried to block out the fear that crept up, focusing instead on the healthy rhythm. I placed him in the bassinet.

Returning to the couch, I lifted Chelsea into my arms and carried her to our bed. She was still fast asleep when I put her down and covered her. It would only be another hour or so anyway before the baby would inevitably wake up hungry.

I ventured back into the living room and was just

about to shut down my laptop and join Chelsea in bed when I noticed a new email had come in.

It was from Elec O'Rourke.

Damien,

Hey. I'll forgive the slightly deranged under-tone of your message. I'm thinking if you have a newborn, you're not getting much sleep, and you're probably just wired. Scramble the letters of wired, you get weird. Wired = Weird. If you're not wired, then maybe you're just a little weird. But that's okay, because weirdness aside, you seem to really love Chelsea. She deserves someone who truly appreciates her.

Anyway, I understand what it feels like to be grateful. I have a son, too. And he's perfect. I have no doubt that things ended up exactly as they should have.

Chelsea is an amazing woman. You're a lucky man. I would say give her a kiss and a hug from me, but I'm afraid you might take it the wrong way, and I'd end up in a body bag.

So, just let her know I wish her the best.

As for you and me, I hope we're cool now, although you can save the big gay kiss.

Happy New Year and congrats on your son.

--Elec O'Rourke

P.S. You were great in The Omen.

WANT TO FIND OUT WHAT
HAPPENED WITH JADE AND TYLER?
Download *JADED AND TYED*, a FREE novelette
for my newsletter subscribers here.
(https://dl.bookfunnel.com/p1b0axreue)

ALSO READ ELEC AND GRETA'S STORY
IN THE *NEW YORK TIMES BESTSELLER*
STEPBROTHER DEAREST
(http://amzn.to/1mFNMeg)

ACKNOWLEDGEMENTS

I always say the acknowledgements are the hardest part of the book to write. There are simply too many people that contribute to the success of a book, and it's impossible to properly thank each and every one.

First and foremost, I need to thank the readers all over the world who continue to support and promote my books. Your support and encouragement are my reasons for continuing this journey. And to all of the book bloggers/bookstagrammers/influencers who work tirelessly to support me book after book, please know how much I appreciate you.

To Vi – You're the best friend and partner in crime I could ask for. Here's to the next ten years of friendship and magical stories.

To Julie – Cheers to a decade of friendship, Rebel cheese, and Fire Island memories.

To Luna –When you read my books for the first time, it's one of the most exciting things for me. Thank you for your love and support every day and for your cherished friendship. See you at Christmas!

To Erika – It will always be an E thing. Thank you for your love, friendship, summer visit, and Great Wolf Lodge bar time—one of my favorite moments of the year.

To Cheri – It's always a good year when I get to see you, my dear friend! Thanks for being part of my tribe and for always looking out and never forgetting a Wednesday.

To Darlene – What can I say? You spoil me. I am very lucky to have you as a friend—and sometimes signing assistant. Thanks for making my life sweeter, both literally and figuratively.

To my Facebook reader group, Penelope's Peeps – I adore you all. You are my home and favorite place to be.

To my agent Kimberly Brower –Thank you for working hard to get my books into the hands of readers around the world.

To Elaine of Allusion Book Formatting and Publishing – Thank you for being the best proofreader, formatter, and friend a girl could ask for.

To my assistant Brooke – Thank you for hard work in handling all of the things Vi and I can't seem to ever get to. We appreciate you so much!

To Kylie and Jo at Give Me Books – You guys are truly the best out there! Thank you for your tireless promotional work. I would be lost without you.

To Letitia Hasser of RBA Designs – My awesome cover designer. Thank you for always working with me until the finished product exactly perfect.

To my husband – Thank you for always taking on so much more than you should have to so that I am able to write. I love you so much.

To the best parents in the world – I'm so lucky to have you! Thank you for everything you have ever done for me and for always being there.

Last but not least, to my daughter and son – Mommy loves you. You are my motivation and inspiration!

OTHER BOOKS BY **PENELOPE WARD**

ABOUT THE **AUTHOR**

PENELOPE WARD is a *New York Times, USA Today* and *#1 Wall Street Journal* bestselling author.

She grew up in Boston with five older brothers and spent most of her twenties as a television news anchor. Penelope resides in Rhode Island with her husband, son and beautiful daughter with autism.

With millions of books sold, she is a 21-time *New York Times* bestseller and the author of over forty novels.

Penelope's books have been translated into over a dozen languages and can be found in bookstores around the world.

Subscribe to Penelope's newsletter here:
http://bit.ly/1X725rj

SOCIAL MEDIA **LINKS**

FACEBOOK
https://www.facebook.com/penelopewardauthor

FACEBOOK PRIVATE FAN GROUP
https://www.facebook.com/groups/PenelopesPeeps/

INSTAGRAM
@penelopewardauthor
http://instagram.com/PenelopeWardAuthor/

TIKTOK
https://www.tiktok.com/@penelopewardofficial

TWITTER
https://twitter.com/PenelopeAuthor

Made in the USA
Coppell, TX
02 October 2024

38030453R00215